JANAMANIA

Novel

Jochen Lobah

The characters and events portrayed in this book are fictitious. Any similarity to real persons, living or dead, is coincidental and not intended by the author.

ISBN-13: 9798429703541
ISBN-10: 1477123456

Cover design by: Art Painter
Library of Congress Control Number: 2018675309
Printed in the United States of America

El rival de Dios no es nunca la creatura concreta que amamos. Lo que termina en apóstasis es la veneración del hombre, el culto de la humanidad

(God's rival is never the concrete creature we love. What ends in apostasy is the veneration of man, the worship of humanity)

NICOLÁS GÓMEZ DÁVILA

Die Anziehung zwischen zweien muss ihrem Dasein vorausgegangen sein.

(The attraction between two must have preceded their existence)

BOTHO STRAUSS

SAUDADE (PART ONE)

It was raining heavily in the endless expanse of the Po Valley. The day before, a strong west wind had put an abrupt end to the persistent foggy November days with their melancholy light. The dark gleam of the wet highway suffused my thoughts with a gentle wistfulness. Leaving the Swiss-Italian border behind, I drove towards Milan's great freeway junction to take the exit to Turin. On the way, I had a short break in Turate, a small but wealthy village in the province of Como, to buy some groceries for the upcoming week. The closed window shutters and Italy's typical hanging lamps, rocking in the gusty wind above the empty streets, radiated a reassuring atmosphere. I stopped my old but reliable Volkswagen Golf first generation in front of a still open, but seemingly deserted supermarket. As I listened to the metallic sound of raindrops on my car, a glimpse at the scattered books on the passenger seat filled me with enthusiasm: what promising reading material to isolate myself from the rest of the world for another winter, this time in a suburb of Turin where nobody knew me. The book selection went perfectly with my eccentric-casual outfit, composed of biker boots, a well-worn black leather jacket and my beloved blue knitted cap I had named with a touch of social sentimentality the 'knitted cap of Neapolitan longshoremen'. All in all, the ideal disguise to hide my introversion and insecurity. Skimming once again the paperbacks, I was convinced that the hardship of my short journey back to Germany had been worth the travel strain to get them in my familiar bookstore at Frankfurt-Bockenheim, not far from the university. First and foremost, I looked forward to delving into the thin but seminal *Discourse on Thinking* by Martin Heidegger. Since my first encounter with the books of this controversial philosopher, I had fallen in love with the meditative audacity of his ideas despite the mainstream of leftist political correctness and a suffocating taboo among my fellow students towards his person and thinking. Most of the aspiring academics of both arts faculties, in Turin and in Frankfurt as well, were fiercely insisting on being considered either leftist or progressive the disastrous end of the socialist utopia in Eastern Europe notwithstanding. Their political bearing was also their unmistakable trademark of identity and Heidegger was undoubtedly their main opponent. Yet the impressive profoundness and beauty of his thoughts irresistibly stimulated me. The unexplainable depth of his philosophy always fueled my desire to gain more wisdom and to strengthen my resistance vis-à-vis the so-called present-day reality which had already been tiring me for a long time. I fervently hoped that the further reading of his late period of thinking would give me composure and rest. This dreamy meditation was supported by the hermetic atmosphere in my car that kept the blustery world outside apart. And while I was sitting motionless, Jana's picture came inevitably back to my mind: Jana, with all her beauty and untouchable grace, with her delicate hands and always carefully red-painted fingernails that she would varnish exclusively for me. That alone made me immensely proud. It wasn't until much later, and not without reason, that I started to get jealous perceiving that she would apply her elegant, perfectly balanced make-up for others. The sense of helplessness I experienced was awful when one evening after an unusual quarrel she silently took her eyeshadow together with her lipstick and left me alone on the sofa of my apartment. The dispute was the starting point of an irreversible crisis because it was obvious that the incident had marked a strange break in our relationship. And indeed, it should be the first hint of the impending end of our surreal happiness.

From the first moment, Jana's beauty had been the symbol of a world that had not yet been disenchanted. Her handsomeness was sheer grace and I was overwhelmed by the abundance of meaning her presence conveyed to me. It seemed that everything that existed had been exclusively created to be an adequate setting for her. Wherever she appeared, she transformed the environment into an appropriate backdrop for her. She had the power to change my idea of existence from scratch. And so, Jana would soon be the real counterpart of my academic research and the boredom of everyday life. Only much later and outside the academic ambience I should learn that there were still thinkers who had never given up their stance of being enchanted of existence and its dazzling beauty, focusing their writing on this experience. They did not care that their attitude did not correspond to the mainstream weltanschauung dominated by scientific reductionism and ideological over-politicization. In the distant past, simple astonishment was the source of thought so that creation's beauty and perfection were the real cause of reflection. And Jana was in my eyes the perfect embodiment of it. I was absolutely sure that neither a famous university professor nor an epistemology would have hardly ever been able to change my mind in this matter. It was crystal clear that love had penetrated with all its power into the depths of my soul.

As usual, I did not buy much, I simply loved strolling through small supermarkets in Italy. It was always a welcome distraction. Delicious food was found everywhere, offered with love and care. I picked up a couple of packets of penne and linguine which I would eat regularly just with a simple tomato-tuna sauce or with butter and grated parmesan. Cooking pasta had quickly become a kind of exclusive evening ritual because

I had stopped having lunch due to my self-imposed asceticism. At that time, I was in dire need of such a self-esthetic to feel still alive. Moreover, I had lost my healthy appetite the moment I separated from Jana.

A long winter lay ahead of me, with lonely evenings I would spend with in-depth analysis of my literary discovery of the year, the Medieval Tuscan literature, especially Dante and Petrarca. Originally, the purpose of my stay in Turin was to deepen the knowledge of modern German philosophy, particularly Nietzsche as a precursor of Heidegger's ideas about nihilism. Turin's university was a center for German thought mainly due to Nietzsche's past in this city. Yet my rising passion for Dante was not at all a coincidence. The protagonist of his works, Beatrice, permanently reminded me of Jana and at a certain moment of my reading, both names could have been easily exchanged since I understood that I had to sublimate Jana's person the same way Dante did with Beatrice. Perhaps that was an appropriate method to stifle my chronic sorrow. And the weekends, pre-eminently Saturday nights, I sought ephemeral happiness and entertainment, through the uptight attempt to dance until attaining a delirious state, trying to deaden all memories of my love affair with her and to overcome my fragile state of mind. But the more I danced, the faster a violent nostalgia rose in me and so I desperately kept on moving until my complete exhaustion. I usually chose the Centralino on a small side road of Via Po where mainly Dancefloor and House music were played. Sometimes I left Turin late on Saturday for the gigantic Ultimo Impero, a real abyss of Deep House music, thirty miles away, for the simple reason that I loved to drive back home through the empty streets at early dawn.

Driving in the rainy weather and wind, I missed the exit to the autostrada Piacenza Torino in the maze of highway junctions in Milan's northwest, but also due to a dreamy remembering of a wonderful December evening we spent together. We were eating a delicious Raclette in her apartment in a pre-Christmas atmosphere. I clearly saw her gracile fingers shoving the Raclette patella into the stove and pulling it out with the same gracefulness moments later, as though it had happened yesterday. The period around that late autumn weekend marked most probably the emotional climax of our magical relationship. Neither of us would have thought at that moment this unity could break up into a thousand pieces one day. Our surrendering to each other conveyed timeless happiness and the romantic winter ambience outside seemed to protect our emotional paradise against all disturbing influences.

I came out on the great Viale Alcide de Gasperi which headed into downtown. It was appalling to see all those young prostitutes standing in that cold and rainy fall eve lined up at the edge of the illuminated park of Lampugnano. As I had repeatedly read in some articles of the Corriere della Sera they came mainly from Serbia and Albania, trying to escape poverty during the bloody civil war in the Balkans. At that time, we had not yet a real idea if it was a confessional or rather ethnic conflict in the heart of Europe. The fact was that the liberation from a unifying socialist dictatorship brought blood and grief over this region. I was seized with a rising temptation to stop the car and to negotiate with one of those young and poor girls, driven by a strong desire to erase for a short while Jana's picture in my mind. So, I was tempted to forget myself and with me all my adventures, hopes, joys and moments of suffering with her at the brink of a dark unpeopled park in Milan through a dirty and in Italy legally forbidden physical relationship. But that was just wishful thinking since I was too shy and too scared to do so. Instead, I continued to search for the freeway exit to Turin, eventually driving into the dark plains of Piedmont.

Although I studied and lived in the wonderful city of Turin, I had developed a certain weakness for Milan with its hidden treasures behind its bustling facades. Whenever the longing for Jana and all the memories of our three-year love affair overwhelmed me, I left my small apartment in Turin's northern suburbs and went directly to the Porta Nuova station. From there I took the hourly express train to Milan and sought refuge in the sober interior of the Basilica of Sant'Ambrogio where I would sometimes sit for hours under the old Romanesque arches with hints of inexplicable crying fits, seeking consolation. After I calmed down, I remained often a good while inside the old nave, observing the coming and going of tourists or the quiet invocation of some pious woman or man. It was always a strange mixture between the mundane visitors and those who sought repentance. I loved the church's simple ambience, mostly free of all the anthropomorphizing illustrations of God and without overstressing the tragic elements which had poured afterwards into Christianity as a legacy of Hellenistic and Roman culture. The majestic austerity of this old house of worship made it the ideal place for spiritual cleansing. That was the reason I appreciated from the beginning of my stay northern Italy's relatively simple churches of Romanesque heritage much more than the southern Italy and Spanish baroque-kitsch which esthetically I could not bear and which moreover seemed to me as the irreversible atrophy of human spirituality. Every time I left this place, walking across the silent inner courtyard of Sant'Ambrogio in the midst of this crowded and stressful city, I was completely relaxed as if I had been treated with an effective anesthetic. It also touched me profoundly that the place had been the environment of the spiritual father of Catholicism, Saint Augustin of Hippo whose *Confessions* I had been reading more than once during my personal crises. His ascetic approach to life impressed me and his autobiography offered me from time to time an emotional recovery from my woes. As soon as I ceased my delving into that book I suffered regularly relapses into my painful reminiscences of Jana and an even stronger longing for finding a somehow beautiful female student at the University of Turin who would be able to replace her and to extinguish my consuming craving. Moreover, that work of late antiquity was nourishing my yearning for a way of existence free of sufferings and a peaceful setting. Augustin's radical soliloquy made unmistakably clear that even the deepest love would be accompanied by the taste of evanescence. His bravery to show that nothing would last and that even life's most beautiful moments were condemned to be dragged down into the lowland of our earthly and ephemeral existence, condemned to disappear with us, suffused me with bitterness and anguish. Nevertheless, I saw in his strict asceticism a fervent zeal to love and to live, so that I was totally convinced he had not exclusively God in mind when he wrote: *you have touched me and I am burning for peace in You.* The sentence sounded not less impressive in the Latin original on the right page of the book: *tetigisti me et exarsi in pacem tuam.* Augustin's *Confessions* had become my intensive reading for many nights, while I was fully aware that the famous Catholic scholar had a radical conversation with himself, addressing his monolog to the most intrinsic part of his being. In doing so he removed all the mud at the bottom of his soul to finally get closer to God. Yet his visually stunning language kept reminding me of Jana's extraordinary beauty and as I devoured that book with unusual attention, I slowly realized I was dramatically relapsing into my emotional addiction. And again Jana's picture came back to my mind with all its spell. Thus, a new phase of enduring desperation set in, a crisis I tried to heal with long nocturnal walks through the deserted streets of Turin's northern suburbs. It was a period I was permanently in need of fresh air and exercise to avoid an emotional collapse.

It was really astounding how the time factor could be the

most effective tranquilizer. After weeks of despair, I started to love going again to the faculty of humanities every morning, resuming my focus on studying, even though in the meantime I had gained a sort of dissident reputation among most of the politically left-wing students of philosophy. But the biggest struggle was still to be fought at the level of the affairs of the heart since I was not yet able to get seriously involved in a new relationship. I knew that the attraction I felt for some of those beautiful young Italian female students was but purely superficial. Most probably I would not have been able to fall in love, but it could have been a temptation to forget Jana at least for a while. A relationship would have been at best emotional numbing of my painful trauma that I had lost her definitely forever and with her disappearance, the real meaning of my life had been buried in a bottomless abyss.

So I spent my time in Turin attending university lectures and strolling around the many improvised libraries under the arcades of the Via Po, skimming almost every day on my way back home all genres of books. After the end of the lessons, late afternoon, I felt most happy since I should never feel at ease among the many students who were constantly involved in fierce political debates. It was strange listening to all these sophisticated discussions and it seemed to me that the role of an intellectual was totally reduced to one who ponders upon a system that would realize total justice for humanity. Yet this was a task for God or a state of the hereafter. In my eyes, there was a deep lack of lessons learnt from the recent collapse of real socialism in Europe's East. Their overt stance to shape society and to impose their doctrine of salvation conveyed to them a presumptuous attitude although all those students had undoubtedly the best intentions. By contrast, my apolitical attitude was provocative and suited the fact that I regularly attended the weekly lectures of Giacomo Cordani on late medieval literature and the modern poetry of Eugenio Montale.

Cordani's melancholic nature with his nostalgic glimpse, full of longing for something that mankind had forever lost or perhaps never achieved, was not only adequate to the lesson's topic but filled me also with calmness. I was keenly listening to his lectures that made me much curious about the anachronistic weltanschauung of the late medieval and early renaissance literature, furthermore, his interpretations of Montale's poetry conveyed a detailed idea of the poet's universe of melancholy. Some students who were engaged in political-revolutionary matters started to make fun of me, of that odd German guy, since they had heard I was attending Cordani's seminars. They sometimes tried even to convince me that the medieval literature of Dante, Petrarca and Boccaccio was not only out-of-date and at best of encyclopedic interest, but also a totally reactionary genre of literature. Gabriella, a fervent and attractive anarchical activist I usually met during the courses on German idealism, preached to me about the deeper intentions of Cordani's choice to teach Montale's hermetic poetry and said to me that it was unmistakably a clear sign of his upper-class affiliation and of his blindness vis-à-vis the context of present-day social problems. Cordani was an academic remnant of sentimental bourgeois weltschmerz she concluded. Her objections she reiterated from time to time never prevented me from regularly joining his lectures, rather they had an opposite effect, namely the idea of being perceived as someone who was not participating in compulsory seminaries had started to please me. Additionally, the stance to flee the political zeitgeist went not only hand in hand with my inclination to shun the academic mainstream, but also with my timidity and chronic uncertainty. That was perhaps also the hidden reason for a directional change in a geographical sense: Milan remained in my eyes that mesmerizing and unconventional city, full of outward beauty and excitements, but I slowly felt a growing yearning for a calmer and more contemplative place. I discovered an hourly train connection from Turin's central station Porta Nuova to Genova and from my first arrival in the former maritime power, I was much attracted by the blue Mediterranean shimmering behind the city's impressing ochre-colored sea of houses. Genova was a real Mediterranean city with few tourists, but with a remarkable community of North Africans from Morocco and Algeria that hinted at the nearby Arab World at the other end of the sea. Whenever a sunny weekend was forecasted in that period of spring awakening, I got up early in the morning, took the books Cordani had recommended us and made the two and a half hour trip to Liguria's capital. After leaving the train at the railroad station Genova Brignole, I usually went on by a local train to Nervi, a quiet and elegant Genoese suburb directly located at the seaside. I had discovered a wonderful small corner of a sandy beach embedded in a rockbound coast where I spent almost all the following weekends till the beginning of the summer. It was there where I immersed myself in Dante's *Vita Nova,* but neither did I show the slightest interest in historically contextualizing this revolutionary book written in Tuscan dialect nor did I show interest in its Christian symbolism. Like Augustin's *Confessions* I was reading Dante's *New Life* exclusively against the backdrop of personal experiences. Delving into its alternating rhythm of prose and sonnets dedicated to Beatrice Portinari's beauty and purity, I lost all kinds of reading distance and easily replaced her with Jana's image. Reading and re-reading the book again and again I was fully aware that I was apotheosizing Jana's omnipresent picture to quench my tormenting thirst for meaning which had undergone an immense breakdown since the end of our relationship. Sometimes I wondered how could I continue to stay in Italy instead of going back to Germany and searching for her proximity. I dreamt of kneeling at her door and asking for her mercy and indulgence, hoping she would promise me to stay anew at my side, at least for one further summer. Over time, I got used to fighting against these forms of endless despair, especially during the weekend and since I was not able to make real friends with my politically over-aware fellow students, I had to spend the Saturdays and Sundays alone. Oddly enough, I noticed that I felt uncomfortable every time I made a long conversation with a female student who evidently showed either an intellectual or emotional interest in me and it was as if I would cheat on Jana even though our love affair had already ended two years ago.

During that period of intense reading, I felt also a rising need to distract myself with primitive activities. After a late lunch, I often sat for hours in a Pizzeria nearby or took a bath in the still ice-cold waters of the Mediterranean Sea. And particularly on Sundays, I found distraction on my way back to Turin in a Bar inside the station of Nervi, watching the soccer matches of Italy's Serie A and sometimes of the Genovese club Sampdoria. Like all other people in that small coffeehouse, I followed the football matches with the utmost concentration, being completely absorbed by the dense atmosphere. The voices of those soccer maniacs and the lively surroundings were the ideal background noise to be relieved from all my craving for Jana and to get rid of my crystalized addiction to her. For this reason, I fell rapidly in love with that Eastern part of Genova and made it a habit of going to Nervi even twice a weekend, returning to Turin only to overnight from Saturday to Sunday, taking mostly the last train from Genova Nervi via Brignole back to Porta Nuova. I did the same on Sundays.

Many weeks later, towards the end of the summer semester, professor Cordani announced the exam date for Italian literature. The Via Po's arcades in the university district in downtown Turin were full of life, its streets full of pleasant anticipation of the upcoming summer vacation. As a non-native-speaker and with regard to Montale's hermetic poetry I was totally relaxed in view of the looming written exam. Before distributing the worksheets, Cordani had informed us that the examination consisted of two main questions: an interpretation of Montale's early poetry, particularly of the *Ossi di Seppia* or *Le Occasioni*, where he tried to free himself from his isolation. With his sad, but never unfriendly glance Cordani added that he considered the second part as more important, namely to write a concise essay on the meaning of literature and the reason for having chosen that field of study even though it would not promise a high income. His explanations had confirmed again all my enthusiasm for him and I looked much forward to devoting myself mainly to the second part of the test. It had a very personal dimension. Then, I quickly noticed that I would be able to write for hours about Montale's early and hermetic poems, fully empathizing myself with his bourgeois loneliness, surrounded by the colorful landscape of Liguria. This was noble escapism as I wrote fervently. What could a sensible man have done otherwise than break out of the devastating atmosphere of the first half of the twentieth century? A period of materialistic unleashing and jingoism, not to mention the era's Promethean claim to appropriate mankind's destiny by the means of shortsighted and man-made ideologies. But writing about three selected poems of Montale had been only a creative warm-up for the exam's second part and the essential question of the role of literature in our life. Without the slightest reluctance and in emotional turmoil I started to write about my love for Jana. The words were gushing out and I could have still written for hours about the dazzling light which filled my existence from the moment I had seen her for the first time. Yet in the same breath, I described the strange awareness of transience overshadowing that incredible feeling of happiness from its inception. I wrote down the entire story of my first vacation with her in Campania, at the Gulf of Salerno, portraying the memorable moment she slept soundly on the beach in the late afternoon while I looked at her beautiful skin and her perfect contours. Her wet black hair and her elegant fingers stretched out on the hot sand bewitched me. Happiness had suddenly no limits at all, being rather a mystical experience that abolished my captivity in space and time, but a strange foreboding of the absolute unrepeatability of that moment was already rising in me. Observing her motionless beauty was as if I would look at a work of art that made me completely happy. A mixture of negative feelings and thoughts about the ephemeral character of that delightful quarter-hour of my life came up again a few weeks later as I thought that extraordinary afternoon owed perhaps all of its outstanding bliss to its illusionary nature. That idea made me infinitely sad and had to be rejected. The profusion of beauty, I continued to write, had been so overwhelming that it could hardly have been the outcome of blind coincidence. So, every single moment I later spent with Jana taught me to take life as such never again for granted. In the course of time, I had ceased to consider philosophy and literature as pure matters of higher education, instead, both subjects had become a relative effective cure for my despair after my futile attempt to isolate our passionate love from the rest of the world.

From the first day of our romantic attachment, I feared that everyday life would drag our love down into the sphere of a meaningless daily routine, slowly stifling our emotional life. At a later time, I explained to Jana my longing for the singularity of our love, articulating my dream of escaping with her. It was the period when she was still receptive to such a surreal conception of love. These had been exceptional days of a foretaste of paradise as I denoted them in hindsight. My whole second part of the exam consisted in expounding the concept of literature as the only healthy substitute for our disappointments in love matters so that writing and reading needed to become an existential attitude which should be distinguished completely from Paris existentialism whose aim was to shape the spirit of the age and to offer political solutions for man's quest for meaning in a world marked by total absurdity. After a short while of enthusiastic reading which had been from the beginning slightly marred by the unromantic and sterile 'love' between Jean-Paul Sartre and

Simone de Beauvoir, I considered later on their existentialism made in Paris rather an attack on the meaning of existence. From then on, existentialism was in my eyes essentially anti-existentialist. Sartre's late works such as *Critic of the Dialectical Reason* and his flirt with socialist totalitarianism alienated me quickly from these coffeehouse avant-gardist-moralists who were paradoxically anti-elitist despite their pampered upbringing in the cradle of the French state. Additionally, I was convinced that French existentialism had been the result of a misunderstanding of Heidegger's early philosophy, essentially of *Being and Time*. That's what I finally tried to explain to professor Cordani with my torrent of words, mixing continuously up my emotional and intellectual experiences, with the conclusion that literature was neither entertainment nor political or discursive awareness-raising, but the ambitious will of searching for the truth. But I knew that statement would have totalitarian and anachronistic meaning and I noticed the expression of unconcealing the truth was a conception of Heidegger's reflection on art.

Two weeks later Cordani told us before conveying our exam ratings that he had been really excited by the prosaic explanation of a German student. I was totally embarrassed and blushed when he mentioned that he had not read such a sensitive essay about literature for a long time. It came as a surprise to me since I had written with an unmistakable radicalism, concluding the exam with the summary that a book that would not change one's life should not have been written at all. It was a pretentious statement, but life and reading should become in my view one zone of indistinguishability. I understood that my attitude towards literature corresponded to a decisive art radicalism that helped me to develop my relationship with literature and philosophy, detaching them from contemporary and secondary issues. It was the intensity of the love affair with Jana that mainly triggered my thoughts and meditations: I had simply to find out if Jana's beauty and my passion for her had a deeper meaning for my existence.

Strange enough that my predilection for literature and philosophy was going hand in hand with a growing contempt for all educational establishments which systematically prevented to my mind the impact of literature's beauty and its pedagogic values on individuals. Novels were not made to classify them into a framework of interpretative patterns or to pin them down into a context of purely historical interest alone. My relationship with educational institutions had always been characterized by a feeling of trepidation. I sometimes could hardly draw a distinction between being a pupil or a prisoner. Looking back, attending school always seemed to me as to serve a daily jail term along with twenty-five fellow prisoners, a sentence of detention imposed on us by the so-called duty to become civilized and domesticated beings. But most of my classmates were so sympathetic that I despised the idea to rival them on the field of school performance. So, I realized that I was not made for educational Darwinism since at that time I was exclusively yearning for having good and cool friends. Thus, I felt totally comfortable when my teachers gave me mediocre grades because then there was no reason for my classmates to be envious. Fortunately, and despite my reluctance to go to school, I had an excellent relationship with them, full of human warmth and solidarity. With some of my male classmates, I even shared a fervent contempt for the majority of our teachers and a permanent anti-authoritarian basic mood. That communal spirit had quickly inspired friendship among us that should extend long beyond our classical period of youth. Regarding my reading habits, I followed the academic curriculum only when the author or the work appealed to me on a very personal level. To read or to study a book because I would be obliged to do so by the Ministry of Education should have no meaning for me, especially later at the university. Reading had to be a kind of radical sensual experience. Only then the heart could be touched and transformed deep inside. But because of this stubborn attitude, I also gave away a significant number of good grades.

Daily university life strengthened my convictions that an intellectual activity would require escapism to flourish and to shape independence of thought. Despite the greater freedom in comparison with my years at school, the masses of students and of prospective elites at the university had shocked me from the beginning. I quickly lost sight of the esthetic dimension and the deeper meaning of literature and philosophy. Worse, I lost the sense for the beauty of written texts and their inspiring rhythms, instead, all that I was perceiving in the academic environment was a discursive clamor, thus I concluded that not discussion but a strict meditative atmosphere must be the adequate prerequisite of philosophy or literary activity. As a result, I left one morning the boring lecture on logic and went straight to the book shop, buying an edition of Max Frisch's *Diaries*. Subsequently, I took the subway and changed into the bus that brought me to the periphery where I always parked my car. It was my beloved month of November that had always touched me due to its conciliatory light and the infatuating scent of fallen leaves. The parking lot was situated right on the edge of the huge forest south of Frankfurt. It had snowed lightly the day before and I entered the white shimmering woodland, completely alone with some blackbirds and ravens that would not leave for the warmer south. The following days should become one of the most wonderful periods I spent in my life since they were completely uneventful, so to say. Every morning I returned to a wooden bench where I was sitting for hours despite the cold, after all, I was warmly dressed. During that week I did not go to university, but I read the entire *Diary 1946-1949* of Max Frisch in the company of already leafless trees. The silence of the coming winter made the book penetrate in a more intense way into my mind, leading me through the text to the solitude of the Valle Onsernone in the

Swiss Canton of Ticino. It made me feel to share Frisch's loneliness and his consuming desire for being loved. The whole week was an excellent exercise for enduring loneliness and for facing the unavoidable insight that all things we deeply love and we exclusively live for will sooner or later vanish with certainty. That was the only accessible truth at that time for me. Neither our parents nor teachers, let alone university professors had taught us how to cope with the ensuing mental ruin. Yet the mild scent of fallen November leaves and the calming grey afternoon light in the midst of this deserted area provided the ideal setting to bear that bitter truth and not to despair.

Lazio Rome played very well against Borussia Dortmund on the European level that evening. The sky blues had a legendary team with two outstanding strikers, Beppe Signori and Pierluigi Casiraghi. A few years later they would win the same year the championship and the national cup with an even better team around Alessandro Nesta and their team manager Sven-Göran Eriksson. They would abruptly end the northern hegemony in Italy's soccer league. Carlo turned to me and asked in his always friendly manner if he could offer me another espresso or perhaps a light dish of homemade pasta.

Carlo and Matteo were two brothers, coming originally from Sardinia, and extremely kind men who had long since considered me as a member of their family. I had started immediately after the high school diploma to work as a private tutor for Carlo's children and it was great fun to support Michele and later his younger sister Valeria in math, German and English. Most probably I would have done it free of charge, but Carlo would have never accepted such a deal, by contrast, he appreciated my work beyond measure and paid me far above the average. His generosity was another reason why I had never had financial problems during my days as a student. And I was not miserly, to say the least, rather lavish.

Whenever I set foot in Carlo's house it felt like a homecoming of the heart. The Italian atmosphere was irresistible and similar to the ambience in their successful and regionally famous pizzeria Porto di Olbia where we were watching the match together with a few guests that evening.

'You aren't a supporter of Lazio Rom, are you?' Matteo asked me.

'Of course not. I have seen a total of three matches of the yellow reds at Rome,' I proudly replied.

Indeed, I walked through Rome's suburbs for days and days, only to visit the setting of Pasolini's early novels, written in the dialect of the marginalized sub-proletariat living there in the fifties. And I went to the beach of Lido di Ostia where he had been murdered during the extreme political tensions of the mid-seventies in Italy, a homicide probably due to his unorthodox leftist-reactionary stance. During my in-depth readings of Pasolini's extremely different works, I was identifying myself in a tremendous way with Rome's sub-proletarian youth, although Italy's social structures underwent such comprehensive changes in the nineties that I could hardly find remnants of Pasolini's idealized youth in suburbs like Centocelle and Pietralata. In the meantime, most of Europe had become a spoiled middle-class world, inclined towards excessive consumerism. Pasolini had foreseen and criticized exactly that development several months before his killing in an open column on the first page of the conservative daily Corriere della Sera. Anyway, I had good reasons to support AS Rome, the city's other soccer club that had its origin in the classical worker neighborhood Testaccio which I knew like the back of my hand as I explained to Matteo.

After returning from Italy to Germany, I ate woodstove-made-Pizza with increasing frequency or drank just two, three espressos in the pizzeria Porto di Olbia with the sole intention of sitting there and enjoying the Italian atmosphere. Already at the beginning of my romantic relationship with Jana, we often ordered Pizza there to go. At that time, we always felt the dire need to be alone. But every time we went by, Carlo enthusiastically welcomed us.

Those were memories of happy days. In reality, the time after my return from Turin was extremely challenging since Jana kept popping up in my dreams, showing herself to me in her knee-high glossy boots and the elegantly applied new makeup she had bought to make herself beautiful. Yet in all these dreams the new rouge she was using for a certain time and her sexier clothing style should have been a clear sign of distancing herself from me. These were nightmares for which I needed at least a day to overcome them. And it always felt like yesterday when I sometimes got absorbed in reminiscences of the disastrous late-night phone call that was so different from all other hundreds of phone conversations that had become our sweet habit from the beginning of our love story. She told me then relatively relaxed she had been accompanied home by a fellow student from a symposium on the treatment of pulmonary cancer late in the evening. My heart almost stopped when I heard with how much fervor she said they had gone with his motorbike. Moreover, it was the first time she used the word friend for a fellow male student since we had come together. I tried not to lose my composure and to avoid any sign of jealousy, but I immediately understood that I was in the midst of a struggle for my much-loved Jana. It meant the Darwinism of desire had come into my life-scenery. Of course, I always feared that she was too beautiful and too attractive for not being wooed by many of her male colleagues and, at that moment, I painfully realized that a new stage of life would begin: a time of suffering and desperation. After that late-night conversation that had left deep emotional scars, there was a strange taste on my tongue, a taste I had never experienced before, but I was already sure that it would be the taste of a dramatic loss. In the blink of an eye, my entire perception of the world had changed, instead of being the appropriate setting for Jana's beauty, it was becoming a hostile place and so my first fragmentary contact with Buddhist thinking came into my mind, now with a seemingly better understanding of the core statement that existence was principally an affair of woes, prompted by illusions and projections as the German philosopher Schopenhauer described it in his long treatise *The World as Will and Representation* two hundred years ago. The following night, I was haunted by pictures of Jana, sitting on the motorbike with her black knee-high boots and pressing her body against the so-called friend to probably feel his warmth. Nobody knew better than me that she was not only a very sensitive but also a very haptic person and it was certainly me who knew best how graceful and beguiling her gestures could be.

The next morning, I woke up early with still the same strange taste in my mouth. A decade later I would much better understand why Muslim mystics speak of taste or dhauq when they come closer to God, corresponding to the strong relationship between sapere and sapore in Latin terms. Unquestionably, to understand was a matter of taste, since for every state of mind there is a taste on our tongue: the taste of love, the taste of joy, the taste of despair and most probably the taste of the approaching death.

When she told me days later, as if everything was not already sad enough, that she would travel directly after our planned summer vacation holiday with a group of prospective doctors to the Netherland's coast for sailing, I was sure I would never bear her absence. I had somehow to save myself from that looming tragedy and I started to wonder how could I best numb the pain of separation. So, I thought I had a real chance of withstanding that plight of the heart if I would only walk for days and days, remaining in constant motion. Running away would be the motto, just run away. And I could perhaps start at Rome and later on take the train to small villages like Anzio,

San Felice and Gaeta in the region's south to the bordering Campania, walking there for hours along the Mediterranean shore. That would be undoubtedly the most effective way to deal with the pain of separation and my consuming jealousy.

I had already begun in late spring the preparation for my so far biggest emotional challenge, booking a room in Rome for the period she would be in the Netherlands. Consequently, our last vacation was characterized by unusual ups and downs, accompanied by an unbearable alienation process, full of mistrust and dying sensuality. And before she set out for the Zandvoort Beach west of Amsterdam with her student friends, I had already reached Rome to get away from her as quickly as possible. I could not stand the feeling that she would leave me behind.

At the beginning of my stay, I took every morning the regional train to Lido di Ostia. An overcrowded Mediterranean seaside resort with an endless suburban beach where I lay around, delving into Umberto Eco's *Il nome della rosa* I bought immediately after my arrival in a bookstore close to Largo Argentina. I choose it after watching several times Jean-Jacques Annaud's beautiful film version, with Sean Connery in the role of William of Baskerville, so I was full of hope the book would give me emotional strength. Furthermore, there were moments I was totally distracted by the search of Pasolini's traces in order to fill his literature and paradox opinions with places and real life. Given the circumstances, Rome was the ideal place for me at the time. A lively city, full of contradictions and chaotic noise, but also full of charming and calm places like the hills of the Janiculum where the lovers could find quiet spots for their retreat. I often took the bus 64 which connected the Vatican to Rome main station Termini, traversing the entire historic downtown. The small studio apartment I had rented for six weeks in the lively station district was simple and affordable. Whenever I did not take the train to Lido di Ostia I got off the bus at Via Nazionale to immerse myself into the streets of the old town and to stroll from one café to another. I liked to listen to the rhythms of the Roman dialect with its long vowels and tried to understand what were people talking about. Since Jana's absence exhausted me physically and mentally, I had hardly any appetite, so during the day I only drank a few Cappuccinos and refreshing lemonade. For almost six weeks I would be gone, Jana had to feel my absence somehow, and I silently hoped that I would deeply hurt her the same way she had hurt me. But thinking that way was the unmistakable sign that love and mutual respect had already come to an end, even though I did not yet have the courage to concede it. And so, I continued to reorganize my life without Jana, coping the best I could with my painful heartache.

The longer I was in Rome, the better I was able to deal with my mental fragility and solitude. I tried to suffocate all nascent thoughts of Jana's vacation, yet I was bursting with jealousy whenever I imagined for a short while how she would redden her lips with one of her carefully selected lipsticks to be attractive for the evening. It had always filled me with a mixture of exuberant joy and pride when I gave her something special, as the expensive brand lipstick after a long dinner a fall evening at my home. With such gestures, I did not only prove to her my deepest love but also the fact she was the most precious thing for me, not to mention that she impersonated the undreamt meaning of my life. And now I was obsessed by the idea she would use that proof-of-love-gift to enchant others. Fortunately, I was getting day by day better at effectively deadening such thoughts.

The mid-nineties were a strange age, an era that still got along without mobile phones. There was no way to succumb to the temptation to dial Jana's number and ask her how she did. Over time, however, I developed a daily habit that made me pretty happy: instead of taking the bus 64 to Via Nazionale or the regional train to Ostia, as I did the first two weeks of my stay, I regularly set in long walks towards the Eastern neighborhoods of Rome, walking the entire morning along the Via Nomentana or the Via Tiburtina in the unmerciful Mediterranean sunlight of August towards the northeastern suburbs of Monte Sacro and Pietralata. What attracted me most was the fragrance of life in these crowded urban districts. And one could, despite the changing times, still notice that once this area had been undoubtedly a melting pot of the new arrivals in town, mainly people from Italy's rural south in search of prosperity. The place had preserved his characteristic, since the district was conspicuously populated by different cultures, notably from Sub-Sahara and North Africa. I often engaged in conversation with peers, asking them with the city map in my hands for a location or for the estimation of a distance, ending often up in an in-depth talk on Roman football and the rivalry between Lazio and Roma. And sometimes I addressed a young and attractive woman on the pretext of asking the time or a street, hoping to reap a brief and tender smile I was greatly craving for. But what I liked most, was to sit alone in an abandoned shabby bar at noon, hanging around and sipping a cappuccino or an espresso, since the hunger would arise only in the evening.

I immediately fell in love with the endless Via Nomentana lined with shady plane trees. This Roman main road led me out of the center and the terracotta-colored apartment buildings became rarer the longer I walked towards the city's eastern periphery. Along with this centrifugal motion, I succumbed more and more to the sweet illusion of being able to escape my painful yearning for Jana. Nevertheless, one of these extremely hot mid-summer evenings, while drinking my third orange soda in front of a small supermarket, all my resentments and thoughts came abruptly back, accompanied by the overwhelming conviction that she had destroyed the stronghold of our exceptional love. It was me who always tried to protect our feelings with a fervent eagerness from the world's unmerciful expediency. While I stared into the void a fit of frenzied jealousy seized me when I again imagined her going out and flirting with all those young males of a future successful generation of doctors. And all at once, that end of the day was about to turn into an emotional hell and I decided to get back to my apartment quickly, searching for the right bus among the many that drove up and down the Via Nomentana day and night. I was not in the mood to make the entire way back on foot, although, paradoxically, the shimmering street lights along with the violet sky as a harbinger of the night made this evening a particularly beautiful one. Suddenly some meters beside an old pine tree, just at a stone's throw from the crossroads into Viale Tripoli, I noticed a young and tall lady with magenta-colored high heels, a very handsome face and long black hair. She was very much made up and walked slowly but directly towards me, for a short moment she seemed to hesitate, yet eventually, she addressed me. 'Hey, how are you, my dear? What are you doing here? There is nothing to see in this corner of the city. Are you from Milan?'

At first, I had no intention of answering her, even though I was flattered she saw me as a northern Italian, but when I looked into her beautiful dark eyes, I could not resist replying, 'I'm just strolling around to discover Rome's history.'

'Oh, what a nonsense,' she said, almost indignantly. 'The sights are elsewhere! So, tell me what are you doing here? I think you are searching for some relaxation, isn't it? I can see it in your eyes,' she added decidedly.

I told her she was completely wrong, but her words touched me deep inside which I was certainly not able to hide from her. She came closer. I perceived her elegant handbag and her pretty slender fingers. Although she was not pushy, she tried to engage me in a longer conversation. 'I will make you a good price and your sadness will disappear for a time, I promise you,' she said. I thought I recognized a slight Roman accent even so she pronounced her words with elegance.

I had always avoided getting closer to prostitutes due to my romantic idea of love and less of moral reasons. Later on, such a temptation was completely impossible due to my pure feelings for Jana. But I clearly felt it would be a relief for me to talk to someone.

'I don't have enough money with me, I am sorry,' I said to her. Yet she was persistent, explaining to me that money was not the most important thing to have a good time with her.

'Please, look how much money you have with you?' she asked in friendly imperative. Even if I had not the slightest intention to accompany her, I instinctively looked in my wallet and naively told her that I had only a hundred fifty thousand lire with me. 'That's quite enough, including a delicious pasta dish, what do you say?'

With an uncertain smile, I replied to her that I had already had dinner and therefore I was not hungry at all. She smiled too and explained to me what a bad storyteller I was since no one in Rome could already have had dinner at such an early hour. The dinner would be served at half-past eight at the earliest she remarked.

'What are you afraid of?' she asked.

'I'm not afraid,' I replied uncertainly.

Almost tenderly she told me to relax and come with her, she would offer me a coffee and I would have time to think about staying overnight. We could negotiate the price in hindsight, she kindly said, stressing that she was always customer-oriented. Towards the end of the sentence, her voice became slightly feeble and less persuasive while I had to admit that her soft voice had charmed me from the first word and all of a sudden, we were going slowly side by side in the same direction as if I had tacitly accepted her suggestion. Strange, but I was following this unknown young woman to an equally unknown place. We walked like a shy pair of lovers along the noisy Via Nomentana, which at this point already ushered into the Roman suburb of Mentana with its pine-lined landscape of hills. After a short distance, we turned into a small but paved side road. There were Tuscan cypress trees and Latium pines scattered around, hosting thousands of cicadas that gave us a charming sunset concert. Finally, we entered into a mixture of an old ocher-colored country house. I was in a complete tunnel of obliterated feelings of the past and a rising tension of what would occur. As she ushered me in, I noticed a wide-open entry door to the right. She told me that it was the shared apartment of three Senegalese students. Subsequently, she went up the staircase and led me to her apartment on the first floor. I was immediately surprised by the elegance of the furnishing and the cleanliness of the rooms since the country house from the outside had seemed rather run-down. And it came to the fore now that I was full of prejudices about the life of a prostitute. She asked me to have a seat and to make myself comfortable on her oversized bed and although I felt rather uncomfortable, I obeyed without hesitation. Both windows of her large living room, which apparently also served her as the bedroom, were wide open. A light summer breeze filled the room with a desire for life and a pleasant heat. I had just sat down when someone suddenly knocked on her apartment door that caused me to panic, convinced that it was the police, but she looked at me through the open kitchen door and calmed me down. 'It's just Mamadou, you must know that I devote men no more than twenty minutes of my precious time, let alone to chat longer with them. You understand that you are privileged, let's say a VIP?'

A confident smile lay on her face as she opened the door and talked to Mamadou. She told him that we could perhaps have a late dinner all together, but she would have to wait for how the evening developed she added with a lowering voice. Sitting upright and motionless on her bed, I felt a little more relaxed after I had heard his voice, which was gentle and sensitive, too. She returned from the kitchen with a tray full of selected soft drinks and sat down next to me. It was the first time I was able to look at her attentively. She had beautiful slender fingers with red-painted nails which I had already noticed on the Via Nomentana and her eyes were dark, almost black like her smooth and wonderful long hairs. Smiling with indulgence she bluntly told me how sad and disappointed I seemed to her, certainly due to a failed love story. 'Your heart is frozen like an ice cube and you are afraid that it could break into a thousand pieces. You are an open book to me, sorry. You are longing for being loved with full devotion.'

Since her remark exactly described my emotional state, I gave way to a wave of self-pity and I felt how tears came to my eyes. I took her hand and started to weep like a child while I suddenly noticed again the abysmal emptiness Jana's absence had bequeathed in me. Embracing me she consolingly pushed my head against her breast. 'My name is Rossana, and you, what's your name?'

I was too touched to answer her immediately, instead, I pushed my head ever stronger into her breasts and let my tears run down my cheeks. Her natural scent and intimacy gave me a feeling of security.

After I had calmed a bit, she told me that Mamadou had come upstairs to propose a common dinner which had become a kind of domestic tradition among the house residents. In a sudden change of subject, she emphasized that most of her clients, fortunately, disappeared directly after she had satisfied their desires. She stressed it was the bad conscience of bourgeois decency since almost all of them were married and totally frustrated by their everyday life. When I heard bad conscience, I thought of resentment as well. Both were key concepts of Nietzsche's late philosophy. So, they could have been a good introduction to an in-depth discussion about at the time one of my most appreciated philosophers. That fragment of idea vanished as fast as it had come to me. But at least my mood was slowly changing for the better, I felt more comfortable in this place now.

She further told me that these three students were all outstanding cooks and it was always a culinary highlight when they prepared their national dish, Chebu Jen. In the same breath, she affirmed that I would not regret to share a late dinner with them and to alleviate my suffering, although I immediately objected with a hint of panic that I had still to go back to downtown this evening. I had not yet finished the sentence when she said to me in a commanding tone to spend the entire night with her, while she silently took my hands with a tenderness I had not experienced for a long time. The gesture made me even sadder because I fervently wished Jana were with me here and now, instead it was a young prostitute in the suburbs of Rome I had to pay later in the day. But for the first time after a long period, I felt something like calm within my heart.

'Come on, let's go down to spend the evening with Mamadou, Assane and Musa. I'm inviting you to our culinary summer night meetings. You'll like it, I'm sure,' she said to me like I was a good friend of hers.

As I looked deep into Rossana's eyes, I noticed the rise of an astounding fragment of feeling: it was her tenderness, although most probably feigned, in addition to her unbiased manner along with her exceptional beauty that quickly captured my mind. There was something surreal about the whole situation, but that unreal element in combination with the human warmth Rossana was outpouring not only touched me, it filled me every moment with more composure. My first intensive social contact after days helped me to break through the self-imposed isolation and self-pity. Time had been long overdue since I knew that I was making most probably a pitiful figure with my apotheosis of romantic and fateful love accompanied by a morbid melancholy.

What then followed was perhaps one of the most wonderful

summer evenings in my life. Rossana and the three Senegalese students formed an extraordinary house community that for sure I would never see again in such a constellation. It was an isolated island of unrestricted solidarity. Rossana had prepared amazingly delicious Spaghetti all amatriciana, one of the most famous first courses in Rome's culinary ambience. Afterwards, these three West Africans made us happy with an extremely tasty Chebu Jen. They had been working all the time in the kitchen, had set the table, but they never neglected to take part in our exuberant gathering with their engaging nature even during the meal preparation. What impressed me most from the beginning of that night was the fact they were laughing all the time, even without drinking alcohol. Rossana, Mamadou, Assane and Musa consumed only soft drinks, later on, they prepared tea and coffee. It was a very relaxed ambience and I felt happiness steadily rising in me, moreover, I had never the feeling they considered me as Rossana's client. Even more astounding was the fact that all three Senegalese were Sunni Muslims as they had described themselves during one of our lively discussions on metaphysics and the meaning of existence. And it was indeed Rossana who triggered the debate, pronouncing in her natural directness the sentence that with the loss of my love I would have lost all joie de vivre and that I would wallow in unhealthy self-pity. Instinctively I wanted to object that she could not have the slightest idea of my emotional state and that she did not know the details about my life. But it would have been a ridiculous statement, especially with the view to how miserable I did only about two hours ago when I hid my tears covered face like a helpless child in the breasts of a person who I did not really know. So, I paused for a moment, instead, I looked deep into her eyes with the astonishing conviction that she was not at all a stranger for me. Her conspicuous beauty and the natural way with which she treated me must have been either the result of very good acting ability, probably a prerequisite for her work, or the result of a mutual attraction. The latter I fervently wished to believe.

I had never expected such kindness and the topic of suffering due to a failed romantic love had sparked soon an oddly open, almost relaxed discussion. It was a wonderful anti-bourgeois setting, a prostitute living together with three Sunni-African Muslims, rather a constellation for a neo-realistic movie of the post-war era even though there was no migration from African countries to Europe at that time. In a certain way, my curiosity of getting an idea of the Roman suburbs as I had become acquainted with them by Pasolini's novels of the fifties and which obviously did not exist any longer had altogether been quenched. Only that those neighborhoods had transformed themselves into a melting pot of different cultures since the intra-Italian migration to Rome had slowly been replaced by African migration. Sitting with them now, I sensed the Mediterranean and cosmopolitan character of the city, despite its distinct fascist history throughout the first half of the twentieth century.

Our discussion quickly unfolded and I was amazed at the ease of the atmosphere the intimate issues we were talking about notwithstanding. The meaning of existence, we all agreed more or less, would be either to gain knowledge or to love. I opted for love, Musa for knowledge, yet he made clear that the deepening of knowledge could not be an end in itself since in this case, it would be bereft of real meaning. It had to lead, he added, to the natural understanding that we were transient beings, brought forth by the Creator. Grasping that reality must necessarily strengthen our insight that the meaning of life would be to worship God, to praise and thank Him. I understood immediately it was the way Muslims found their raison d'être. I would agree in so far as philosophy too was an art of preparing for death and of acknowledging life's transience. That was rather a platonic approach commented Mamadou and the result of traditional forms of wisdom, still lacking strong moral principles and the concept of Judgment Day. I was struck by their naturalness in discussing such existential issues while Rossana remarked that we were dealing with luxury topics that ignored real life. But it was a discrete objection that was based on her experience of organizing her life without asking others for their well-meaning and missionary advice. She stressed that everybody must develop his philosophy on the basis of personal experiences in order to cope with his mental challenges, traumas and daily issues. All four were indeed good examples of self-determined lives. When I saw the carefully folded prayer rugs next to me on a small Moroccan style divan, I bluntly told them I always thought it was perhaps a problem for Muslims to live with someone like Rossana. She smiled at me and said with an undertone of slight contempt that I was not much better like the rest of the world's mediocre population that viewed prostitutes as well suited for quick use, but not as human beings with dignity. I blushed and tried to apologize, quickly adding that I found it extraordinary and amazing how they lived here. Assane assured me not to worry, Rossana liked me, otherwise, she would not have invited me to remain for dinner, being undoubtedly a privilege and so I was reminded she had told me the same words a few hours ago. I blushed anew and wished to vanish off the face of the earth but Assane relaxed the atmosphere serving me more of the delicious Chebu Jen. We continued the debate and Mamadou explained to me that in Islam, especially in its Senegalese version, mercy must always prevail. 'We have to show in every moment compassion and leniency towards our fellows, especially with regard to their everyday mistakes and negligence. Showing mercy is a moral duty for Muslims, even though Islam is often not perceived as a religion of mercy, but rather as a religion of strict regulations and punishments. On the other side, we Senegalese Muslims have to admit that even in our country as well as here in our small mosques in Rome we are experiencing a very strong wave of puritanism. It has to do unfortunately with the identification of many Muslims with modern political ideas like being fit for the striving for power and ruling. A concept borrowed by the West to adapt ourselves to the political hegemony of the Western world. But these puritans confuse the concept of surrendering to God with power and they are totally convinced that they can bring the real Islam since in their eyes the implementation of true Islam has been prevented so far by the West's outward forces. For example, colonialism and post-colonialism, with their stupid doctrines of mankind's emancipation and material growth. Yet the truth is we Muslims bear the responsibility for living in backwardness and far from the Islamic principles of social justice and peace. Almost all Muslim societies are deeply divided, the opposite of what pristine Islam teaches us, namely to be an indulgent community of solidarity. And you see, that you too, have perceived us rather as people who would mercilessly exclude others who are different. And that is really no reproach at all.'

Assane's comprehensive analysis and distinct self-criticism regarding the Muslim community surprised me and made me more curious. He resumed his explications. 'In a certain way, this wave of enduring puritanism was at the end the result of a geopolitical clash of bigger dimensions. Since the end of colonialism and until the end of the eighties Muslim countries had been under the influence of pure secular, or worse, socialist regimes. Much of the oil revenues of the Arab kingdoms that staunchly resisted this political pressure were being invested in religious purist propaganda to tackle the wave of a Promethean ideology like the communism and socialism. Countries like Saudi Arabia spent much money to promote this uniform purist approach, at the time with a certain naivety and good intentions. They overestimated not only themselves but underestimated also the Muslim's greed for political competition and worldly power, changing strategy only when Saddam Hussein invaded Kuwait and declared the end of the Sabah's family rule, celebrating prematurely the end of the Emirate Kuwait. And, in the beginning, purists like the Muslim brotherhood enthusiastically welcomed that step and supported Iraqi troops, although Saddam had been rather a purely secular and, moreover, a brutal ruler. Later on, the Muslim brotherhood developed its own political agenda and emancipated itself further from traditional models of Islamic ruling. Modern Islam or better the political Islam of modernity was born and we can feel the impact also in Senegal and here in the Roman surroundings. Many of our brothers and sisters define themselves as guardians of Islam, but they often neglect their own spiritual and moral efforts, instead, preferring to reprimand others. Consequently, quite a few of our generation are becoming Pharisees, requesting the realization of strict moral rules in the public sphere, but don't omit any possibility to bypass these rules as privileged ones. I think this has nothing to do with Islam, at least our religious upbringing and context did not teach us such an approach. Today you can see that especially the young Muslim generation finds itself within a deep identity crisis, being obsessed by the distinction of halal and haram. They sometimes are unable to deal with the habits of everyday life, although Islam is a religion that aims to ease mundane affairs. That problem is paradoxically the result of the intrusion of modern ideas into traditional Muslim thought. We are coping now with extremely complex identity issues.'

Musa added they did not have any problems with Rossana and she did not have the slightest problems with them. 'She is very tolerant, she allows us even to pray,' said Musa while all were laughing. 'You have no idea how important she is. She doesn't only share delicious food and drinks with us but also supports us with many of the administrative challenges we usually face here in Italy. I think it's due to her patience in working with our dossiers that we all got our residence permits and have access to higher education. She is in a certain way definitely our counsellor-of-law.'

It was only a matter of time before our discussion turned finally to Jana and my suffering. Again, an inspiring debate started as we all had different ideas of love. For the Senegalese, it was irrevocably linked to marriage. Rossana straightway made it clear that she appreciated neither the legal framework nor the romantic version. Her remarks regarding love were rather sober and disillusioned. Shortly afterwards, Musa asked me why I had separated from Jana if she was my great love. I was helplessly exposed to this question, sincerely replying that I did not know it exactly. Perhaps there were too many disappointments, in other words too many unfulfilled expectations in addition to too many misunderstandings. Perhaps another reason was the fact our love had been too much passionate from its inception, full of surrender and dissolution of the self. And consequently, there was too much jealousy from the start, particularly on my part. On the other hand, I could never cause any jealousy in her, since she was my entire universe of the heart. I had only eyes for her. We would have needed, as it had always been my dream, a completely isolated ambiance, a remote area where we could have lived out our deep love in calm and without social life and pressures. Yet our world had not been made for such a luxury of feelings.

They listened carefully to me, probably due in part to my unbridled storytelling and the fact I was sharing very intimate details of my relationship with Jana. Musa argued that romantic love could be a trigger for a lasting togetherness, but the deeper objective of a partnership was something different, namely to build up a family and an economically as well as emotionally stable community. Pure utilitarianism enriched with traditionalism I thought not without a slight contempt. Nevertheless, I kept attentively listening to their views and ideas. I defiantly replied that our modern everyday life suffocated in the long term our sense for beauty, for our real values and longings. Although I had not thought for some days on philosophical topics neither had I read in one of the essays I took with me, among them Sartre's essay on *Baudelaire* and Chestov's *Potestas Clavium*, I explained emphatically that Heidegger's philosophy had always been fascinating me, especially his detailed polemic against the concept of the everydayness which leads in its last consequence to the oblivion of being. It was a state that darkened the world and our surroundings. This brief philosophical digression suddenly bubbled out of me, best describing my then worldview which was undoubtedly a result of my own state of mind. Completely alone in Rome. Isolated. Without Jana. Without friends. Escape or agonizing delay of the impending end of our relationship. I concluded with the statement that love was a sacred affair.

'Only God is sacred,' replied Assane kindly with a smile on his lips.

'You are right,' I told him, 'but God has created love, it is our entire source of happiness,' I remarked.

'It's rather one of many sources of happiness,' Musa interfered in the conversation. 'It's first of all the love of God and the adjustment on our part to His intentions with regard to His creation which is the primary source of happiness for man. All the rest like balance, optimism and kindness towards others follows from that attitude.'

I was speechless for the moment before I went on with the comment that the Christian monks with their aristocratic spiritual attitude had always preferred world-negation to reach happiness and composure. Their stance corresponded in a certain way with the Buddhist approach that the created world could not be but a source of suffering and disenchantment. And undoubtedly because of the shattered romantic illusions of my love for Jana I added, almost annoyed and in a simplistic way, that mankind's history was the best evidence for that conclusion. Not enough, a good example, I continued, had been illustrated by the history of my German compatriots themselves: a high civilization as a pretext for barbarism and annihilation of others, moreover, ephemeral prosperity through war and production of weapons combined with extreme political aggressiveness. The recent history of Germany was nothing else than a crazy frenzy in an age of so-called rationalism and modernity. Apart from that, to believe in peaceful humankind was anyway a naïve kitsch idea and history was always the same somber affair. The best way to cope with the hubris of man and history was to escape, trying to build up a happy even though transient paradise. And this was also the reason that I had always shunned wider political participation, much less political mass events at the university. Now Rossana with her black long wonderful hair and her incredibly beautiful deep brown eyes looked at me and asked kindly if this wonderful love story had helped me to successfully deal with my everyday challenges. ‘Sorry that I have to ask you, but have you been happy with that experience of a so-called passionate love? I only see that you are totally disappointed because you had tasted the fruit of ecstasy, but every fresh and delicious fruit is quickly be consumed,’ she said and immediately assured me with a moving smile that she knew how it would feel.

Finally, we did not agree at all on most of the points concerning love and relationship, but we had at least a weak but common denominator, namely that love had a somehow anagogic, even healing sense. Despite all the discoveries in the field of neurosurgery love would forever remain one of mankind’s mysteries.

During the morning hours, Rossana took my hand and led me upstairs to her stylishly furnished apartment. ‘It’s not worth leaving,’ she said, ‘lay down and relax.’

It was unmistakably an order that I obeyed, overwhelmed by emotional and physical fatigue. She pulled carefully off her magenta-colored high heels. Her feet were extremely slender with red painted toenails, simply exciting. Rossana disrobed further except for her red colored stylish lingerie. As she lay down beside me, I asked her timidly if she would allow me to embrace her. I put my right hand on her brassiere, noticing that she too put her hand over mine. It was a very tender touch, exactly what I longed for. Yet it felt completely surreal.

The price I had to pay for this wholesome distraction was extremely high. As I walked along the endless Via Nomentana the next morning, Jana's picture in combination with a deep feeling of loss and guilty came back to my mind to emotionally inflict me in a tremendous way. I did not even notice the deafening traffic noise around me. The people who rushed to work seemed to me like the disinterested background of my personal tragedy. Rossana apparently had left early in the morning, putting a small paper on the table, with a short note: It was a lovely evening. Take much care! I put all the money I had with me on her nightstand.

The Roman summer heat grew stronger. Full of despair, I took the bus in the direction Roma-Termini. What would Jana think of my moral failure? This was the question that permanently obsessed my mind. My whole body was filled up with pain and unbearable longing for her and I had the impression that the loss of Jana was now definitive and irrevocable. What made my state still worse was the conviction that she would feel totally at ease without me as if the last three years had not occurred at all. Our auspicious love had come to an end and even the sweetest memories would soon begin to fade away. It was just a common illusion of every first and intense love to consider itself as something special. And our love was certainly no exception.

As I went back from the main station towards the apartment near the Piazza Indipendenza the surroundings seemed to isolate me, to bury me alive. I clearly realized that I could not find meaning in existence unless I would entirely exist for a woman. This woman had to be Jana I had lost forever. My desolation could not have been bigger, but Rome's impressive beauty and its chaotic life impulse were both intensive enough to slightly soothe my frightening state of suffering during the upcoming days.

ESCAPISM (PART ONE)

My stay at Turin had built me morally and physically up, despite a persistent fragility on the emotional level. In hindsight, I considered my love for Jana as 'the wonder of my life.' My deep and sincere feelings for her had from the beginning a kind of metaphysical bearing, constantly underpinned by the ease of surreal happiness.

The mixture of study and escaping from the settings of our relationship gave me new hope. Actually, I expected that Turin would open up a new perspective of my life and perhaps an opportunity to fall in love again. But Jana remained far too present in my mind, thus I was completely unable of starting a new love affair. I left Turin after a year-long stay to go definitely back to Germany and to finish my studies. Prior to that, I had the idea to call my beloved Italian friends Luca and Adriana in the Marches. In this guest family, I had deepened my Italian skills several months before I went to Turin. Since then, we had always been keeping in touch and both were equally enthusiastic about the idea that I wanted to pay them a visit.

I looked much forward to driving again on the Autostrada del Sole from Milan via Bologna to Florence and immersing into the Tuscan countryside which abruptly merges at the mountain pass at Sansepolcro into the green-hilly and dreamy Marches. The landscape there is an almost perfect mixture of the more Mediterranean Tuscany and the hillier as well as woodier Umbria in its south. The region is not densely populated and even its capital Ancona, despite a relatively important seaport for the eastern Mediterranean, is rather a cozy city with small and sober Romanesque churches.

I spent much of the summer in a very relaxed manner in the small town of Urbania, in the midst of light green hills and sunburned fields. Adriana's and Luca's daughters had already left home for studying in Milan and Rome, the elder one, Alessandra attended an English intensive course in Cornwall while the younger daughter Nicola was on a trip with her fellow students in the United States. I felt a strong heartache when Luca uttered the sentence 'with her fellow students' during our phone call so that for the rest of the day I had to try hard not to fall back into the consuming longing for Jana.

Luca and Adriana were two down-to-earth persons, full of human warmth and both politically left-wing, mixed with a strong anti-establishment attitude. They shared a very critical stance toward the extreme conservatism of the Catholic Church and Italy's society in general. In Italy's central regions like Tuscany, Emilia and the Marches a political leftist mindset was not unusual particularly among the educated middle-class, representing a moderate and entrepreneurial left far from having totalitarian dreams or repressive inclinations. As expected, those were happy days. We had lengthy dinners with intense discussions about contemporary social and political issues. Apart from the terrible Balkan wars, our nineties had been a time of incredible liberties in central Europe the rising unemployment notwithstanding. Italy had the best soccer league worldwide and the European success stories of AC Milan and Juventus had become a kind of national pride throughout the decade. Yet a critical observer of society like Luca noticed that the European and especially the Italian society was entering a period of cultural decadence due to their excessive consumer-oriented values. During his fervent criticism of the social conditions in his country, I often felt uncomfortable thinking about my political idleness. I was reading few works with as much enthusiasm and continuity as *Les Fleurs du Mal* and my persisting passion for Baudelaire's poetry confirmed in a certain sense my conviction of being implicitly one of the representatives of that second European decadence after the fin de siècle. Nevertheless, I had become acquainted mainly through Pasolini's oeuvre with the ideas of Italy's outstanding communist figures like Gramsci and Berlinguer. But even if their theories sounded always promising, I feared the opinion compulsion and dogmatism within a political group dynamics or student movements, not to mention political parties. However, I began to reflect more intensely on my personal life, especially on the idea of a political commitment that could help to cope better with my private challenges and to get out of my emotional bubble. But was it not already a political commitment per se to get involved with a person, to be permanently at her side, while pondering on the issue, I lost my composure afresh and saw myself and Jana anew drowning in a timeless flood of happiness hormones. In the end, I was convinced that it was a healthy sign of humility not to engage in politics and to pretend to have solutions for the endless problems of humanity since solutions generally made problems worse. The idea gave me peace of mind and I recalled Heideggers' *Letter on humanism*, where he stated that thinking was already a form of acting. And love? Love as a form of politics? A noble idea that enthralled me.

One evening Luca explained to me that the rise of the media tycoon Berlusconi to a political leader was threatening the entire democratic system in Italy. His campaign had triggered a deep socio-political crisis that would certainly end up in a widespread anti-establishment attitude. Berlusconi's success was in his eyes a consequence of the end of the classical left-right polarization which was not limited to Italy alone. It would soon become a global phenomenon. Those lively discussions after dinner and in this cozy atmosphere with the long-bearded Luca as a constant source of conversation, accompanied by his keen indifference vis-à-vis the majority and clerical opinion in the small town, were always inspiring. But what I loved most during that month-long stay were the late evening walks along the northern hillside of Urbania, looking southwards the green valley. It had become a recreating habit to walk one or two hours before sunset between the dense green holm oaks forest until I reached the totally calm clearing of the monastery Santa Chiara. I always sat on a small wooden bench daydreaming, contemplating the quiescent mediaeval center of Urbania in the evening light. While I was staying there for the third time consecutive, taking a healthy distance to all my memories of Jana, I perceived again a monk, leaving the monastery. He had already greeted me the day before with a cordial smile, but this time his salutation was still more intimate, almost as he would recognize an old friend. At the same time, he drew closer to me and said, 'Good evening! It rarely happens, especially in midsummer that people come up here to enjoy this magnificent view.'

I explained to him that in the last days of my stay in Italy I was enjoying nature's tranquility and beauty before I would return to Germany to end my fruitless studies of philosophy. On his skinny but noble feature, an even warmer smile became apparent as if he would have received some good news. 'Oh, precious philosophy, I think you can't go wrong studying philosophy since human beings are not only creatures with a destructive and hubristic will, but also endowed with intellect and capacities of insight. The ability to strive for knowledge is a very distinctive and noble human trait.'

He added a compliment about my fluent and elaborated Italian language skills which flattered me much, but felt good before he continued. 'I can feel your love for this language, isn't it? And love is a beautiful thing. *L'amor che move il sole e l'altre stelle,* you certainly know the last sentence of Dante's great *Divine Comedy.* Mandatory reading for learned theologians and philosophers,' he said with a gentle smile.

I was struck by his statement and had difficulties hiding my tears of emotion. He noticed it and introduced rapidly himself as Giuseppe, proposing to continue our conversation during the next days before sunset, provided it would suit me, adding that he would be curious to know how things went on in Germany. He told me further he had previously lived and studied in Frankfurt for a few years. As responsible for the book inventory in the archdiocese of the greater region, he would be working in the upcoming weeks to update Santa Chiara's huge library.

Two days later I was sitting with this anachronistic man in his Franciscan monk robe on the same bench in the peaceable sunset light. During that second meeting, I was still more impressed by Giuseppe who confirmed my feeling that I was speaking with an exceptional personality the longer our talk lasted. He never lost his humble voice while he told me about his doctoral thesis he had written at the elitist theological institute of Sankt Georgien where I had grown up nearby. I could not believe it. And although we were speaking almost the entire evening Italian, from time to time his excellent knowledge of German flashed. How elegantly he pronounced the odd German words Arbeitsbeschaffungsmaßnahme or Aschenbecher which he deemed extremely beautiful, explaining to me that he admired the putting together of all nouns to get one substantive and to avoid complicated genitives.

There was no further getting to know each other necessary. We had an informal and warm conversation from the beginning. He asked me how I had managed to stay for one year in Italy and why did I choose to study philosophy abroad since Germany was together with Greece the cradle of philosophical thought. I told him in detail it had been a combination of reasons, first of all, due to my deep love for this country and secondly due to the possibility to get a fellowship from the University of Turin which was a partner university of Frankfurt. It was strange that he immediately noticed it was only half part of the story. So, I quickly added that one of the reasons was also the yearning memories of the long summer holidays I had spent with my great love Jana in her father's vacation house in the south of Italy. There was no reluctance on my part concerning the revealing of these intimacies because he radiated so much trustworthiness and human warmth from the very first moment we met.

'And what is your great love doing now?' he asked gently.

He seemed slightly disappointed as he heard that I did not know it and that we had lost sight of each other. With a touch of melancholy, he said:

'My impression is you haven't yet overcome your deep-seated disappointment that stemmed from the loss of your great love. It's likely that this love had suspended all the disenchantment regarding our contemporary age of cold rationality. Nothing against rationality, but it's bereft of meaning when there is nothing above or behind a rational pattern and when it becomes totally hypostatized, as the sole binding truth.' He resumed after a short silence. 'With the setting-in of your love story the entire world around you had been starting probably to transform its face. Earthly existence was all of a sudden full of meaning and beauty, far beyond the ordinary acquainted measure, not unlike a metaphysical shock underpinned with sensual revelation. And there is indeed no meaning without the perception of beauty, of harmony, and I presume to say that the beauty of the world represented the extended mirror of your love's beauty and your beloved partner.'

Again, there was a short break in our conversation. I did not comment on his interpretation, but I was surprised how much his description matched my then situation. Motionless I looked into the distant landscape, entranced by the evening light.

'And you have searched here in Italy for the remnants of

your happiness, perhaps you were full of hope to reestablish it through memories? You are struggling to maintain your emotional balance, isn't it?' he asked cautiously.

'Right,' I agreed with a faint voice.

'And you are perhaps disillusioned by the fact that philosophy and the spiritual life both can never convey to you this intense meaning of life you experienced during the time you had with your greatest love.'

'Her name is Jana,' I told him quickly as if I were afraid to pronounce this word.

'And now not even philosophy and literature can help you to give your life a real meaning back. I apologize my dear friend, but it reminds me of Romeo's frustration in view to his unfulfilled love and the impossibility to find comfort elsewhere. You might remember Shakespeare's verse: *Hang up philosophy! Unless philosophy can make a Juliet, displant a town, reverse a prince's doom, it helps not, it prevails not. Talk no more!*'

For a moment I was speechless, especially by the circumstance that this impressive man who did not really know me was able to read in my mind like in an open book. He added with his calm and generous voice that I should not be worried and in the end, my soul would become stronger and more mature by this painful experience which must be considered as part of my destiny.

'The proverb *Time heals all wounds* is fortunately not only a stereotype,' he continued our talk. 'Don' think that due to my seemingly withdrawn life I wouldn't know about passion and love. We are all created beings, full of longings as a result of our imperfection and the limits of our earthly existence.'

It was time to leave for both of us since the sun had already set. Luca and Adriana were waiting for me. They had invited some friends for dinner. But that was not the main reason for I was in a good mood, I was particularly looking forward to meeting Giuseppe the next day at the same time on that bench again as we had agreed.

During the following days, we always met in the late afternoon in front of the Santa Chiara monastery for Capuchin nuns and he had asked the chief nun if he could invite a friend into the monastery's quiet garden, a not less anachronistic place than Giuseppe's personality itself. While he was continuing his speech, I was fully aware of the privilege and the outstanding moments I spent with him. Giuseppe confirmed to me that he had known that intensity of passion and he had feared as a young man to become addicted to this feeling. 'I had often the impression that I would only love for the sake of love itself. Beauty attracted me like cocaine – we both smiled when he uttered the sentence – and I had never been with the same girl for long. To avoid misunderstandings: I wasn't a Don Juan, since my upbringing was too conservative and therefore, I was rather afraid of erotic attraction. But I fell in love too often which caused me pain and suffering. The studies of theology and philosophy would certainly change my mind, at least I hoped that. Of course, it took its time until I was really decided to dedicate my life to monasticism and in a certain way to a spiritual retreat. In Frankfurt, at the Jesuits of Sankt Georgien, I had learned so many important things. It was in that lively and modern city I deepened the way of our famous brother Bonaventura and his spiritual tenets were undoubtedly the trigger for my final orientation, although he had lived some seven hundred years before. Among my friends, not to say family members, no one took me seriously. Yet, there I started the real *itinerarium in mentis deum*, a difficult attempt in the aftermath of the rebellious social climate of the late sixties. Today I have to admit that it was, to put it bluntly, a kind of conservative rebellion mixed with spiritual dandyism. Going against the mainstream and the establishment had always attracted me, from the time of my late adolescence. I feared becoming a slave of life's conventional claims, in other words, to become a decent consumer and to build a house, to raise children and so forth. Perhaps I think different today, but I know it's too late now and things are not reversible at all. It is good to keep attached to one's principles also there may be moments where they are doubtful and contrary to the contemporary mindset.'

While he was telling me all these intimacies of his life, I had the strong impression that an ally in spirit was opening his heart to me. He replied without hesitation to my inquisitive question why he had not become an intellectual engagé or a person committed to politics, expounding that what he was doing was undoubtedly a commitment to his community, to his brothers and sisters in spirit. So, it could be quite considered as a political stance. Life as a monk required, he continued, a certain clear-cut political attitude albeit it differs a great deal from the present-day understanding of political participation and had lost in our contemporary context all its appeal. Politics today was linked to the pursuit of power and the aim to offer people a model to satisfy their individual needs. Or it was characterized by pure opposition, the reverse of the medal which identified politics with power. 'Politics, I think, mainly means to serve other people and the community you live within instead of pretending to have the wisdom and tools to guide them. Of course, it's easier for us, monks of the Franciscan order or convinced Christians to serve others because we have a timeless framework or an anachronistic dogma to which we surrender, although the church constantly tries to meet the requirements of the zeitgeist. This is a wrong strategy in my eyes and will harm in the midterm the Church's authenticity and its spirituality as well. The very sense of spirituality is to understand that we've been all thrown into time and our stay here on earth is short. Therefore, our claims for power and perfection certainly turn out to be senseless vanities. The only way to perfection is sincere humility, prayer.'

Giuseppe's serene explanations made me enthusiastic

for thinking and philosophizing as I had not experienced for a long time thus, I started to tell Giuseppe about my wonderful time in Turin. I told him about my studies on late middle age literature with Giacomo Cordani and my research on Heidegger's late philosophy with the famous Gian Piero Cavagliano and how his celebrity prompted overcrowded auditoriums totally lacking a philosophical ambience.

I continued to disclose details of my relationship in a rush of passion, not without vanity, yet I was totally aware that fate had been gracious to me. Or how could I have better described the feeling of happiness with which I was walking nearly every evening tightly embraced with Jana through the calm streets of the suburb where she lived. There was no doubt that I had been a chosen young man beside a diva, chosen to be her first real love the way she had been herself my first real love and so my entire life had been subsequently drowning for three years in a flood of happy moments. In the same breath, I told him that it had been almost impossible for me to reorganize my life after the end of our love affair. It was a wonder, I stressed, that I had not given up my studies and I concluded that at the end of the day it had been an enormous privilege to live and study in Italy since the stay had undoubtedly changed my mindset and identity. But I also emphasized that I did not consider myself a prospective philosopher, not to say an intellectual, because I was not keen at all to attend debates or ethereal talks. He immediately interfered that it did not matter to depend on clichés as how an intellectual must live; the essential was to find a climate, a surrounding which would favor the unfolding of thought and spiritual activity. The present-day intellectual was a relatively new invention of mass communication in his eyes so that a philosopher should generally not be reduced to a figure of a well-briefed newspaper reader, constantly participating in public discussions to comment on political events. And with an unmistakable emphasis, he added, 'You should be aware that the deeper your thoughts are, the lesser is the probability to have potential interlocutors. Especially in our modern-day context with its subaltern chats, it's most important to understand that deep thinking and a critical analysis do not depend on discursive quantity. In this age of hypostasis of quantity quality alone can make the difference. And first of all, today quality ought to remain unnoticed. In other words, imperceptibility should not be a negative indicator of quality in the realm of thought.'

Giuseppe's words assumed the sound of a severe sermon to encourage my intellectual activities. But I asked him what he had meant by spiritual activity to understand better the difference between intellectual and spiritual. He made from the onset of the following debate clear that all intellectual activity would remain subaltern in comparison to spiritual activity. 'Spirituality always focuses on our creation's origin, the source of existence and only there we are able to find the true meaning of life. You can train your mind or intellectual skills, reading, for example, Descartes, Spinoza or Kant, and consequently, better understand the history of philosophy, but you can also delve into Bonaventure's works which will be a totally different thing. His approach goes so much further than all philosophy because it dissolves the contradiction of thoughts and deeds and therefore the fragmentation of our personality. Real spiritual activity usually claims to bring all elements of life, the mind and the body in one harmonious unity. Therefore, spirituality must directly come from the acknowledgement of God's existence as the source of creation. Ideally, your actions need to reflect your thoughts, without the slightest dissociation. That's the meaning of spiritual life and I know it sounds pretentious in today's context. Here, the great Muslim thinker al-Ghazali can be seen as an outstanding example. In the beginning, he was a very orthodox scholar who taught Islamic jurisprudence in Nishapur, today's Iran, towards the end of the eleventh century. Later on, he abandoned his academic positions and public life, dedicating himself exclusively to meditation and to the search for truth. His book the *Revival of the Religious Sciences* is a masterpiece with regard to the reconciliation of orthodoxy and the way to perfection of God-consciousness on an individual level, called Ihsan by Muslims. But after trying to read the preface to the voluminous work and learning Arabic, I gave up after two years. Moreover, I had to face unfriendly critics from the Church's administrative hierarchy. In their eyes, I had been dealing too extensively with Muslim thought, although it was a Franciscan tradition since Francis of Assisi met with the Muslim ruler al-Malik al Kamil.'

It was not at all clear to me why this extremely smart and charismatic man had withdrawn from this world. I tried to find it out since, like him, I was longing for harmony and peace of mind. Now it was my turn and I told him that I was not able to get along with the present-day setting characterized by a society in permanent turmoil and motion. The good manners we had been taught during our upbringing were slowly transforming into monstrous hypocrisy, disguising our subtle warfare on the individual level. Despite our wealthy and relatively equitable societies, mankind, so I concluded generalizing, was unfit to overcome its primitive principle of Darwinism or in other words its eternal fight due to social jealousy. Former rivalries between social classes had been in my eyes effectively replaced by rivalries between individuals, at least in the context of the so-called emancipated societies in the West. We were in a permanent need of yielding new and particular lifestyles in order to maintain a consumer-oriented dynamism without asking for its deeper meaning. But this kind of particularism was pure conformism and had nothing in common with liberty. And I asked Giuseppe what to do if one had no will and not the natural disposition to assimilate himself to this paradox machinery which fosters competition, but at the same time was holding tight to socio-mania and opportunism? Was my desire to avoid masses and people an unmistakable sign of misanthropy? Was my attitude perhaps unsocial and inequitable vis-à-vis society? Or was I rather unsocial because I was a social person within a profoundly unsocial society? I had no idea at all.

'These are issues of mankind's nature in general and if we take a look upon man's history there are indeed no indications to be optimistic. That's the reason for our moderate seclusion from the rest of society because we are bound to unrestricted solidarity, flowing directly from the acknowledgement of God's existence and certain patterns which cannot be changed within the framework of our created existence. And such solidarity is not be found in wider social constructs due to the lack of absolute principles which could be able to socially unify us, instead, our contemporary model of society and politics in the West has been based on competitive political ideas. This modern idea is generally sold to us as the pluralistic version of political reality, but this approach is completely devoid of metaphysical principles, not to say of a notion of truth. All these products are the outcome of intellectual speculation on a purely subjective level and of the pseudo-faith that man's will, wishes and deeds are sovereign. Here, the difference between intellectual and spiritual is evident. Spirituality must be committed to truth or higher principles that are in a certain sense open to interpretation but can never be changed in their essence.'

I objected that our present age did not suit such an outdated approach to reality and social contexts.

'I'm afraid you are right. Today's creed in materialism and individual emancipation, regardless of one's political orientation, is continuously eradicating the traditions of true spirituality. It became clear for me during the post-68-period at the beginning of the seventies. I had the feeling that we were at a point to slide irreversibly into a period of materialistic anarchy which confirmed my choice to study theology and later on joining the Franciscan order.'

Giuseppe's voice became more and more a friend's voice, although we had only known each other for a few days.

When I came back shortly after sunset into the Via Torquato Piccini I disclosed most of the details of our previous conversation. I noticed that Luca developed sympathy for Giuseppe while I was revealing him particulars of my in-depth talk with the Franciscan monk, despite his general antipathy against the institution of the church. Luca was in a certain way the perfect embodiment of a north Italian leftist, holding an important position within the state's administration in the neighboring municipality of Sant'Angelo in Vado which made him a well-off bourgeois. He took a fervent ecological-socialist stance as it was widespread in Italy's leftist strongholds. Yet his character was too independent to get involved in party politics, his political mantra was rather individual or civil society resistance.

I loved those moments when we spent the entire night discussing until the upcoming dawn in the spacious kitchen of that typical Italian apartment in a well-maintained building of the late Renaissance. He kept rubbing his long beard and was listening attentively to me, meanwhile stirring thoughtfully a new variation of Pasta sauce. Usually, we waited for his wife who came back late from her work as a cook in a nearby restaurant, so we always had dinner around midnight which was a good time on those hot summer days. The ambiance helped me to forget Jana for hours sometimes. But whenever Luca was revealing, during the long and almost contemplative preparations for dinner, the secrets of the different manners of Italian cooking and the diversity of Italian types of pasta, I began to dream of bragging to her with such knowledge. While listening to him, I regularly succumbed to long fantasies about a conciliatory meeting with Jana after my return to Germany. I dreamt of preparing her the simplest but most delicious variations of pasta and of telling her about the history of the former royal Neapolitan Pasta di Gragnano with its short and long kind of types of pasta. And when we would sit together, sharing a delicious meal and a fruity red wine, she would surely fall in love again with me the same unconditional way she had always loved me throughout our three years relationship. It came as a relief when Luca asked me to take a stand regarding a political or social problem so that I was obliged to interrupt these dreamy meditations.

After these long dinners, I was not able to fall asleep immediately due to the coffee we still drank late at night and so I made it a habit of reading Tolstoy's *Anna Karenina*. A perfect setting for silent dawn reading, although the book's intrigues, especially the upcoming adultery, were causing anxiety and despair in me. I finished my reading with the chirping of the birds that lulled me into a restless sleep.

The end of my stay in Urbania also meant the end of my year-long stay in Italy. My last and long conversation with Giuseppe was characterized by warmth and inspiration. I told him I had started reading Tolstoy which made him not only extremely curious but showed suddenly his comprehensive knowledge in matters of literature. Thus, the subsequent discussion made unmistakably clear that he was not only a real librarian, apart from being a Franciscan, but also a great expert on Russian authors. Tolstoy rapidly became the issue of an inspiring talk and Giuseppe expounded why he considered the Russian writer to be one of the most outstanding novelists of the world's literature. In the same breath, he emphasized that no other novelist had described with such an esthetical strength the meaning of repentance. All of Tolstoy's books were extraordinarily intense, especially his late works exclusively revolving around questions of human destiny and eschatology. He added that one could directly experience Ivan Ilyich's hopeless sufferings and the role of the impending death as a crystallizer of all our deeds by a mindful reading. Giuseppe affirmed that reading Tolstoy was a moral shock therapy since no one could remain the same person after a serious devotion to his masterpieces. And in his eyes, the Ukrainian philosopher Shestov was right claiming that Tolstoy was, in reality, a fervent preacher, a trait which came to the fore especially in his radical late works like the *Kreutzer Sonata.* This oeuvre was of utmost interest for one who would try to lead a pious life, yet Tolstoy's position in the *Kreutzer Sonata* had long ago lost its meaning, particularly within the context of our emancipatory modernity. In the end, he focused on morally doing good without exception. What was most interesting about Shestov's in-depth analysis of Tolstoy's preaching was his statement that it was not enough to do good, one had to go beyond the principle of good and seek God. Giuseppe melancholically remained silent for a moment. After a short while he sighed softly and wondered how one could live without having read Tolstoy, Dostoyevsky and Shestov.

It was a cloudy and muggy evening after a very hot summer day and from the mountains in the south, belonging already to Umbria, dark clouds announced an impending thunderstorm. The ambiance during our last evening was quieter than usual, the swallows flew low and chirped excitedly. I resumed the conversation, asking him what he meant with the statement that the content of the *Kreutzer Sonata* was no longer of interest regarding our modern or a rather contemporary mindset?

'Sexuality has lost its sacred dimension,' he said thoughtfully. 'It might sound strange but it has lost its erotism and here in Italy sexual activity has turned into a fitness program. In our busy world in constant motion, there are only a few people who do not have a lover or an affair. In the realm of erotic stimulants, almost everyone has become replaceable. But perhaps the extension of our lifespan due to progress in science and healthcare urges us from time to time to search for new stimulations, new adventures and sexual relations. I understand that today one has many periods of life, with different partners. It is only a too human desire, yet it divests sexuality of its intrinsic beauty and higher aim, namely to be the source of total happiness and life.'

Giuseppe smiled tenderly and continued, 'I shouldn't be so severe with Italy. It will be more or less the same in all other modern and so-called enlightened societies. Sexuality has been drawn into the consumption trap. Today, most things are perceived as an object of consumerism according to the prevailing weltanschauung that is purely utilitarian. And it is only all too obvious that this kind of pseudo-doctrine of salvation penetrates the interpersonal relationship as well. You see, I am starting to preach, the same what Shestov said about the late Tolstoy, and I know that I am sometimes too harsh, we should never exaggerate our moralizing attitude leading to moral tyranny nor would it fit with Franciscan spirituality that is dominated by forbearance and comprehension. And if one is well-versed in the history of the church, he knows only too well that the clergy is least suitable to launch a moral discourse even though it should be its main task. But clerics are only humans too, we should not expect perfection. Apart from the extreme condemnation of sexual intercourse which is not insignificant for a monk the figure of Pozdnyschev is one of the most interesting in world literature. He is a distinct anachronistic character and his pure personal experiences made him a non-conformist regarding public opinion. As the pardoned murderer of his wife and with his extravagant persuasions he had no choice but to be a misfit within his social context. Yet his painful existential crisis led him to a deeper insight than that of his average contemporaries and he is always ready to defend his knowledge and intellectual stance. Pozdnyschev's bearing should be considered exemplary for a critical mind today. The same can be said of Shestov, whose *Potestas Clavium* is still inspiring in our time with its detailed polemic, not against reason, but against the excesses of present-day rationalism and its unyielding pride. It has long since replaced humility and healthy modesty.'

After another pause for thought, looking in silence at the dark clouds in the distance, he resumed his speech, 'But for most of modern mankind, these words are no longer meaningful, or at best only of historical importance. Paradoxically, in a certain way, the need for seclusion has perhaps never been so relevant as in our present age characterized by pure entertainment and expediency. And to be honest, I do not suppose that a society based on the perfect intertwining of consumer totalitarianism and entertainment can still be considered as a human society. I think we are no longer able to uphold the inflationary talk of humanism. As a specialist of Heidegger's philosophy, you know better what I mean since he considered the term humanism as unsuitable to describe the essence of man.'

We sat in silence for a good while then he said in an amused voice, 'Since you are young, you might think that we Franciscans are the perfect fun killers, but is it really desirable to be addicted to entertainment or to spend money on subaltern items? Happiness through consumerism is a totally ephemeral state of mind. An illusion to maintain the balances of the masses and to assure social peace. Envy is a tolerable by-product here and the greed for consumption is sold as individualism and self-realization. We are living in a new phase in the history of political ideas, namely the creation of an anti-political ideology. I am convinced that the monstrous advertising machinery will drown us sooner or later, it is just the beginning of a so far unknown extent of illusions, a dictatorship of unreal pictures. I know, my dear friend, now I am preaching like the late Savonarola against the Medici and their tainted era in Florence. Instead, one should rather be thankful for the achievements of our time with its human rights, affording me to criticize harshly our epoch, without running the risk to be publicly burnt alive to death which was unavoidably Savonarola's fate. You see,' he said laughing, 'it suits me to live in seclusion, so I disturb neither the public opinion nor the establishment. This is more of a task for intellectuals and philosophers, participating in talk shows and trying to correct our wrong outlook on life. I prefer the companionship of my books, the devotion to God and to care for my brothers and sisters in the archdiocese. It's finally a question of humility and humility cannot be mixed up with political or public ambitions. This, in turn, would mean that I could offer others a solution-oriented philosophy, an attitude that is undoubtedly intellectual or could be better described as intellectual pride which has been one of the most challenging problems within the history of thought. Our history of philosophy as you know better is very colorful but fortunately the result of fallible human beings. Therefore, we should neither apotheosize individual ideas nor hypostatize present-day rationalism with its seductive energies of self-righteousness and over-pragmatic utilitarianism. I consider these phenomena as the worst plight of our existence and it is completely opposed to our Franciscan spirit which is best reflected in Saint Francisco's work *Cantico delle Creature* where nature is represented as the most positive reflection of God's creation. The whole poem is a homage to creation's beauty and the incomparable beauty of its Creator.'

With enthusiasm, he remarked that the Franciscan order despite its strict abstinence refers to nature's harmony as the source of insight, hence Franciscans were all great esthetes. And with an undertone of serene resignation, he stated that we could hardly find sense in life without perceiving beauty everywhere, but the recognition and the anagogical sense of beauty had long been replaced by Cartesian rationalism with its unmistakable tendency to disintegrate a holistic vision of creation. Since then, our concept of reality had been more and more reduced to simple fragments and unhealthy material growth. This historical process reflects, as Heidegger had diagnosed almost half a century before, a form of nihilism as a remnant of occidental metaphysics itself. It was certainly the peak of cynicism and despair of man's history. Giuseppe recommended that I read Shestov, one of the most independent intellectuals within the history of thought. A philosopher who fiercely polemicized against the spirit of the fin-de-siècle. Shestov saw in the overemphasizing of rationalism and dull empiricism the biggest threats for human awareness. Along with Nietzsche, he was the first thinker predicting that modern rationalism and science would become objects of meaningless adoration. The salient results of this truly anti-intellectual attitude, as Giuseppe named it, were two world wars with their incommensurable human disasters. And it followed as if this wasn't enough, the development of a so-called advanced technology that was able to extinguish mankind.

Slowly and consciously, he continued his philosophical reflections, emphasizing that thanks to our materialistic achievements at least in most parts of the Western world man were able to live peacefully and to be satisfied with his integration into the steady flow of productivity and consumerism. Yet he wondered if this way of life could be considered as sensible. What we called until recently rational had harmed in a historically incomparable way not so much our natural, but, worse, our mental environment. If the natural environment was suffering, it was simply the outcome of our fragmented awareness, creating enormous dissonances within the pattern of God's creation. Today, mankind would invent other rational approaches in order to cure these aberrations. And although this endless process was generally labeled as progress, it was but a vicious circle.

Despite his extremely critical remarks, Giuseppe was full of serenity. 'And who can dare to speak of progress when our patterns of mindset are bound to superficialities and concepts. They are deeply harming our psychology as the fragility of most of the modern people living in the urban areas clearly proves. The materialistic achievements of our epoch do not only dazzle us but imply a further growth of our self-adoration, thus opening the doors for continuous self-destruction. So, the best sign of our fellow man's confusion is his longing for a strong state which cares for everyone and everything, with ever more detailed laws and regulations. But all these requirements of legal guidelines are to my mind the outcome of mankind's deeper disorientation.'

His speech took an unexpected turn when he suddenly added that he was living very well here in the midst of the Abruzzi foothills, a landscape with its small villages and which had been undergone a more natural change in the course of time. The society's transformation in this region of Italy had been more adapted to the requirements of its natural and cultural environment. There was a slower transition to consumerism here. He reiterated unmistakably that his philosophical attitude was characterized by a decisive disillusionment towards all forms of social utopia. In the Middle Ages, as he elucidated, there was always a social or familial reason to become a monk. Instead, a monk's life today was a remnant of a spiritual ideal and therefore in a certain sense much more idealist than during the climax of institutionalized Christian culture in medieval Europe.

'Of course, dear friend, I must admit that I am most probably a very weak creature not made for Darwinian struggle or to pursue social status. Monasticism is a kind of resignation in the face of man's unquenchable ambitions, a retreat from the manifold ideas an individual can bring forth in order to save mankind. But at the same time, I have to concede that this lifestyle is perhaps a sweet illusion and can therefore be considered as the opposite of reality as well. But who could still say what reality essentially is? Do we still have an idea about reality? And if there were no God and no source of existence, who could dare to speak of reality at all? Well, my friend, in one word, my life here in the borderland between Umbria and the Marche is pure escapism from modern society's event rush.'

He looked at me as if I were a trustworthy old friend, placing his right hand on my left shoulder and added, 'Our young and upcoming philosopher, what will you do with your painful remembrance of your beloved Jana? Is there perhaps the chance to revive your relationship?'

'I think it's excluded! Things went wrong and with hindsight, we had burned the resources of our deep love too quickly. However, I can't stand the thought that one day she will have the same feelings for someone else since I was totally convinced that we had been meant for each other.'

'I believe I can fully understand you. I apologize dear friend, but this romantic relationship seems to me like a political utopia, initially everything is promising, everything is possible, but the longer you must adapt to social reality the more difficult the constellation becomes. The painful thing is that you are still very jealous which means you are still full of love for her.'

'And in a certain sense, your remarks on monasticism made it totally clear for me that my year in Italy was nothing but escapism too from a painful reality, namely that our love has definitely come to an end. At the outset, I hoped that Italy's beauty, the majesty of its landscape you spoke about, would not only comfort me but also be an appropriate remedy for my mind. However, most of the beautiful places reminded me of Jana's beauty and of my addiction to her. Nevertheless, the fact of her physical absence was soothing my mind so far that I was able to pursue at least my studies and to focus a bit on new things like Italian literature. But to be honest, I would never claim to study literature or philosophy in order to become a scholar. I would have nothing to say, that's for sure. I think my studies have been only entertainment or distraction, in one word, just escapism. Simply to escape from the weltschmerz, from lovesickness.'

Giuseppe smiled indulgently and said:

'Well, there are different forms to assuage our existential suffering, normally through alcohol, excessive sexual activity or entertainments of subaltern character. But you use high literature to distract yourself and to escape reality. Perhaps you are closer to reality than you think in reading Dante, Tolstoy and all the usual suspects of world literature. And I can't see why reading shouldn't be a cure or a mental sedative. The more you understand reality, the quieter you become and the more you live in peace with yourself and your surroundings. It's almost Franciscan spirituality. The soul harmonizes with the beauty of nature. But Franciscans don't need reading to struggle for this state of mind, they need prayer. Constant prayer. Because without prayer existence is meaningless, my friend. Life had taught me this irrevocable certainty and that's why I became a Franciscan.'

Since it was already getting dark, it was time to say goodbye. And it would be a definite goodbye. I wanted to leave Urbania the very next morning. Giuseppe seemed to me like an epiphany and the encounters with him in the past few days filled me up with incredible strength and serenity. He told me that he too had to go back in order to join the vesper service, adding that I knew now where I could find him and insisted whenever I would come back, I was obliged to visit him. Stretching out both of his hands, he tenderly took my right hand and told me after a while that my love for Jana was full of meaning, but first, time had to go by to understand better. 'Appreciate your time with Jana as a gift, as pure mercy of God. A deep love has much in common with fervent prayer. Both are keys to realizing the beauty of existence. Take so much care my inspiring friend.'

I was moved to tears and gave him a strong hug. He smiled warm-heartedly when he saw tears running down my cheeks. Giuseppe walked away, but turned around again and waved to me one last time. While descending the trodden path through the walnut trees, his farewell sentence was constantly hammering into my mind. Monastic and spiritual aristocracy, I thought. A timeless and Dantean anachronism, like Giuseppe's entire physical appearance itself and with his thin figure which could be noticed even in the simple Franciscan outfit he was akin to an elegant line in the landscape.

I stayed awake for a long time that night. It was now the moment to summarize my stay in Italy. I came there with the intention of studying German philosophy with the famous Gian Piero Cavagliano, but I finally ended up in the small seminar on Italian literature by Gianluca Cordani. And that intense conversation with Giuseppe during the last days of my time in Italy confirmed to me there was no conventional way to gain knowledge. Yet as I had told him, at the end of the day, studying signified only a welcoming distraction for me since I was still completely absorbed by morbid sentimentalism and pathologic longing for Jana's body and soul. Fragments of images were still coming into my mind. Jana's underwear scattered on the floor, the elegant bathrobe in front of the shower stall; and again, the beauty of her long black hairs and her dark noble eyes of an Arabian princess, as I often had called her, although she had never been happy with that designation.

I should ponder on Giuseppe's impressive parable of prayer and love for a very long time. Love and prayer, both seemed to me as the noblest forms of escapism, with the difference that prayer would not entail suffering like love. It was clear to me that love as an escapist alternative would be off the table for the time being. So, I had no other choice than to focus on reading as suitable means of avoiding a clash with daily reality. Since I was not keen to become a professor or a teacher, there was no need to share my insights through lectures or public debates with others. Reading would be pure joy, in short, deluxe-reading, without the slightest need for conventional interpretation. But it was sure that my particular form of escapism would not be those of a monk, at best it would be a semi-urban or paradox monasticism. In addition, monasticism without prayer.

SOLILOQUY (PART ONE)

I left the Via Foligno in Turin with my full packed Volkswagen and turned right at the first crossroads at Corso Lombardia towards the Novara Milan highway. Waiting at the traffic light, I looked to my right at Café Fiore where I had spent so many mornings reading soccer match reports in sports tabloids. The anaesthetizing effects of delving into Italy's traditional sports newspapers like the Gazzetta dello Sport, the Corriere dello Sport and Turin's Tuttosport had always been astounding. I passed hours therein, especially Saturday and Sunday mornings, studying meticulously almost all articles about the most renowned Italian football clubs like Juventus, Milan and Inter and furthermore discussing with the young talkative barkeeper Nino the newspaper's club alignments. It became evident that the Gazzetta, edited in Milan, had more sympathy for the AC Milan. Tuttosport, edited in Turin, was the sport daily for Italy's most successful soccer club Juventus, and with the Corriere from Rome also the capital's traditional club AS had its own voice. Instead of thoroughly reading the cultural and political pages of the conservative-intellectual Corriere della Sera, which every advanced student of philosophy would surely have done, I studied the detailed forecast of the impending Sunday matches. At a certain point, I stopped counting how many latte macchiatos I had ordered from Nino before noon because they were my constant physical sedative during my analyses and I comforted myself from time to time by saying that I was at least a militant non-smoker. What a nice time in the end despite the loneliness and suffering. Ciao Nino and take care I thought sadly.

Before I abandoned Turin, I had bid a warm farewell to my homeowners, a wealthy couple in their middle age who had been kind enough to rent this furnished apartment on two levels to me. It was perfectly integrated into their detached villa, yet attractively located in the midst of the lively neighborhood of Borgo Vittoria in Turin's north. They had adopted a boy from Peru who was carefully raised by his step-parents as I had noticed in the course of time. I had contacted them by phone in early December due to my inability to endure any longer the atmosphere of my first lodging, the Villa San Gregorio which was a well-organized boarding home for students in the midst of Turin's beautiful southern hills. My first stay had been brokered by my professor of Italian literature at the University of Frankfurt, Paola, since she was the first to have the idea that I could continue my studies in Italy. She had felt from the outset of our first meeting in a seminar that the topic bored me very much: the preoccupation with the literary avant-garde of Italy around its core author Eduardo Sanguinetti. Never should I feel later on that words and texts could be so far from reality and sensuality, completely alienated from their destiny. At least, that had been my instinctive reaction, although this kind of attitude was certainly due to a lack of intellectual sensibility on my part. But Paola was kind, sharing my exaggerated veneration for the freethinker Pasolini; moreover, she was able to deal with my rebellious solitude, obviously reflected in my shyness and self-imposed protectionism.

It was thanks to a generous offer from the University of Turin and the department of literature that I could stay there for an entire academic year. Fortunately, this study stay had not been organized by an official academic exchange program. I had wanted it that way in order to feel freer and not to be squeezed into a collective to-do schedule. Thus, it had not lasted too long before I started to feel increasingly uncomfortable with regard to the daily rituals and the rigorous organization within the Villa San Gregorio. I was struggling with the prescribed times for eating and obligatory gatherings as well as with a kind of curfew that prevented the students to have access to the building after ten o'clock in the evening. To go to a concert by the famous Eros Ramazzotti in Milan I had to seek a special permit to get the key for the main door because I would not come back before two o'clock in the morning. However, that exemption provided me with a stigma for the rest of my stay: From then on, I was considered as someone who disregarded the common rules. The concert itself was torture for me since I was standing in the midst of ten thousand Italians and, due to the sweetest memories of the summers I had spent with Jana, constantly being overwhelmed by tears. The remembrances were triggered by key songs we had listened to on the radio during our summer holiday in her father's Mediterranean vacation house. It filled me with resentment that the students in Villa San Gregorio thought I would be privileged, instead, I was suffering and struggling against the most stupid conventions and discipline. But at the same time, I was fully aware it was an unfair judgement. Almost all students were in reality extremely kind and non-conventional, although most of them stemmed from relatively well-off and conservative families. They usually studied engineering which promised wealth and status. Despite having the right to stay there an entire academic year, my desire to be independent gained the upper hand already at the beginning of December. I was lucky that the first appointment I had in order to search for a new dwelling was immediately successful. Even though I was dressed provocatively casual with my black leather jacket over my preferred close-fitting green shirt, biker boots and my beloved blue knitted cap, they immediately assured me to give me the apartment until next summer just as I had wished. They offered me to pay rent only from January on and to move in instantly if I already needed lodging for December. On the following day, I signed the contract and received promptly the keys. A new feeling of freedom seized me.

Now, I was able to leave the Villa San Gregorio as soon as possible. And here again, my cowardice knew no limits at all. Instead of saying goodbye to the rector Michele, an extremely lenient clergy, or to say adieu to my French acquaintance Hugo and the film buffs Antonio and Matteo with whom I went several times to the arthouse cinema in the Mole Antonelliana, I dragged clandestinely all my belongings shortly after midnight into my old Golf and left the facility a few minutes after the doorman had opened the main gate around five o'clock in the morning. At the end of the day, I felt too humiliated to start a farewell conversation, I felt too fragile and too disoriented, because at that time the yearning arose to return home, to go to Jana's apartment, ringing the doorbell and fervently beseeching her to come back to me and to be with me again. I knew that these were transient illusions, triggered by a badly wounded heart and that I needed solitude, giving to my heart rest and peace. Avoiding too many social contacts was now the most important thing and the new apartment seemed to be the ideal place to realize this strategy of emotional recovery.

Opposite the Café Fiore, I glimpsed again the phone box at the corner Corso Lombardia. I did not count how often I went in and dialed Jana's number, just to hang immediately up the phone since I was completely aware I could have never endured her news. It would have been a nightmare and jealousy would certainly have aroused to a level that had harmed again my mental balance. To imagine her walking with her new lover through the tranquil streets of the neighborhood where she lived was an absolute anathema for me. These short but extremely powerful emotional relapses ended mostly up with long phone conversations I had either with my friend Mirko or Olaf. Both were always able to build me up and fill me with new energy. After having reached again a certain composure, I regularly continued my late evening strolls in Turin's northern periphery with its extensive green areas. There was soothing silence there which became more and more my appreciated companion in the night. And the peripheral setting was the kind of urban structure that attracted me most. It was there I found the air to breathe and space to move. Hence the apartment in Via Foligno was the perfect point of attachment between the city and the outskirts that opened up to nature. During the day one could see the nearby Alps and I often went to the natural preserve of La Mandria where I was lying within an endless meadow, skimming superficially through the many books I had taken with me, interrupted by long reminiscences of wonderful moments with Jana. Moreover, the sublimation of my sufferings needed not only intellectual food but also physical activity. My reading and thought meanderings were steadily accompanied by physical training, hundreds of sit-ups and push-ups and since I ate only two times a day and had no fat at all, my muscles were growing quickly. It was undoubtedly a narcissistic paranoia that ought to prepare me for an esthetical war against Jana and her potential new partner, in case I would meet them sooner or later in New-Isenburg or its surroundings. A possible encounter with Jana had become my persistent obsession. Every time I tried to imagine such an unforeseeable scenario with her, my fingers started to tremble. Then, it was the same excitement as within the moment I had touched Jana's fingers for the first time and caressed her cheek during that surreal summer evening in Italy. An instant which was rooted in my mind like a very personal myth: years ago, but nonetheless a determining element of my life that would be present until my death and perhaps beyond.

Going back to Germany made me desperate and sad. Already a few kilometers from Turin I painfully felt how much I would miss the city, despite my continuous tendencies to quit it whenever I was able to do so. How often did I leave Piedmont's capital for one or two-day trips to the Mediterranean shores of Liguria or the northern Toscana, only to come closer to the south and to be more inside Italy, just as if the country's heart could protect me from something. I did not really notice it during my one year stay how softly and discretely Turin welcomed me, whenever I came back late in the evening, either on the autostrada Genova Alessandria or arriving on the last train from La Spezia Centrale or Genova Brignole. And with the ending of the winter, at the beginning of March, people were strolling around until late at night under the arcades between the Via Po and the Corso Regina Margherita, filling the city with a moderate rhythm, quite unlike the busy Milan. I loved walking back the seven kilometers from the main station Porta Nuova to my apartment in Via Foligno. Relaxing night walks that soothed the pain of my memories. The mild spring breeze slowly blew away all forms of despair. And suddenly I realized how good it felt to be back in Turin if it hadn't been for my upcoming return to Germany which lay ahead of me like a threat. It would be an enormous challenge to integrate me again into the setting where Jana probably was still living. I had never dared to use the simple term being together with regard to our relationship since I had denoted that time span as *the* three years where a genuine *meaning of life* had unexpectedly filled me with so much intensity, so much optimism and magic happiness.

And so finally, I got angrier and angrier about my own weakness of will and the unmistakable fact I did not really have the strength to leave my past behind and to start a new life at a place I had fallen in love with. I could have finished my studies in Turin, my Italian was good enough by now, or I could have searched for a simple job also without a master's degree. It would not have mattered what kind of work, the essential would have been not to return to Germany and to let definitely fade my memories of Jana. It would have been imperative to avoid the place where we had spent so many wonderful moments and I was sure that was a necessary prerequisite to look ahead and to resume life.

After a three-and-a-half-hour drive, I left the A7 Lugano Luzern at Airolo, a small village with still Italian characteristics at the southern slopes of the Swiss Alps. The place seemed abandoned despite its oversized rail station where trains were connecting central Europe with the Mediterranean region via the nearby Gotthard pass. There were no passersby and the entire station gave the impression to be out of service. On the equally deserted main drag, there was a tiny and simple Osteria with four workers, apparently employees of the Swiss Federal Railways, having a late lunch. The waiter presented himself as the owner in flawless Italian, nearly without an accent I did not expect in a mountain village at the foot of the Alps. The four guests made a completely relaxed impression and did not seem to regard me as an intruder into the social order of the village or their lunch break. Rather, they hardly took notice of me. The owner kindly told me that there was no menu card, but he could offer me today a Minestrone alla ticinese followed by the main course, Risotto ai mirtilli, a southern Switzerland delicacy of rice with fresh blueberries. There was no objection on my part and I accepted willingly. During the whole trip from Turin on I had been lost in nostalgia and sometimes it was astounding how simple I overtook other cars and changed tracks while being immersed in a flood of hazy memories. The calm and isolated ambiance of the Osteria was further boosting that wave of impressions, prompting the relapse into one of the most dramatic feelings of crisis I ever experienced. My mind was full of uncontrollable and disordered fragments of the past and I felt more than ever that I had to use my life to make the past the present. How many days had I been happy at the beginning of our love story I suddenly wondered? Immediately with the inception of our daily routine after the first infatuation, my heart was seized by a deep fear of losing the source of my happiness, a fear of losing all the moments that would lay still ahead of us. Sometimes it went so far that I spent the mornings and lunchtimes completely inactive and missed my university lectures. At least I worked with my students as a private tutor in the afternoon to make money which indeed gave me the illusion to be relatively free and to think about what could I do in the evening with Jana, what could I offer her. And from the start, I made her unmistakably clear that she was the sole source of my joie de vivre.

What suddenly frightened me was a deeply rooted fear of death, the fear of sudden disappearance. And so, despite the current state of happiness, a certain and strange presence of emptiness slowly rose in me. I got the impression that the apprehension of death had been gripping my heart the same way as the love for Jana. On a rational level, I had no tool and no idea of how to balance that intense, meanwhile existential love with the rising fear of total annihilation. Sometimes an utterly impenetrable veil enveloped not only the immediate surroundings but also my whole personality, leading for moments my entire life ad absurdum as if I would not exist and instead move in an enigmatic dream. In addition to that, I had the feeling the surreal happiness of being together with her spoke from its inner dimension to me, with the single aim to inform me about the ephemeral character of happiness in general. As if the deeper reason for swimming on a wave of ineffable bliss was only to unambiguously remind me of the fragility of existence. And the message that hammered from then on continuously into my mind was that death alone, that nothingness alone would triumph at the end. As a consequence, my concerns about how to deal with my love, how to build up a life together with Jana and how to preserve these feelings and days of happiness, were vain and senseless since in those moments, existence had no meaning at all. Worse, it was the period when I started to feel real physical pain, fearing that a mortal disease had already been taking possession of my body, threatening to set an end to my life which had just started. Beyond, the time I spent without Jana was totally empty time, the vibration of an inner void so far unknown to me. More and more aspects of my active life seemed to become irrelevant, even reading started to lose its meaning, let alone the concern for my individual evolution. At that time, I preferred not to attend too many seminaries and lectures at the university, because I did not feel the necessity for social contacts and conviviality. Paola, my sympathetic professor for Italian literature who later helped me to get my scholarship at Turin, addressed my isolation and reticence during a private conversation in the university's cafeteria. She criticized me for my frequent absence, especially a colloquium on the late works of Pasolini, and was, rightly so, very much vexed about my sudden lack of interest. This friendly Italian lady knew best of my great passion for the Friulian intellectual. Instead of pursuing my studies, I merely wrote a term paper and took two oral tests at the end of the semester, investing only a minimum. I much preferred to go to the faculty of medicine every weekday only to shyly walk up and down in front of the sterile building where Jana was attending her lectures. The feeling of being physically close to her gave me peace of mind. Sometimes it happened that we could not see us for a day and that meant my fear of death would emerge again, even in the midst of Frankfurt's crowded main shopping mile, the Zeil. And sometimes the same occurred while I was waiting for her phone call in the evening, in the mid-nineties mobile phones were still completely unknown, so you had patiently to stay at home. Hence, the early days of our love relationship were characterized by a radical emotional up and down for me: either I was together with Jana and completely isolated from time and space, in a state of paradisiac happiness, or in a state of total despair, full of dark thoughts, accompanied by various clinical symptoms. It was a relentless law that the more beautiful our first autumn days were, the deeper became my suffering and the more pronounced were my physical symptoms. Or to put it another way, the more I loved her the more unhappy and lonely I felt. I understood that it was all a question of sense, starting to observe others and to think about how they lived and where they would find the meaning of life. But no matter how I looked at the issue I could not discover any meaning in my existence apart from the unconditional love for Jana. Love was the only sense of life, not philosophy, not literature and still less a bourgeois life within a daily and well-structured rhythm of pale habits and subaltern pursuits of senseless wealth. Yet I was totally aware that it was most probably emotional kitsch of a fragile mind. Therefore, I rapidly became jealous of people who had ideas and convictions to which they dedicated their life with enthusiasm. All I had were my recurring, even terrorizing thoughts that *everything will be obliterated. Everything will be drowned in nothingness.* Our love and its beauty as well. I wondered how one could just continue to live with such a weltanschauung? The conclusion was quite clear: it was pointless to think further about the meaning of existence. Transience was the sole reliable reference and there could hardly be any real sense of life that would not belong to the sphere of illusion. Thus, a period set in when everything I undertook seemed to be threatened by an overwhelming illusionary character, no matter what I did. And it dawned on me that my feelings for Jana had indeed reached a climax that would surely be followed by a period of sobering disappointment. These thoughts were incessantly penetrating into my mind and I feared the moment this emotional downward movement would start. My main concern at that time was not to weaken our relationship due to my mood changes and tremendous anxieties. The only lasting feelings were my depression and my physical pain, my hysteria and my hypochondria. That was my sad reality, despite a heart full of love and consuming yearning.

The owner suddenly showed up and kindly asked if I would like a dessert, saying he could offer me a combination of a delicious homemade tiramisu and the usual Italian coffee. I meekly accepted since I wanted to stay as long as I could on the southern side of the Alps to enjoy the still Italian ambience. I knew it would threaten my mental balance not to stay away from Germany and to come again physically closer to Jana. South of the Alps was now that geographical part where my longings resided and where I could neither lose someone nor recapture a period lost forever. Strangely enough, during my stay in Italy, I had the feeling to possess Jana definitely, enclosed in my heart, because my time spent with her was like a bare fact transformed into an enduring dream which could never be challenged. It was a perfect virtual reality to put it in a paradox formula.

While I sipped the café and spooned my tiramisu, I thought anew back to the initial period of our love. The time when my heart was completely mesmerized by Jana's mind-blowing beauty, her fragrance and the taste of her lips. I would never forget the moment when I was waiting for her in front of her parents' house in that idyllic byroad of the small close-to-the-airport town New-Isenburg. She often had dinner there although they paid her a small but elegant apartment nearby. The swarms of swallows were staging their daily evening concert and my heart almost burst with happiness and joy. It was as if my everyday struggle with all these emotional ups and downs and persistent pain of her absence had been only the prelude for what was to come now: There she was, stepping out of the front door and gracefully approaching me with all her elegancy. That was the moment I could finally drown myself completely in her presence, in her fragrance, in her arms, after a long day of unbearable deprivation.

That state of unearthly happiness had lasted for a relatively long time, more or less until the beginning of the following spring. Our ritualized greeting kiss still had the same vibration as our first kiss at the beach of Acciaroli. I am sure I will remember the taste of her then lipstick for the rest of my life.

During our first year she often presented herself to me in new clothes and was always stylish, especially in summer she wore new high heels and I knew that she would only put them on for me. My fingers trembled every time she came out of the front door and went along the small path from the entrance to the garden gate. We often made a long stroll for staying together as long as we could and we walked to the main road with its shops and cafés where we sometimes ate Italian ice cream or drank a cappuccino in the ice cream parlor Venezia. There, we chatted with the waiter Alberto about our recent holidays in Campania where he originally came from. He admired us, a couple who had come together in Italy and we could feel that in his eyes we were the perfect fusion of a pair of lovers. Even the mobile flower seller from Bangladesh who regularly went through the Venezia to sell his botanic goods always ceded us a red rose whenever he met us, but he never accepted money. It was a flattering gesture that filled us with a slight pride, confirming our impression that our love was something extraordinary, particular. That sweet routine became our weekday art of procrastination because afterwards, especially on Friday and Saturday, when we were free of the daily engagements, we would either go to her or to me and spend the night together. To describe these nights would be a senseless and too mundane undertaking. It was an emotional ecstasy that left no memories which could have been adequately articulated in forms of grammar and context. At that time, we rarely met our close friends, and it was not until much later that we went to birthday or university parties together. And we always felt that the eyes were on us either with jealousy or admiration, but in the end, we did not care since we were too much busy with our infatuation. Hence, whenever we spent time together during the first two years, we had the tendency to isolate ourselves from the rest of the world. For example, we never went for a long walk during daylight, rather, we yearned for the twilight or the night, simply to let the darkness envelop us. We craved for staying intimate. Yet we were not able to escape natural law, and with the slight decrease in our passion, we had slowly started to break through our isolation and attend more get-togethers of friends or fellow students. One of the first bigger social events we joined was Mirko's birthday party in December, exactly fifteen months after we had come together. He was one of my best friends, a passionate character who struggled during that period to continue with his law studies and had invited many budding lawyers, handsome and extremely self-assured. Mirko wanted to take the opportunity to strengthen his network and to go against his dwindling motivation. It was the first social event we commonly joined, and as the evening progressed and the alcohol consumption increased, I perceived from a certain distance that Jana was chatting and laughing with a charismatic young male guest. I was not able to understand the content of their lively conversation due to the loud music of George Michael songs, but it was clear that they were much amused and had certainly found the right topic for an amicable or even intimate debate. Suddenly he touched Jana's right forearm several times while he continued telling her something apparently exciting. As I saw that he touched her wonderful forearm again, this time longer and more intensely, I immediately used a pretext to interrupt my superficial debate with a young female doctor from Croatia to leave Mirko's birthday party cowardly and unnoticed. I felt brutally attacked and it seemed to me that someone had rammed a long and very sharp knife deep into my heart. It was as if I should faint. Holistic helplessness seized me.

I walked for many hours through the dark and threatening streets of Offenbach. When I reached my small apartment at dawn, I saw that Mirko had called me several times, leaving different messages on the answering machine, expressing sincere concerns regarding my disappearance. And there was a sentence that sounded like a paradisiac melody, namely that Jana had been much worried as well and had wept all the time. Olaf, another close friend from my school days, had accompanied her safely at home as Mirko said. Jana herself had called me a few times and had left three frantic messages, roughly half an hour before I got home. When I heard her voice, I started to cry too, stammering into the empty rooms of my apartment that I loved her so much. It was a childish crying, full of despair and imploring. It took us a few days to overcome that first crisis, but I understood that it had been the first sign of the disintegration of our inviolable and unearthly love.

My decision to leave the place and to pay the bill had been preceded by a long hesitation. I knew that as soon as I would read Luzern or Basel on the road signs, I would return to a broken and forever lost paradise. And I was much afraid of the idea to reorganize my life without Jana at a place that was totally filled with memories of her. To be back in Offenbach and especially New-Isenburg meant to reintegrate me into a context where only the reminiscences of my love for Jana alone existed. Again, I understood that my studies of philosophy and literature had been but a snobbish pastime since I had no idea of how to live. How soothing the elegance and easiness of life in Turin seemed to me now.

CRAVING FOR SENSE

As soon as I got back, I quickly became addicted to a row of inconspicuous houses, lush green trees and melancholy curved street lights. My beloved New-Isenburg, the small suburb of Frankfurt that administratively belonged to the nearby cosmopolitan yet grey-post-industrial Offenbach. That was the small town where Jana lived and where I had spent the happiest years of my life, thanks to her. I was sure she still had her little and elegant duplex apartment nearby her parent's home. In short, my emotional relapse after coming back from Italy where I had only lived to create a certain distance was tremendous. Almost every place was still being coated with sweet memories, but fortunately, I started to feel somehow a kind of healthy detachment inside. So loss and lovesickness had slowly been replaced by more balanced remembrances which, to my amazement, evoked feelings of lightness and timelessness. Also, my obsession disappeared to hold Jana responsible for most of our disputes or for terminating our relationship and even my then insane jealousy seemed a very distant, quite unreal emotion. Astonishingly enough, whenever I thought back to Jana, my life was still full of meaning. And sometimes during long late-night walks surrounded by the scent of the lime trees which lined so many small streets nearby her apartment my heart was filled again with overwhelming joy. It was now totally clear that Jana had become my personal epiphany, my sole and perfect dispenser of meaning in my life. Despite a more or less successful reintegration into the daily habits, a period began which could be best described as the time of sweeping memories.

At the end of the day, I had to admit that I was a lucky PhD-candidate regardless of my chronic unhappiness in love. Not only had I found a very handsome and affordable apartment but I got also a fantastic job, despite my ongoing flashes of memories. So, I was relieved that I could cope with everyday challenges.

I was not good as many of the female students who had applied for the position of an advertising editor at the Frankfurt Gazette, a social-liberal and relatively independent daily newspaper with leftist and already environmental leanings. The chief of human resources told me later on the phone that they would need two editors for its large weekend advertising insert and they opted definitely to hire also a second male candidate, of those I had been the best regarding the typing test. That was extremely good news because it was nearly the perfect job for one who had the intention to write a dissertation. A two workdays week was scheduled, Wednesday and Thursday, but that kind man also added during the call that I would often work until early Friday since the enormous advertising insert for the voluminous weekend edition had to be printed by Friday afternoon at the latest.

Our team was usually busy two workdays from five o'clock in the afternoon until two o'clock in the early morning. All of us were mostly students, the older among the team had abandoned their studies to tackle financial pressures resulting from failed relationships and subsequent maintenance payments for children and ex-partners. Towards the end of the nineties, the working conditions within the printing industry were extremely good. Mainly through night work, we earned a lavish shift allowance. The job enabled me to furnish my small apartment at the outskirts of Offenbach stylishly but discreetly. First, I established a huge library in my light-flooded living room where I brought order into all the books I had been acquiring during the years. They were giving me shelter and security, protecting me from a hostile reality outside, from people's greed for noise and quarrels. These were my nightly thoughts as I sat in my reading chair to recover from everyday trivialities. Backed by the Wednesday and Thursday late work rhythm, I was falling in love with the silence of the night. People were peaceful due to their sleep, their transitory death. The omnipresent calm set my memories and my imagination free. It was a blessing to my soul and a pure balm to my heart.

The working atmosphere within the advertising department was pleasant which I did not really expect. The overall ambience corresponded completely to my need not to be exposed to constant competition since the entire surrounding was characterized by discrete mutual solidarity and relaxed working conditions. My colleagues were mostly leftist students who thought that the meaning of life was to show full solidarity with others and to fight for an imperialism of equality. For this attitude of life, it seemed they needed neither metaphysics nor religion, in short, fully emancipated human beings. Thus, every week I was surprised anew at how good I felt among these female leftist colleagues. There was a second male team member, Simon, who had studied orchestral music, but abandoned long ago the environment of professional music. Simon was a pretty cool guy, totally unpretentious with excellent knowledge of German literature. It was interesting that he had been a former member of the communist party but was reconverted to a more independent state of mind after he had realized the missionary and overbearing character of his communist peers from whom he had been soon alienated. In course of time, we would sit next to each other, sharing effortlessly common interests of conversation during our long working evenings. One early Friday morning he told me details about his addiction to a young Russian woman who lived in

Frankfurt. It had been a desperate love story that took him a lot of time to overcome. I was moved to tears as I listened to him, but he did not notice as he was focused on typing the ad. From that day on I considered Simon tacitly as my close ally.

During a conversation on literature with Simon and two other female colleagues, I even dared to tell that the *Swelling He-Goat Song* of Botho Strauß had been my recent literary discovery despite its general characterization as an essay of a reactionary author. They immediately showed interest in the topic and did not attack me which was in my eyes quite astounding. This social liberal working ambiance was a very important refuge of security over many years for me. And the huge amount of work during the long Wednesday and Thursday nights was always carefully divided with great solidarity in our female-dominated team.

My Master of Arts in philosophy at the University of Frankfurt received still a good grade thanks to my above-average performance in German and Italian literature with a focus on Goethe's pantheistic worldview in his early works, especially in *The Sorrows of Young Werther*. Fortunately, the examining board was also happy with my relatively unconventional interpretations of Pavese's last work *Il Mestiere di Vivere*. But in philosophy, the major subject, my Master of Arts paper caused a vast polemic because my professor, the conservative Hermann Rotter I had always appreciated, did not agree at all with my interpretation of Nietzsche's conception of the eternal return. He started his final assessment of my thesis with a disparaging remark concerning the quote of the later French Nobel Prize laureate Jean Marie Gustave Le Clézio that I had thoroughly chosen and prefixed to my work: *Mais heureusement on ne vit pas logiquement*. I should have known before that for a bourgeois professor of philosophy and his meticulous scientific spirit such a statement would constitute pure feuilleton style and nuisance. Moreover, my sources of reference were mostly those of the French avant-gardist philosopher Gilles Deleuze and Pierre Klossowski, an independent painter and author who lived in Paris. In both their monumental work they stated that Nietzsche's conception of the eternal return was but a selective method to unreservedly affirm the moments of happiness in life, eliminating at the same time all negative feelings and deeds. In their view, Nietzsche's idea was the establishment of a new samsara which would not lead to nirvana but to a kind of enduring culmination of existence without elements of negativity. Thus, Nietzsche's thought had been a comprehensive attack on Hegel's idealistic philosophy with its hypostasis of lifeless inwardness and absolute rationality. Professor Rotter offered me kindly to repeat the paper with a more thorough and comparative approach to better meet academic standards and to avoid getting a bad grade. He had undoubtedly good intentions, yet I considered the ideas of the French reception of Nietzsche much convincing and so I preferred the bad grade in philosophy. But with an overall grade of 'good' I would perhaps still have the possibility to find a professor for a PhD and indeed, only a few weeks later I met Gerhard Gardner, a relatively young and left-liberal professor who encouraged me to work out a dissertation on E*ccentric Thought in Modern Philosophy*. Gardner was very open to my creative approach to philosophy, even if that was sometimes at the expense of scientific accuracy, yet he was convinced on the basis of my exposé that I would be able to unfold a profound polemic against modernity's rationalism and its totalitarian structures. He considered my suggestion to refer to the four great skeptics of rationalism, namely de Sade, Kierkegaard, Nietzsche and Heidegger, much promising. During the first meeting with him, I reiterated my view that philosophy as the search for the right ethic or rather the right lifestyle in the light of the truth had been completely distorted by the impact of modern rationalism and empiricism. And I made clear that philosophy was the timeless art of thought and had nothing in common with positivism or contemporary science. This was a reactionary thesis said Gardner, but if I could prove it with scientific arguments, it would certainly be an interesting study on the illusionary character of reasonable thinking in modernity.

With this project, I was totally happy and I eventually subscribed to a philosophical stream that most of my fellow students would term perhaps not exactly reactionary but at least conservative or anti-intellectual. And to that rhythm of life, consisting of readings at home, memories of my past life with Jana and the work with the advertising team of the Frankfurt Gazette, I still added a two-day afternoon job as a private tutor at an institute of homework supervision. I never set foot again in a university's library, rather I bought all the books I needed although it was an expensive undertaking. Reading and dreaming, in that way, I would spend the rest of the seemingly peaceful nineties at the end of a frenzy century. Meanwhile, all my close friends remained the same, there was Olaf and Emre from school and Mirko, my old dear companion in sports whose talent I had discovered and who subsequently won regional athletic championships several times. He knew that I did not appreciate at all rather his mother's choice to study law and to transform himself slowly into a wannabe star lawyer. I was sure the failure of this path was predetermined since it would not correspond to his consuming yearning for living beyond conventions. And finally, I was happy with the independent leftist Simon of our Gazette-team to have a further colleague whom I referred to as a friend, even though we saw each other only twice a week during work.

During the long reading sessions in the silence of the night, my longings and emotions constantly overwhelmed me. Above all, I felt Jana's closeness and so, the small suburb New-Isenburg became rapidly a tranquillizing haven for me. Only there, I was able to find peace of mind. I often went there after work, during Thursday or Friday mornings before dawn, or after the research for my dissertation late at night.

In this case, I turned the floor lamp out and took the car driving along the suburb's Garden Street until its end nearby the huge but always empty parking lot in front of the public swimming pool and the local Tennis club. The place was bordered by dignified old oak trees accompanying the seasons and the constant return of remembrances of our three years relationship. Despite a relatively organized daily rhythm, my life was completely focused on returning to the place where she lived. I would have never dared to disturb or to observe her, the opposite was true: my sole intention was to evoke exactly the feelings I had when walking along these streets with her countless times. And whenever I set out for my customary stroll through New Isenburg's calm and pretty side roads, my heart was filled with bliss. I usually approached her apartment in Fountain Street nearby the parking lot, but I always avoided directly walking past the house. Instead, I turned into Jahn Street where she often parked her old white Volkswagen Golf at the sidewalk. Sometimes I glanced over to see if lights were on in her apartment and when she was at home, I continued my way calmly and relaxed. What I did not avoid, however, was walking directly past her parent's home, a bourgeois single-family house at the quiet end of the town's western part. Almost every evening and even late at night the floor lamp's dim light in the living room was on and I knew well that her father was sitting there to read in one of his books about comparative constitutional law or in one of Thomas Mann's late works. Her father Rolf, an unconventional professor for constitutional law, and her mother Alina, who fled as a student what was then Czechoslovakia to Germany during the Prague Spring in 1968, had loved me from the beginning. Nevertheless, at the outset of our relationship, he once told me that his daughter Jana had to focus on her studies instead of yielding to the inclinations of the heart. Fortunately, there was a friendly and slightly ironic undertone in his exhortation.

Both of her parents were cultivated and extremely warm

people. Since the first official encounter as Jana's boyfriend, it had always been a very unconstrained being together whenever I picked her up at her parent's home or dined with them. The spectrum of her father's interests barely knew any limit, we talked regularly about soccer or music or German literature of Swiss origin, mostly Max Frisch or Dürrenmatt, his preferred authors alongside Thomas Mann. Their house had always been a home for me and I was happy there with Jana. Every time I left her parent's illuminated house during these silent walks behind me, my heart was seized by a kind of ecstatic tranquility while I further made my way through the quiet nocturnal side streets. And so, a long history of a compulsive motion of repetition set in spending almost every free moment at places where I had touched Jana, where I had laughed together with her and where I had still the impression to smell her body's irresistible scent. Whatever I did, whether I was studying, working or dating old school friends like Olaf and Mirko, I was permanently longing to leave the place where I was and to go back to New-Isenburg. It was there we always went out for long walks tightly embraced and being completely happy as long as we were together. Nearly every day had been a celebration of happiness and we had lived within the sweet illusion that this moment could remain forever isolated from the constraints of time, isolated from other peoples' jealousy. And I really believed that we could remain outside of what I had considered in my youthful enthusiasm as the silly pursuits of work and the senseless striving for lifeless, material goods. In fact, since knowing Jana, I had lost all sense of rationality. And whenever I could not see her for a few days for family or academic reasons, I immediately lost my elixir of life. In the meantime, she had become a female doctor and was surrounded mostly by ambitious people who focused on their professional life with clear goals in mind. During my long and lonely walks, I remembered with an astonishing composure that she had been more and more absent toward the second year of our relationship, undoubtedly due to the beginning of her career and her new social environment. Though she had always explained the reasons to me in the most undramatic and convincing way.

Those quiet streets with their detached houses of that unknown and unspectacular neighborhood gave me the certainty that there was something I could never lose again: my memories and intimate identity. An identity that was completely irrelevant for others and could not be perceived from outside. I clearly understood that memory was the real existential sword that would be able to cut man from its vulgar and simplistic biological meaning. And my ambitious aim was to live within positive memories alone, removing all negative elements of the so-called everyday life. Nietzsche's philosophy had probably left his imprint. Over the next few months, I learned that yearning for a place could be as intense as the yearning for a woman if only that place had transformed itself into a unique symbol for a flawless state of happiness.

So, it was not a sheer coincidence that *weltschmerz* poems became my favorite reading of my post-Jana period. Moreover, they suited exactly my philosophical research on Kierkegaard, Nietzsche and Heidegger. Despite the influential German romanticism with its main representatives E.T.A. Hoffmann and Novalis, it was French symbolism, namely Baudelaire which attracted me most. Together with Huysmans' narrations, Baudelaire's poetic universe helped me to revitalize my own private dandyism which I denoted with an oxymoron as proletarian dandyism, due to the fact that I despised conventionalism and the idea of being perceived perhaps as an overdressed wannabe. Hence, the money I earned through my two jobs was either invested in books or in a mixture of elegant and casual clothes like torn jeans with Italian sports shoes. I was keen to find my own style of clothing, but in reality, there was only one reason why I carefully focused on my outward appearance: I was steadily full of subliminal hope to meet Jana in an unforeseen way, perhaps during my usual walk in her surroundings in New-Isenburg or even on my way to work in downtown Frankfurt. My real dream was that she would appear and yearningly look at me, only to realize that our biggest mistake had been our separation which was the unique reason for both our enduring unhappiness in love affairs. These exciting thoughts came into my mind with the fervent desire she would finally grasp the unmistakable fact that I would be her destiny, her fado and that such an intensity of love was nothing else than pure grace. Yet these dreamy ideas quickly gave way to the sober knowledge that we would certainly never come together again. My outfit could be at best an armor that would prepare me for a sudden battle, to stand against Jana's new partner who would be undoubtedly a very elegant and handsome guy, a successful young doctor-to-be, a lawyer or a laid-back stock trader. And just the thought of her happiness shared with a new partner threatened to become a permanent source of my own unhappiness.

Fortunately, my inclination to withdraw and to search for inner peace increased steadily and while others would drown their grief in excessive drinking, I anesthetized myself entire nights with the recitation of Baudelaire's *La mort des amants* or *Semper eadem*. But my general disposition to socialize would never make me a real example of isolation since I was cherishing an intense relationship with all of my best friends and I still met up with them regularly. I understood that my romantic idea of friendship was also a reason for my relative emotional stability and for the balance I upheld within my daily struggle to cope with the irretrievable loss of Jana. And it was not a question of the encounters' frequency, but of mutual trust, the intensity of talks and profound solidarity in sharing our common sufferings. Our meetings were always a balm for the soul and the source of hope to overcome somehow in the future my post-Jana period.

My experience with grief and lovesickness was not an exclusive one. The opposite was true since all my friends tasted more or less the same bitterness at the end of their first real love affairs. We had left our days of innocence and youthful enthusiasm behind and were slowly becoming more bourgeois and pragmatic, exactly as the course of time would foresee it. But amongst us, we maintained this defiant and restive stance that had been characterizing us so far during our youth in Offenbach, that cosmopolitan melting pot nearby Frankfurt. The city was certainly the opposite of an idyllic place. Furthermore, it was not only me who had a romantic conception of friendship, we all were always able to give us mutual consolation and to build each other up. For I was by his side when Olaf's emotional comfort zone collapsed abruptly because his great love Valeria had a banal one-night-stand, a completely ephemeral and at the end worthless spasm of pleasure, the first weekend she spent without him. And she did worse, she confessed everything in detail to Olaf as soon as she was back. For what reason? Perhaps to underline her authenticity and liberty? To trivialize her infidelity? Or to dramatize it? To ask forgiveness or maybe to strengthen the feeling of being desired? We pondered over it for an entire night, opening one bottle of over-expensive Barolo red wine after another, but we were not able to find a reasonable answer. Before that, I had seen my physically strong friend totally humiliated and distressed, yet it was astonishing how quickly he recovered afterwards from this negative experience, although he had considered Valeria definitely as the love of his life. Just a few months later I noticed that he was rather relieved by the end of that love affair, and as he said, due to his chronically fragile relationship with Valeria's parents, two psychoanalysts, or to say it with Olaf's words, 'two awareness manipulators'. In his opinion the worst of all professions, a view that I totally shared with him, especially after a fervent reading of Deleuze's and Guattari's *Anti-Oedipus*, a work of an avant-gardist philosophy of the seventies, undoubtedly influenced by Nietzsche's conclusion that the psychoanalysts were the priests of the modern age. Olaf often told me that during many of the debates that both had with her parents, Valeria herself lost sometimes orientation since they talked about life as if it were a kind of complicated math problem that could only be solved by applicating the right formula. And that formula itself was characterized as the method to reconcile the concept of reality with individual desires and wills. Once, I told him in a very provocative and perhaps overbearing way that their method of education was committed to blind anthropocentrism and helping to promote a new era of social apathy since they would reduce reality to a mélange of contexts and arbitrary ideas. Life was a game in their eyes, without outward correctives and the rule of the game could be changed according to the needs and moods. Such an approach was simply a remnant of Cartesian hubris I said and the false promises of Renaissance which had been fostering so long man's illusion of being the unrestricted sovereign. In that way, both parents were perfect role models of modern individuals.

My friends played a salient role in my life. They were the port to where I could return anytime and breathe for a moment fresh air beyond the quotidian worries. And whenever a relationship of one of my close friends broke up, I fervently tried to de-dramatize, especially with regard to their then ex-partners and I attempted to find out why one of my best friends was so much in love with his respective girlfriend; yet there was not much to discover, at first sight; most of their female partners seemed to me pale and faceless, without the slightest sex appeal. But that was obviously a result of my biased subjectivity, moreover, Jana had left a too strong imprint of the ideal of feminine beauty in my mind, a totally idealized creature of flesh and blood. Still years later, whenever a feeling for a woman was looming on the horizon, I would compare every single trait with Jana's ones. How unfair that was. Nonetheless, she was the archetype of female attraction that was deeply rooted in my mind I would certainly never get rid of.

By far the worst experience we all had was with our dear friend Emre, the brilliant later on analyst for Middle-East-politics. He was extremely handsome and his intellectual appetite, apart from international politics and European-Mid-East-relations, was keenly focused on cinematic history. We spent legendary Saturdays together since he was regularly coming around to watch the afternoon's Bundesliga matches with me, followed by a totally unhealthy to go for dinner at a nearby fast-food restaurant. Afterwards, we started our movie nights and it was Emre who led me out of my ignorance of cinema history familiarizing me with the great filmmakers Luis Bunuel, Luchino Visconti and the newer generation like Martin Scorsese. I did not remember how often we had watched Visconti's *Gattopardo* and its legendary scene of Alain Delon's and Claudia Cardinale's waltz. Emre had experienced his real intellectual explosion during a one year stay at the University of Paris. The city and its culture changed him completely. Years later, he wrote in the foreword of his dissertation that it had been the happiest period in his life and the memory of it helped him to get over his long grief of a rapidly broken marriage. Yet from the outset, all his friends, wondered how this marriage had come about. Most probably, it had been a kind of identity crisis and the longing for lost cultural roots that drove him towards the obsession to marry a young lady with Turkish background from Graz in Austria. At a certain moment, we all stopped counting the humiliations Emre had received prior to the marriage by the spouse's father. His insults reached for all taboo zones, namely religion, identity and descent. Although her family had been completely socialized in Austria the impending wedding caused them a radical backlash on the level of the most rudimentary and primitive instincts with regard to the otherness. In the end, we all participated in Graz in this sad ceremony, eating silently our half-chicken with French fries and drinking liters of unhealthy sweet lemonade. With her family, we bandied only a few words that did not go beyond the ritual courtesies. As close friends of

Emre we were full of resentment towards his wife's family. Since we had all grown up in Offenbach, that melting pot of a hundred nationalities, the sentiment of distinguishing one on the basis of his descent, nationality or race was completely foreign to us. Moreover, Emre was himself of Turkish origin, coming evidently from a region against which her family harbored a deep prejudice. What had gone wrong, we often asked ourselves, since he was not even a Kurd?

We had never seen our friend Emre so totally out of place as during that memorable weekend in Styria's state capital, even though he had been surrounded almost exclusively by people of his original cultural background. In retrospect, that moment marked the beginning of his mental and physical decline, as he and his wife started a life dedicated to culinary indulgence, so far as we could perceive it from outside. The visible effects of that gluttony were the loss of Emre's intellectual keenness and the inception of serious weight and health problems. His condition depressed me and I tried to find out the deeper reasons for their craving for food and creeping misuse of alcohol. I did not come to a clear conclusion and within our contemporary context of prosperity and crises of meaning, they were no exception at all. Somehow, they were missing an important element of the elixir of life.

We regularly invited Emre and his wife Birsun under the pretext to watch a top European soccer match or simply to have dinner due to our common feeling that he would appreciate being in the company of his old friends. On these occasions, Emre always drank so much that with the advancing of the evening he slowly lost control of himself. Only a year later, he suffered from a pulmonary embolism and that illness marked fortunately a turning point in his life. Months before, he had not only started to search for mistresses, but also confessed to me later during a meeting in a coffee bar that he had never felt real love for Birsun and was filled with much resentment towards his wife. He had entered a phase of life in which frustration and unhappiness had replaced carefree youth.

For that reason, I was moved to tears when I read in the foreword of his brilliant PhD thesis on a late November evening that the memories of his wonderful time in Paris helped him to overcome the too long period of the divorce. So, he had wasted the most precious time of his life to separate from a wife he had never felt love for, I thought. And what was about me? What was my approach to life and to reality? Wasn't I wasting my own time too in an abnormal nostalgia and the ever and ever repeated walks through the empty and nocturnal streets of that small suburb nearby the big Airport of Frankfurt, searching for something that no longer existed?

Sometimes, whenever I was awake long after midnight and preparing a further tea in order to continue my readings and enjoying the silence of the night, I stood up and started to go back and forth in my small but elegant and sober furnished apartment; and I often uttered loudly like a maniac the name of my friends, not because I was missing them so much at that moment, rather because I was completely suffused with sudden happiness that I had the privilege to have them as close friends. And like a maniac, I would call into the empty living room the names of Emre, Olaf, Mirko and later on the name of Ricardo, that gentle Italian dissident who would become one of my most intimate friends. Subliminal despair and solitude, deepened by the nocturnal silence, had prompted that reaction since I was in need to convince myself that I wasn't alone in this endless, and in the eyes of modern science, totally meaningless cold universe. The dimmed light of the anachronistic designed floor lamp in my small living room which I considered rather as my library soothed me while I was continuing to walk slowly back and forth. I was totally aware that I could, whenever I needed them, call Mirko or Olaf in the midst of the night and ask for help. It gave me a feeling of security and at the same time, I realized that it had become so complicated for me to establish new ties to other people. However, I had no real need for it. With my books and old friendships, I was just fine, at least for now. With regard to new relationships, I was undoubtedly a stubborn reactionary, despite my young age, and probably a hopeless case. I always looked back with fervent nostalgia.

Ruth joined me at my desk and asked me if I would like to spend the break in the Italian ice cream parlor nearby, which was still open. With her usual kindness, she explained to me that she wished to talk to me for a short moment. We were both sipping cappuccino and as deputy head of the advertising newsroom, she inquired how I felt in the editorial team. I immediately understood that it was a kind of obligatory appraisal interview to which Ruth with her customary politeness had given an informal character. She was in advanced age, probably in her climacteric period, with traces of life experience and permanent smoking on her skin, since whenever she could, she would smoke her cigarettes and assume a thoughtful expression. She said she was very happy with both quota men, me and Simon, embarrassedly adding that this characterization from the Human Resources was complete nonsense, moreover, the entire team had long ceased to consider us as quota men. And, though it didn't correspond to her character to oversee permanently the quantity of our edited advertisements, it was of course her professional role to thoroughly evaluate our work outcome. Her voice was full of an apologizing undertone, while she was continuing to explain to me that our results, even she didn't like the expression, were excellent. I was profoundly touched by her positive appraisal, replying that it felt totally good to hear that and I confirmed to her I was happy in her team and with my male colleague. Simon was a very interesting character and intellectually extremely stimulating. My response seemed to satisfy her and I was sure she could perceive my pleasure to have her as a direct superior. This reflective and balanced woman remained one of the most polite and caring persons I had ever met in my life. Besides, Ruth was really the first fervent leftist person that I came to deeply appreciate. Of course, she was a typical do-gooder, a politically hyper-correct person, but unlike most of the other leftist minds, she never moralized on others neither felt superior nor showed resentment if someone differed sharply from her view. Her gentle and caring nature flooded every Wednesday and Thursday evening in our open space office and that was the time when my longings for Jana mostly disappeared, at least for a few hours. In those moments I had the impression to be ready for a new life. We finished our cappuccino in a relaxed silence before we went back to work which lasted until long after midnight. Late that evening Simon started telling me in fragments about one of his most disappointing love stories while we were both mechanically typing ads.

We opened another bottle of the finest Barolo. Although we didn't earn much money and were certainly far from over-average salaries, Olaf and I never saved when it came to good food and red wine. It was enough to eat a piece of delicious Parmesan or Apulian bread, accompanied by a balanced red wine to spend an inspiring evening with a friend that had always been at my side. And I knew with certainty that he would always be nearby as long as I live. Of course, there were periods when we were busy with ourselves, going through adolescence and becoming adults, especially after he left our class in high school to repeat voluntarily the twelfth grade. But fortunately, there were never longer phases in which we had in one way or another no contact or made no plans for a short trip together, since, in the end, we always knew how precious and deep our friendship was. As he took a sip, he smiled at me. 'Do you remember what did you say that summer evening when I wasn't sure at all whether you were still together with Jana? I had a vague foreboding of your relationship crisis. You had been recently not as talkative as usual and it seemed to me there was a heavy burden on your heart.'

'I remember well how desperate I was then during that period. I could not stand the idea that I definitely would lose her or that I had already lost her. Olaf, believe me, I had absolutely no idea how to continue to live without her. The world had become a cold place like a burned-out comet. Everything lost its meaning. My studies, my friendships. At that moment we had been together for three years what usually seems a long period for young lovers, but I swear to you that my love for her had still the same intensity as during that marvelous vacation we spent in Acciaroli.'

'I felt you had no idea how to cope with all this. And I was so helpless at the time. The only thing I could do was to give you a strong hug and to press you against my breast when we met.'

I smiled at him and was moved to tears, waiting for his conclusion because I had exactly every detail in my mind like Olaf who continued.

'I have never seen you so downcast, so depressed. You were completely exhausted with jealousy. The thought of losing her terrified you. Yet, you had to separate from her! You had to leave her! That's what I had already told you weeks before! You were completely addicted to Jana! your life was completely focused on her, on her beauty and grace. Understandable somehow, but it was already a kind of idolatry. Inside your mind, there was nothing beyond her.'

'And I know only too well what I answered you that evening we spent in the Yellow Bar until sunrise: that I would kill her if I would lose her. These were exactly my words,' I replied with a melancholic undertone and we both laughed now in relief.

FADING SPELL

The road from Acciaroli to Agropoli along the Cilento Coast was winding and the hinterland had been totally yellowed by the merciless summer heat of July. A few Mediterranean country houses stood stray in the midst of the hilly land. Olive groves and lonely pines lined the horizon here and there in contrasting green. The late afternoon light coming from the nearby seaside suffused the entire surrounding with a timeless atmosphere.

We were both totally happy and full of expectations of what was to come next. My body was flooded by a wave of happiness hormones and this was undoubtedly the reason I was driving like a daredevil with excessive speed along the bendy road. Jana was not afraid at all, from time to time she stretched her right arm out of the car window as if trying to feel the headwind still more intensely. Some hundred meters before arriving at the small village of San Marco the Carabinieri stopped us. They explained to me that I had exceeded the maximum speed and that I had to pay an on-the-spot-fine of thirty thousand Lira. With a pleading undertone, we said we didn't have such an amount with us and that we were poor students from Germany, taking a vacation nearby Acciaroli. One of the carabinieri suddenly became more lenient as we started to use some Italian words for confirming to him that it had been an error and a danger to drive with such a speed. The next time, he said sternly, he would seize my driving license in case I would not pay. Jana apologized as well although she had nothing to do with my breach of law. 'Scusiamoci tanto,' she said kindly.

As we drove on, relieved, Jana smiled at me and put her left hand on my right forearm. 'We were lucky,' she told me.

I looked at her slender fingers and red painted fingernails reposing on my arm electrifying my entire body, then I withdrew my underarm to take her hand tenderly. She returned my gesture with the same tenderness and without the slightest resistance. Time was dissolving before our eyes, and a surreal bliss took hold of us.

Hours earlier we had set out for Agropoli's Saturday market to buy the groceries we needed to organize a barbecue on the wonderful terrace of her father's house, overlooking the Gulf of Salerno. Jana's friends, Katerina and Jenny, promised to make a mixture of pasta and salads while Olaf, Mirko and myself assured to organize a delicious variety of antipasto and to broil regional beef steaks. As Jana knew the region best from the many stays in her family's vacation house, she proposed to go with me to Agropoli where we would find an excellent choice of vegetables, fruits and cheese. All others, it was clear from the beginning, would spend the day until afternoon on the beach. It was pure destiny, I thought the same evening lying on my bed and listening to the singing of crickets, that we should go together grocery shopping the next day. Sleep was out of the question that night.

We left Agropoli early in the afternoon. It was hot, but we spent the entire day in an exuberant mood, choosing delicatessen and deliberating on the dessert and side dishes. On the outskirts of Agropoli on our way back to Acciaroli, there was a huge supermarket where we still bought the rest, especially the pasta and cookies. At the entrance, there was a small and inviting café where we sat down and ordered water and espresso. It was pleasantly empty in that heat and Jana started a conversation while I tried to hide the secrets of my heart. But I was not able to avert my eyes from her beauty, from her black smooth hair, her seemingly black eyes and beautiful cheekbones. Her voice was soft and she was speaking with consideration, with elegance, but never with arrogance. She told me about her medical studies and the pressure she had, saying that she needed to focus on what she would specialize in and where to find a good place for an internship. The greatest flaw would be her impatience, she said, since she couldn't wait to finish her studies and start to work. After a short pause, she resumed, 'It is very much different with you, I think. My father told me that you are studying philosophy and literature and, what is worse, that perhaps you are an anarchist.' She laughed and added immediately, 'He didn't say this that way, these are just my ideas on philosophers, moreover, you don't look like an anarchist.'

I understood it was my turn now, the only chance I would have and so I said, 'If they love the truth, originally the deeper meaning of the term philosopher, much more than the commonly known friend of wisdom, so, if they really love the distinctive truth, they are also obliged to love beauty. So, a philosopher must permanently be in love with beauty or at least in search of beauty, precisely because he is in the quest for truth. Sense for truth and beauty go hand in hand with ethics and esthetics. The great Danish philosopher Kierkegaard had known this only too well. If there are still true philosophers, they had to lead mainly an esthetical existence that shouldn't be mixed up with luxury. Yet due to the fragmentation of philosophy by positive science and epistemology, such a concept of philosophy does no longer exist. Thinking is more primordial than science and doctrinal opinions.'

I was delighted about my prompt and snobbish response, while I noticed that she had carefully listened to me. 'So, you are a fervent anachronist,' she replied amused and said further, 'How much patience you must have to read all these books and to ponder on topics that are not of great importance in the context of our everyday life. At least at first glance. Maybe you will, later on, become a journalist writing book reviews or even political commentaries. But I think it's hard to have access to the media world today. There are many who would like to become journalists or opinion leaders, and I am not sure if the quality is always the touchstone. But if you finish your studies in philosophy, you might at least become a professor at the university. Would it be an option for you?'

While she was talking and speculating on my fate, I looked all the time at her discreetly. A distinguished sense of taste seemed to belong to Jana's natural disposition and it corresponded perfectly to her stunning beauty. She wore cream-colored high heel sandals with a simple white summer dress and, for a medicine student, a rather expensive divers watch, yet she had diligently chosen an understated version which fitted perfectly to her slender wrists and to her graceful forearms. Her toe- and fingernails were both painted with the same unflashy red shade that made an extremely beautiful contrast to her oriental beauty. But most of all, I was impressed by how she talked about the issue of philosophy and how she could easily follow my argumentation. It flattered me that she was so much interested in the details of my life. As I took my cup of espresso, I remarked my hand was trembling. But that was not a new phenomenon, whenever I was close to her during these vacations, I always noticed that my knees were weak and my hands got wet quickly.

'Perhaps I can become a cab driver,' I resumed timidly the conversation with a stark ironical undertone. 'So I will have a calm life and may read many books outside my working hours or while waiting for clients. Wouldn't it be good?'

She looked at me and her gaze penetrated my whole body. I asked her if she wanted to drink one of these delicious San Pellegrino lemonades before we had to return to Acciaroli. An excellent idea she said since she was very thirsty, too. I immediately ordered two of San Pellegrino Lemon and asked the barista to bring us some cookies and something sweet. – Vi faccio qualcosa di buono. Non vi preoccupare, ci penso io a la bella signorina e Lei!

For a brief moment, we silently observed both the few customers coming and going. Shortly afterwards, the lemonades and a selection of small Italian cookies were brought to us with the gentle smile of the courteous barista. I resumed the conversation, even though I had the feeling to faint the next moment. 'Jana, would you really like to know what I am dreaming of?' I said with an astonishingly calm voice.

'Sure!' she replied, looking at me expectantly.

'I'm dreaming of staying with you, to be at your side and not to return to Germany. To stay here, at the beach, even in winter when all places are totally abandoned in this region. I would like to cook your meals and make your laundry. And I would like to contemplate you when you sleep. Anything else would have no meaning at all. No more philosophy! No more useless epistemologies! No more pondering on all the cruelties mankind committed in its so-called history of civilization. Completely uninteresting! I'm dreaming of creating an island outside human civilization, only for you! Jana, I love you! I love you since I have seen you for the first time. The evening we paid your father this three-week stay and had tea with him, do you remember? I couldn't wait for this vacation to begin and to see you again since your father had mentioned to us that you would stay here nearly the entire summer as well.'

Jana totally blushed for a moment and lowered her gaze. Thoughtfully she touched with her elegant fingers the San Pellegrino Lemonade that stood in front of her. Then she smiled, saying, 'You must be crazy, dear philosopher!'

'Not at all! I simply love you! I love you, Jana! I apologize, I don't want to embarrass you while on vacation. But I love you so much!' It had been a desperate confession and again another moment of total silence followed before she resumed with a gentle but serious voice.

'There is no reason for apologizing! But you would quickly be bored with me. Believe me,' she added this time with a slightly feeble and tender voice.

'That's excluded, Jana, utterly impossible. Love doesn't know the concept of boredom.'

We paid the bill and went to the car in silence. She walked at my side in her unmistakable elegant way and I felt every step of her vibrating in my heart. Then, we made our way back to Acciaroli. It was now a surreal afternoon with enchanting light from the West and an endless blue coast to our side. I felt like in a dream from which I wished to never wake up again.

I met Jana for the first time in her father's house in New-Isenburg. A few days earlier I had read an advertisement in the column 'vacation houses' of the famous *Frankfurter Allgemeine Zeitung.*

Elegant apartment in countryside villa near Acciaroli / Campania / Italy with a stunning view of the Gulf of Salerno. Terrace, 2 bedrooms and fully equipped kitchen, park*ing lot and use of the garden for 1500 DM weekly. Please contact 061002 / 80894*

Olaf, Mirko and Emre, we had decided to spend relaxing vacations at the seaside together. Although we were still students, we all were lucky to have well-paid part-time jobs in the Frankfurt area. Our favorites had been Portugal, Spain and Italy. After searching for the place on a map and ascertaining that it was a small town in southern Italy, a region with promising beaches and much beauty of nature, we did agree the same evening to contact the owner. It was quickly done and he invited us already the following evening to come to the nearby New-Isenburg. He kindly asked us to prepay the two weeks, since the demand for his apartment was very high, but at the same time, he obliged us in a very cordial way to stay for dinner. We didn't think twice.

Jana's father was a handsome man with excellent manners, attorney at the Higher Regional Court as we came to know during our conversation. His wife, Alina, that classy and slender lady from Czech origin had a small painting studio nearby as she told us without any extravagance. And as we touched on the subject of literature in between, she was delighted that I knew Milan Kundera. She appeared intellectual and balanced, but was also very caring, serving us not only tea but insisted to taste her home-made Pizza with simple Mozzarella di Bufala and tomato sauce, to get the perfect foretaste of the vacation area. We would just wait a moment for her daughter Jana and her friend who had announced they would also come for dinner. That warmhearted lady added that it would be a good opportunity to know her daughter because she would probably stay for almost two months in the countryside villa together with a small group of friends to recover from the strenuous exams at university. After doing the payment and signing quickly the short rental agreement we talked about anything and everything. We were all impressed by their open-mindedness and sociable approach to us, an unknown group of young testosterone-filled men from the nearby Offenbach, a city of dubious reputation. Jana's father inquired with lively interest also about my studies and he proved to be a well-informed conversational partner with regard to philosophy and literature. I was yet more impressed when he told me that Italy was his clandestine and second love in his life, with a twinkle in his eyes in the direction of his wife who shared obviously his love for this Mediterranean country. He said to have unfortunately no idea about contemporary literature in Italy but in return, he was still a keen reader of early modernity, especially Pirandello, Montale and D'Annunzio. The fin de siècle was his literary passion and so I liked him from the start.

The evening had already advanced when Jana came almost silently in and introduced first her girlfriend Valeria, then herself. My friends and I certainly all had the same thought in mind: God, what an enchanting beauty! And we all had the same difficulties resisting Jana's gentle and challenging gaze with her sparkling deep brown eyes. Both took a seat at the table while Jana congratulated her mother on the delicious pizza whose scent had been perceivable even in front of the door as she said. This young lady had black straight hair and she had discretely applied elegant makeup with an understated shade of red on her full lips. She wore a simple but relatively close-fitting white T-Shirt accentuating her well-shaped breasts. Even then, I was immediately overwhelmed by her confidently and stylish taste that completely matched her natural appearance. Besides, she was wearing well-worn blue jeans with elegant white high heels sandals. With a mischievous smile, she asked then her father if it would be a good idea to rent the apartment to a group of other students, since together with her girlfriends there would be already enough young people in the countryside villa. Her father smiled indulgently at her and replied that he had already mentally adjusted to maximum chaos which would certainly reign in his beloved vacation home this summer. As we left late in the evening, I felt strange happiness which was nothing else than the exuberant joy of seeing this lovely young lady again soon.

As we prepared dinner, we told our friends the story of the Carabinieri who had stopped us due to excessive speed. Olaf jestingly remarked that they had only had the intention to consider a totally in love couple from close. All laughed except Jana and me. I avoided her eyes but saw she was blushing like myself, yet we continued to focus on setting the table while Mirko and Emre prepared the beef steaks and Valeria with Simone dedicated themselves with utmost devotion to the Mediterranean starters. Most of the time I was under the spell of Jana's caring for details. I discreetly observed how she put the flatware, glasses and napkins on the table, noticing that everything she did was done with love and due accuracy. She was completely absorbed in her gestures and I immediately connected the resulting ambiance with a romantic dinner exclusively for us: the lovers, here on the vast terrace of her father's countryside villa, surrounded by Olive trees whose leaves were still gleaming in the twilight. There was a light breeze blowing from the Gulf of Salerno. What a perfect setting for the beginning of our love story if only we were here alone, I thought dreamily.

There are probably rare moments in life where we feel totally at peace with ourselves, our fellowmen and our natural surroundings. That evening was exactly one of those unique moments of my existence. Its intensity was indelibly burned into my heart.

Jana understood her role as a perfect and attentive host since she considered us as guests in her father's wonderful Italian vacation house. Her kindness was overwhelming. She kept asking attentively if we wanted more Pellegrino water or a sip of Primitivo red wine or some green salad or other accompaniments. From time to time, she glanced at me and although being a fleeting moment it was yet a meaningful look, penetrating deep into the unknown depths of my heart. Twice she gave me my glass back after she had poured fresh water in and I wasn't sure at all if it was a coincidence that our fingers touched each other tenderly each time or if it would be the prelude of our passionate love.

It was totally obvious the entire evening that especially Jana and myself were in an extremely good mood, moreover, it was evident too that Jana gave me particular attention so that I had difficulties hiding my nervousness. But it was also the moment I could deeply feel that I had the best friends one could imagine since Mirko, Emre and Olaf were playing their role with the greatest solidarity, realizing I was madly in love with her. I promptly knew I would never forget in my life how much they were by my side that evening.

Our dinner came to an end while we were sipping espresso and eating Sicilian cannoli that we had meticulously chosen in a small patisserie during our stay in Agropoli. The dessert was extremely delicious and Emre, our gourmet, had the right idea, namely to accompany it with a second espresso he made for us. But all were slowly overcome by tiredness and after clearing up the table we agreed to meet at the beach in the late afternoon of the next day. As the voices of Simone, Valeria and Jana lowered more and more in the apartment next to ours and hearing my friends already snoring in their bedrooms, I went out again in order to breathe and be alone. My heart almost burst with longing for Jana. As I stood on the terrace and looked in direction of the Gulf of Salerno which presented itself deep in the night as a black hole without traces of fishing boats' glimmer of light, I perceived somebody coming from the other side of the terrace. Like in a bizarre dream, Jana stood with her slender and graceful figure in front of me. She came close to me, and none of us dared to move for the moment. I already smelled the typical scent of her skin, accentuated by an oriental amber fragrance she loved so much as I came to know weeks later. A total and timeless silence of the night surrounded us. Despite the darkness, I felt determination in her eyes and in all of her demeanor. There was no need for words or further confessions. Our hands fervently sought their counterpart and our lips touched one another in tender expectation. It was like being reborn fully conscious.

When we left Italy's south after this three-week stay, Olaf took attentively care of me during the entire eight-hour trip from Battipaglia via Salerno, Naples and Rome to Milan as I was constantly overwhelmed by crying fits. It was the first time in my life I felt how painful longing could be. With every mile we drove away from Jana it was as if oxygen would decline and as a result my heart, my entire body was becoming heavier. And it was as if I had been pushed out of a so far unknown paradise that I had unexpectedly discovered, but which was already lost forever just a few moments later. Only in the late afternoon nearby Milan, I was able to drive and relieve Olaf who had been so considerate the whole time. My hope was to finally get home and start waiting for Jana who would stay in Italy for at least one month together with Valeria and Simone. She was waiting there for her parents and would return with them at the end of the summer. In the midst of the nineties, there were not yet mobile phones which would have connected us with each other regardless of the place. Of course, we had exchanged our landline numbers and sometimes I was able to talk to her in the evening. International phone calls were very expensive at that time, yet our short conversations were suffused with expectations and the yearning to meet up soon.

It was the time of the discovery that walking for long hours in the fresh air gave me peace of mind. And it was also the period I repeated my walks nearby her parent's house only to feel somehow close to a place Jana knew and where she usually felt at home. In that way, I could share in her everyday surroundings, even though she was still absent. So, I had started to assuage my agonizing longing for her by walking through the streets and environments where she normally lived. It was indeed an effective sedative for me. I went there twice a day, taking my car in the early morning and parking it nearby Garden Street which ran through the entire small town of New-Isenburg. Then, I made my round always passing the house of Jana's parents where I had met her the first time. During my morning walks, I always took a break at Café Nolde where I drank a latte macchiato and bought the Neue Zürcher Zeitung.

It was a luxurious situation since I didn't start working

before the early afternoon at the Pedagogic Institute in Frankfurt, even during the vacation period where I cared especially for male youths who had learning problems. And sometimes I spent almost two hours observing the people's coming and going in that cozy coffeehouse, at the same time reading almost the whole feuilleton and all about international politics, particularly the Arab World which I was greatly interested in without understanding the deeper reasons. Curiously enough, weeks later, with the beginning of the fall and my fourth semester at the university, I started to learn Arabic at the famous Orient Institute just nearby the faculty of philosophy in Dante Street. The proclivity for Arabic should be a sign of fate which I wasn't able to grasp at that time. Reading the newspaper and sipping my latte macchiato on a backstreet totally relaxed me. Then, I came back again in the late evening, and during my strolls, I often saw that Jana's parents had their lights on and sometimes her father walked back and forth in the living room with a book in his hands. According to Jana, her parents would be leaving for southern Italy soon for their summer vacation and joining her. But a few days later she called me surprisingly after midnight, telling me with a voice full of enthusiasm that her parents had well arrived and she had immediately asked them if she was allowed to leave Italy and to return home. Moreover, her friends, Valeria and Simone, had also finished their four-week stay and were back in Frankfurt. She told them she had no intention to further stay there and had made it unmistakably clear to her parents it was an urgent affair since she was missing me so painfully. Jana added that she had confessed to her parents she was in love with me with the words 'my first serious love. A strong love. Real love.' That was mind-blowing news for me. She also told me that her father had smiled at her in a very melancholic but understanding way while her mother had made no comment, yet seemed to feel calm happiness for her. As she hung up the phone, I was so much touched by the joy that tears ran down my cheeks. Unable to sleep, I opened Sartre's book on

Baudelaire and read it until dawn.

It was on September 6, 1994, when my phone rang around eleven o'clock in the evening. I was sitting in my reading chair and was trying to concentrate on the famous paragraph 40 of Heidegger's *Being and Time* which professor Rotter had recommended me to work through before vacations as the key text for my upcoming intermediate examination. For a moment my body consisted only of heartbeat since I knew instantly it was Jana. As I answered the call, I heard her voice full of joy saying, 'I'm back! I'm finally back from Italy!'

Before she could add another sentence, I hastily asked, 'When can we meet?'

'Immediately,' she answered. 'If it only suits you!'

'Are you kidding?' I said breathlessly with excitement.

'I will be waiting for you in front of my parent's house, sitting on the stairs, it's a wonderful mild summer night. Made for us! I have just arrived from the airport by cab.' Her sentences sounded exceptionally disorganized yet full of enthusiasm.

'Really? And we can meet up now?' I still asked with a slightly doubtful undertone.

'Look, my dear, I apologize, I was just in the mood of jesting with you, that's why I am calling you in the middle of the night,' she added ironically, but with an infinitely gentle and expecting voice.

I knew that I would carry her words 'my dear' the rest of my days within the luggage of my memories just as the sentence 'my first serious love. A strong love. Real love.' These were the words she had uttered days before on the phone. 'Give me a few minutes, Jana. It's dark outside and probably you won't see much of me, but I have to look good for you'

'Don't worry, but come quickly! Do you still remember where my parents live?'

'Of course! I was permanently walking past their house the

last five weeks.'

Already half an hour later, we strolled around in an intoxication of happiness along the abandoned side streets of New-Isenburg the entire night until dawn, holding each other so tightly just as if we had constantly to reassure that the other was real and present. She did not ask whether I would stay overnight, but we both knew that this moment was close and that we were keenly yearning for it. As I drove the short way back to Offenbach during sunrise, I listened to my George Michael tape. I had lost all the sense of time and space. And I had no sense of the speed I went the short distance on the federal highway back home. But I had the certainty that the still green leaves and trees, as well as the sunlight of that wonderful impending September day, had been created exclusively for this moment's sake alone. For me, for Jana, for our love and nothing else.

The early period of our relationship was characterized by perfect happiness. We didn't need the slightest entertainment or socializing, all that mattered was being together and loving each other fiercely. Despite long days at the university and part-time jobs, secretarial labor at a diagnostic laboratory for Jana and my coaching for young pupils mostly in the afternoon, we were able to keep up our everyday rituals and cultivate our emotional dependency. On weeknights, we used to meet in New-Isenburg at her parent's house where she often went for dinner. As a result, I was regularly invited and we spent amusing evenings with both her liberal-minded parents who had accepted from the beginning that we were lovers. We normally set out again late in the evening for a long walk through the empty streets of this bourgeois neighborhood which belonged administratively to Offenbach but was much closer to Frankfurt. From New-Isenburg train station Frankfurt South could be reached in two stops with the express train, with tramway 21 after twenty minutes. The aviation noise of the nearby Rhine-Main-Airport, a hub of international aviation, was lowering during our late evening walks, although it should forever remain the timebound background noise of our relationship. From time to time, we dreamily looked at the low flying airplanes trying to guess from where they came. It was astounding how little we needed if only the longing of our hearts was fully satisfied. I enjoyed Jana's appearance every evening anew, always different, always characterized by extraordinary care for my sake which immeasurably flattered me. She meticulously selected her shoes wearing the perfect footwear regardless of the weather conditions; makeup and lipstick were carefully matched. Jana was not only an epiphany of beauty, I quickly understood that she was an epiphany of meaning as well since she gave me an entirely new reason to live. And due to our anesthesia by happiness hormones, we had been anyway both fallen out of the conventional time frame. Sometimes, especially when it was raining, we were sitting in the Venezia Ice cream parlor at New-Isenburg's main road and the Italian ambiance there remembered us of our bygone summertime in Italy's south. Alberto, the Italian waiter from Apulia, was apparently a fan of us so to say. He bluntly told us several times with his unmistakable open Italian character trait that we were a wonderful couple filling up the café with light and beauty and we both subsequently blushed given this romantic and flattering comment. But in a certain sense, that delicate compliment of an outsider had confirmed the unmistakable vibrations of both our hearts and it filled us with silent joy. I should never forget Alberto's countenance when I went to the ice cream parlor again with a friend many years later and he immediately inquired after Jana and our common destiny. I was deeply moved when I saw the unvarnished sadness in his eyes after my short and unequivocal answer.

The ice cream parlor Venezia had become our common relaxing place for almost three years. Especially in late fall and winter, we would sit here to interrupt our ritualized walks. There was a mobile flower seller from Bangladesh who was already smiling from far away heading towards us whenever we sipped our tea or coffee there in the evening. He had soon ceased to sell me red roses for Jana, instead, we always invited him to have tea with us and to tell us more about his difficult journey to Germany and his life as an asylum seeker without a work permit. Arish, that lovely young man, was always full of hope and of positive energy which both of us profoundly absorbed. His kindness and candor, despite the daily hardship he told us about, inspired us every time we met him anew and in a certain way, it strengthened our sense of not letting the moment of our harmony and happiness slip away. In his presence, we felt that living like us was a sheer privilege.

The first time I realized that this feeling of existential happiness would not bear discontinuity was during a short trip to Paris. Kai, my ex-classmate, a student of literature and more a close friend of Olaf than mine, had the idea to organize a short trip to the Ville lumière. Both were kind enough to ask me if I wanted to join them because they knew that I had a passion for French literature, especially for Parisian existentialism. Since I had a relationship with Jana, I called Olaf less frequent, but he understood very well that I had to spend my time with her and that I was totally in love. He had witnessed the beginnings of our love like no other during the summer vacation in Italy and therefore, he would never reproach me for neglecting our friendship. From the start, I agreed to travel with them even though I did not have a good feeling about it.

In the meantime, our emotionally and also physically dependency increased more and more. We often made love passionately in her small apartment after having dinner in her parent's house just a stone's throw away or we spent the weekend in my apartment in the southeastern outskirts of Offenbach. Sometimes she had to study for her exams while I was much more relaxed in my academic research because I had no professional ambitions and pressure at all. I just had to write a few short essays on a particular subject which were in a certain sense of no importance for the world. So, Jana was not excited about the idea of going to Paris with my friends for some days, yet she was completely aware of my passion for literature and did not make a negative comment on it. But her disappointment was clearly visible in her eyes which hurt me a lot. Some days before we set out for Paris, she had even bought me a literary guide with a special focus on existentialism and surrealism. I was so happy with this generous and typical Jana gesture which gave me a sense of relief. For a moment, I had the impression I would perhaps enjoy this trip with Olaf and Kai.

Even the nighttime bus trip from Frankfurt main station to the Gare de l'Est had been a nightmare. I painfully felt Jana's absence and from the inception of the journey, a deep and strange sadness had seized me. I did not enjoy seeing Paris and sitting in Sartre's and Beauvoir's Café Flore the next day with both my friends, drinking an extremely delicious, if overpriced, French café au lait. Instead, I had lost my humor and only pretended to laugh at Kai's jokes and his efforts to entertain us. I was in dire need of Jana's lips, her scent, her presence. While the feeling of her absence was terribly intensifying, my vitality was withering slowly away and replaced by a hermetic emptiness. As a result, my emotional and physical deficiency state was worrying and I had not the slightest idea how to cope with the upcoming stay in Paris. Although we strolled through the most interesting neighborhoods after our arrival, namely the Montmartre, Saint-German-des-Prés and afterwards Montparnasse, I could not really get in touch with this wonderful city, and worse, with my close friends. The same evening, we went to La Coupole for dinner, another generous concession of my friends to my passion for Parisian existentialism. As I poked around lethargically in my food without appetite, Olaf and Kai stared at me in shock for a brief moment, then Kai, with the presence of mind, put his napkin on my lips. I lost much blood but, apart from having a warm feeling around my mouth, I did not feel the blood streaming out of my nostrils. It took a good while until the bleeding stopped. And although both insisted to accompany me back to the Hotel, I convinced them that I would return alone and go to bed earlier this night hoping I would be better the next day. It was important for me they could enjoy the evening in Paris, and for that, they had absolutely to get rid of me. As soon as I was back in our cheap run-down three-bedroom I dialed Jana's number, telling her in a weak voice we had spent a good day and were all much tired now.

'Are you sure? Are you all right?' she asked apprehensively.

'Of course, don't worry,' I told her tense, 'but I miss you so much, Jana! My love for you extinguishes everything else, it has burned even my love for the Parisian existentialism and Jean-Paul Sartre, can you imagine it?'

My sense of humor suddenly came back again because while I was still expressing my farewell to her, I knew exactly what to do after that short conversation. I put the money to pay my share for the accommodation expenses on the table and added a note with a few sentences: *Please enjoy Paris! Thank you for your forbearance! I have to return to see Jana! I'm sure you understand, dear friends! See you soon!*

So I took my bag and left the Hotel, heading directly to the nearby Gare de l'Est. At one of the few opened ticket counters late in the evening, I was able to get a ticket for travelling back to Frankfurt via Cologne. Towards midnight shortly before definitely leaving Paris, I wondered if Olaf and Kai had found my note and if they would have been disappointed and upset with me. But both would fortunately never make a fuss about my sudden disappearance in Paris. I would love them all the more for this noble leniency.

Time is unmerciful and the everydayness of our emotional comfort zone slowly began to crumble. There is rooted negligence in our nature tending to vulgarize at a certain moment also the noblest of our feelings and intentions. We aren't able to live in a cocoon of continuity isolated from the ruthless desire to live and the craving for broadening one's horizon. The strength of our romantic feelings was turning into our long-term dilemma, namely the permanent effort to keep up this emotional intensity which had felt like a potential foretaste of paradise for almost two years. Since pure feelings are not a reliable quantity, they have to be replaced at due time by a value, shared interest or strong common goals which Jana and myself were not able to find at the crucial moment. Our passionate love was exclusively an end in itself and I knew it would never culminate in a quiet middle-class life. It was especially true for me because I had no vision of what to do with my life apart from the luxury to escape reality through books and a dreamy estheticism. But Jana, at a certain moment, had a clear objective on how to proceed after the studies of medicine and how to build a prosperous career. As a result, during an exchange of ideas with her about how to manage the challenges of the future and to find a smooth transition from the student life into the bourgeois lifestyle, I was the totally irrational counterpart in that debate. The question of what would I wish to be or to become sounded so ridiculous for me that I could never deal with it seriously, even though I was aware of the fact that my attitude in this respect seemed pretentious, if not to say surreal and arrogant. I had never the strength to define my life in professional terms and I told Jana one evening in the Venezia ice cream parlor that life could never be professional. It might be experimental or desperate or hopeful or romantic, but never professional. I touched her beautiful slim forearms while I told her my vision of life. She tenderly smiled at me and replied that one can combine both or more since life was not one dimensional. When she asked me how would I like to earn money I answered that I was already making money as a tutor for students. But I understood that she was asking for my long-term perspective with regard to my professional life, so I smiled at her too and told her, 'You know, my dream is to become an unsuccessful author with many scripts in his drawer, earning his money as a cab driver in Rome or perhaps in Paris. I told you that two years ago in Agropoli. Do you remember?' I was so much afraid of all these thoughts about how to organize a conventional life that I was a very bad dialog partner even for my beloved Jana.

In every relationship there is the point where it opens up to others, sharing with them a kind of intimacy that at the beginning of the romantic attachment is out of the question. The natural desire for privacy and solitude prevails. We definitely reached that point during and after our third summer journey to Italy, as a group of Jana's fellow students at the faculty of medicine were spending their vacations in her father's holiday home. The thought alone hurt me beforehand, as the place was magically connected to our love. It was a small group of ambitious and confident students, observing us curiously all the time. And it was not long before they started to challenge our intimacy and, in their eyes, a kitschy relationship. At the outset, their conversations had been witty and ironic, but the following days they adopted a more aggressive and smart-aleck undertone in their long morning conversations during breakfast. After a few days, I withdrew, starting to walk out alone in the late evening and to seek the paths where we had strolled in love during the last two summer holidays. A heavy melancholy seized me while Matthias, Janine, Leon and Kathrin were enjoying their stay as Jana's guests. And she was of course the expected impeccable host.

In the meantime, Matthias had started flirting with Jana before my eyes, lavishing wide-ranging compliments on her.

My isolation increased day by day and already after getting up in the morning Jana noticed my bad mood and could not change it for the better. Fortunately, I had many books with me, including again Heidegger, and I tried to identify the influence of Husserl's in my view pretty boring phenomenology on the early philosophy of Germany's most controversial philosopher. But my general mood was not set for such a research project and so, at least, I pretended to be busy with such questions in order to prepare for the looming exams next year. It was a ridiculous pretense, but philosophy was fit for this purpose. Yet the more I withdrew the more I became the target of the others' maliciousness. Jana was helpless because she had to care about her so-called friends and had no means to re-integrate me, to re-socialize me into this group to which I sensed a deeply rooted aversion. It was exactly the time, philosophically speaking when I started to despise all kinds of social utopia, a stance that from then on I would cultivate with growing intensity. This personal attitude to which I had always had a slight inclination crystallized more and more this summer since I was considering Jana's so-called classmates as brutal invaders. They were slowly and consistently destroying our relationship with the means of lewd commentaries. Besides, they were constantly attacking with their remarks about Jana's sex appeal all our inner and outer harmony. For the first time in my life, I felt that my resentment was slowly transforming itself into a kind of hate, blind and atavistic resentment, causing inner unbalance and disharmony. One night, sitting on the terrace while Jana and the rest were sleeping, I discovered an ugly thought, a totally repulsive sentence which had slowly begun to take shape in my mind: They were staining this place and, worse, our hearts. They were lowlifes and dregs. Still, I had enough sense to understand that my perception of the current setting was completely blurred by my jealousy and my excessive love for Jana. The only appropriate action would have been to leave the place, to spare all of them my moody presence and to let them enjoy their summer vacations. But I wasn't able to do it. I would have never left Jana alone with them. And what had hurt me most was the fact that it happened all at a 'sacred' place for me and her. A place where we had spent the most wonderful moments of our life, where we had learned about intimacy, about the articulation of our deepest feelings, in short, where we had discovered the fusion of our hearts and souls.

It was the self-confident and always joking Matthias who cheekily asked me one evening after the usual common dinner on the terrace if I would be sure Jana was a faithful partner, after all, she was flirting all the time at the university. Jana was not amused about that slanderous comment and gave him an angry look yet I took it very personally and went straight into confrontation, calling him – a fuck knuckle! He had not only succeeded to hurt deeply our most intimate life but also slandering Jana and bringing still more tension between us.

All my usual shyness and salient introversion were suddenly gone. From then on, I was always out for direct face-off and therefore, destroying the rest of the harmony between me and her. At least, we agreed to avoid too much socializing and common initiatives with her so-called fellow students for the rest of these summer days. It took us months to overcome this 'incident', yet we silently knew it was the beginning of our end.

The melancholy which had seized me since that unfortunate clash of three was slowly being replaced by sadness and a comprehensive disappointment about the fact that as a young couple, we would share the general fate of almost all first love affairs in our modern context: initially carried by an overwhelming passion which would be exhausted or changed into an irrevocable resentment over time. It was dawning on me that the ecstasy of passion would, later on, leave a bitter aftertaste due to the disenchantment of feelings, slowly transforming itself into an existential disillusion. Indeed, I had sometimes a strange foreboding that we had perhaps to pay a high price for the sublime elation of romantic love. First of all, we had to conform anew to the standards of mass society with its deeply rooted mechanisms of normative behavior and predictable thought patterns after a period beyond conventional time and space. But the biggest disenchantment was the insight that two individuals could never go for a long time together in the same direction, with the same aims, the same feelings and the same emotional rhythm. For many months I had the feeling that Jana had perhaps enjoyed in a certain way the shabby comments of Matthias, perhaps as a kind of flirt, since I never felt that she somehow understood my morbid jealousy. At the same time, I was quite aware that my illusionary expectations regarding our relationship had not been able to produce a sound and sober judgement. Of course, it was also possible Matthias had felt very much at his ease with us and it had been only his particular manner to kid in this way and to appreciate our extraordinary love. But the truth was that I could not stand influences and troubles coming from outside, rather, I considered them as foreign aggressive invasions into our small and intact universe. And there was finally a remarkable difference between me and Jana: she had a sound and very natural approach to living and to upcoming events, so she was always ready to advance and to follow the natural path to develop her personality. The more intensive events were, the more I needed to withdraw myself and isolate that experience. Despite our three years of lasting privacy, deep inside, she was of opposite character: translated into conventional and contemporary sociopolitical terms she was progressive and open-minded. By contrast, I was very much conservative, not to say reactionary, since I was permanently looking back and drowning in the beauty of past events. Consequently, I could not bear unforeseeable interferences in our relationship at all.

It was a spring evening in the midst of the week and I was laying on the couch in my small apartment, listening to a selection of best fado songs. My thoughts of how to prepare for the upcoming written exams and two presentations on the conception of doubt in the philosophy of Descartes and the meaning of substance in Spinoza's *Ethic* were permanently interrupted by the steady echo of Jana's voice. She had informed me earlier the day on the phone that she would not be with me at Easter, rather she would attend an organized trip of prospective doctors to southern Spain, not only with Matthias and his friends but worse, also with a so far unknown guy. Of course, it was the one who had brought her several times home on his motorbike from university as she suddenly told me a few weeks ago. His name was Ralph as she had mentioned it once, furthermore, she had often assured me that it would be a sheer coincidence since he was living in New-Isenburg as well. What a wondrous fate, I thought. Perhaps he lived just around the corner and paid her regular visits in her cozy apartment which had been so long our pure intimacy sphere. My thoughts rapidly transformed into a total obsession and I saw them loving passionately each other before my eyes. When I noticed that my mouth was completely dry as a result of these obsessive pictures hammering into my mind, I hastily left my apartment, took the car and sped to Jana, despite telling her earlier on the phone I did not want to meet her tonight. Instead, I drove as fast as I could to her home in less than ten minutes, passing two red lights in the reckless hope to cause a fatal accident that would have abruptly ended my suffering. I was sure she was not there, yet I saw light in her living room. She opened the door a short while after I had rung the bell but immediately went back to the black sofa in the living room where she evidently had been sitting, surrounded by a mess of paper and medicine books. Suffused with tremendous jealousy I explained to her with so far unknown aggressivity that I had discovered all and that I would know well about her waning feelings for me and her new enthusiasm for this 'jerk' Ralph. With a furious voice, I further added that it would be the worst nightmare for me to see how they would sit as a harmonious couple on the motorcycle, driving through the streets of Frankfurt and that I would certainly smash his fucking face if I met him. My hands were shaking caused by a deep existential fear of loss and the shocking awareness that precisely at this moment I was destroying the most precious in my life: my love for Jana. Our love. Meanwhile, she had desperately started to cry, relatively silent, yet more and more tears were running down her cheeks while her eyes had not lost any of their beauty, her intense weeping notwithstanding. Strange enough her tears did not touch me at all, only hours later, when I was walking emotionally exhausted through Offenbach's empty streets at night, I realized that I had extinguished the flame of two hearts in the same moment. The following days, I didn't count how often I apologized for my unappropriated tantrum. We only met twice more after this dishonorable incident. It was a shame to risk the end of almost three surreally beautiful years in that way. She needed time as she said which was a moderate, almost reconciling way to end this love story without hurting both of us further. But these two remaining meetings were indeed strange encounters since we basically wished to restore our relationship. I had the impression that Jana was really willing to start from scratch and to resume the idyllic rhythm of our romantic love affair. And yet all the doors for reconciliation had been definitely slammed, for the tenor of events did not allow us to change destiny. And fate, the fado that had been extolled in these Portuguese songs I loved so much, had already decided that for the rest of our life we would go on into different directions and that the unique remnants of our unreal love story could only be found there: in our intimate memories, buried at the bottom of our naked souls.

SOLILOQUY (PART TWO)

Death is incomprehensible, yet the sole key to understanding existence. Sometimes I saw the entire universe collapse in my daydreams and all creatures wiped out. It required an immense effort to uphold this paradoxical thought since everything was totally obliterated in my imagination. Literally, nothing remained. But neither fantasy nor intelligence are made for pondering on nothingness. It is at best a straight way to despair, without a way out. But the question remained how to understand life when there was not a key to grasp the unique certainty of life, the sole event that depends not on destiny but rather completes it, namely life's end. I had not yet understood if one could make out in death the very sense of existence or rather a senseless event of monstrous dimension which makes our earthly sojourn an incommensurable absurdity. Were all our personal sufferings, joy, even our conformism and social adjustment, not to say our moral principles and hopes and disillusions eventually for nothing? Were they completely senseless on the individual and the collective level? Meaningless. Illusionary as Schopenhauer explained in his masterpiece the *World as Will and Representation*. The meaning should have been restricted only to the ephemeral moment? Was that the religion of our zeitgeist? Impossible. It was pure thought terror and academic philosophy was unable to provide a remedy.

The post-Jana and the post-Turin-period continued to

be a time where all my private meditations resulted in exasperation. To avoid losing my memories of Jana and the time spent with her, I began to further intensify my constant walks around Garden Street and Station Street back to Hugenotten Avenue in New-Isenburg. I usually parked my car at the same quiet place in a side street, exactly where I had parked for the first time during my desperate waiting for her return from Italy. And now, years later, the priorities of my own life had not undergone any relevant change. Only that, in the meantime, I was convinced that I was suffering from a kind of mental defect because the sole meaning I could find in my life was the reminiscence of these happy days with her. There was absolutely no way for me to find sense beyond. I was not capable to give meaning to other activities or ideas or projects in life. They all frustrated me quickly and made my life seem empty. Instead, the ability to remember fragments of our being together and to evoke past feelings while strolling around the places where I had been happy for nearly three years still filled my heart with calm and peace.

During my long walks Nietzsche's Aphorism 125, *the madman,* of the *Gay Science* often came into my mind. That man who searched for God, but could not find him anymore, at the same time warning the people surrounding him to be careful with the erasing of such an enormous horizon of meaning. While looking contemplatively at the old linden trees that lined the road on either side, I often associated that aphorism with Jana, or better, with the question of what sense could life have without her, without all these beguiling memories? It was these which made my life into an existence suffused with beauty and happiness, moreover, I was completely aware that it was not worth searching anew for another source of joy because I would have never been able to find it. Living a contented life meant living in memories, and I clearly had the feeling that I would never experience again such a period, instead, there would be the risk to lead a mediocre existence, going to the office every day and striving for material wealth. A life completely adapted to the zeitgeist. Why should it be different for me? Sometimes I smiled at my insights which were ridiculous and kitschy for a real academic philosopher, but I was deeply convinced that the dignity of life would exclusively depend on the presence of beauty, even if this beauty existed only in memories. Existence without dedication to beauty was a sad mediocrity. I had read too many books not to understand that this was just a repetition of the fin-de-siècle approach and that my mental universe had been shaped by Baudelaire, Huysmans and D'Annunzio. Was I ashamed of my esthetic weltanschauung stemming from reactionary thinkers? Undeniably, I was too much a child of this second and totally over-politicized half of the twentieth century not to classify my stance into a political context. In any case, it was painfully true that I would not really fit into the leftist mainstream of my fellow PhD students who made me feel to be devoid of any serious intellectuality. My approach to existence was a pure esthetical one, although I never gave up the hope to draw through that vision sooner or later deeper and more intellectual conclusions. So far, my sole concerns had been how to shun the daily routine or what is usually called 'the real-life' and how to avoid positioning myself within the hierarchy of the social construct. I did not want to fit to the exigencies of the smoothly working social fabric. The tenacious reluctance on my part to adapt to a more rational lifestyle was perhaps pretty trivial or even childish and undoubtedly unworthy for a philosopher of an academic level. But, to be frank with me, I had long since stopped placing hopes in philosophy. Instead, over time I had to recognize that my inability to find meaning beyond my love story with Jana was only a veiled sign for a deeper-seated longing in my heart that could certainly never be satisfied.

Worse, I was permanently aware that my daily life was characterized by mediocrity, despite my daring doctoral thesis on eccentric philosophers like Heidegger, Nietzsche and Kierkegaard. These were all thinkers who thought beyond conventional scientific terms. Yet the days passed in the same pale rhythm. And if the Frankfurt Gazette would not have outsourced the advertising department due to urgent austerity measures, I would probably never have searched for another job since the free time this kind of employment offered me during the week was seductive to delve into contemplative and melancholy life. I was content to keep further reading relevant books for the dissertation a whole day and to leave the apartment about half an hour before sunset for I was totally in love with the early evening light as a sweet allusion to farewell. Later in the evening, I passed by Jana's former apartment, although she no longer lived there, and passed also by her parent's house, still recognizing the glimmer of light of her father's reading lamp behind the cream-colored shimmering curtains. Coincidentally, we sometimes met during my long walks which obviously surprised him but he had the necessary discretion not to ask me what I was doing in New-Isenburg late the evening. Because he was a sensitive and very intelligent person, I was convinced he knew why I was walking through the empty streets: namely caused by a fit of consuming yearning for the place where Jana and I had been happy for such a long period. From the beginning, he was very much aware of our passionate relationship and he never reproached me anything, neither addressed issues of our intimacy nor gave me the feeling that his daughter had wasted her time with me in all these years. Rather, the few times we met in the calm streets of New-Isenburg, he was the same kind and likeable man conveying a sense of old friendship, explaining to me that he was in need of rest to ponder about difficult court cases. So, he had to go for a walk alone. His voice sounded like he justified himself to me and I felt that he was slightly embarrassed to see me in this lonely condition. Before he kept walking on, he told me in a warm voice to take good care of myself. He carefully avoided addressing issues with regard to my former relationship with his daughter. During all our bygone conversations it had always become clear that he liked me and appreciated much my interests in literature and philosophy. Jana's father was one of the rare adults except for my professors and mostly leftist fellow students who showed great interest in a philosophical approach to life. After these random meetings in the streets of New-Isenburg, I continued my walk with a feeling of existential ease. It was as if my Jana period had suddenly come back and as though I had left again for at least a short while the dimension of space and time. New-Isenburg's quiet streets then assumed a kind of timeless beauty and zero gravity, inundating my heart and body with a nostalgia which immediately turned to pure joy, the joy of existence and joy of having known Jana. It was for a moment a kind of absolute, total happiness, something which did not really exist and was, therefore, of unreal and dreamy character. Yet this kind of experience made me subsequently ever more addicted to my cherished daily habit. Weeks or months would pass without such an elation, but they were moments where such a state of mind came back emotionally at full tilt, also without meeting Jana's father. Then, quite suddenly my heart became light and happy anew and one day while I was looking at the falling leaves and walking towards the town's western parts, I clearly realized that this kind of walk was nothing else like a prayer. I was a pilgrim, a pilgrim to my own memories, to my own tiny and insignificant universe that took shape through this concrete place and through every daily step I took. It was a simple pilgrimage to my inner self. And that endless abyss was sometimes suffused with a never experienced beauty.

Is there perhaps such a thing as an unholy prayer? I could not really grasp the meaning of my daily rituals and the looming peace and harmony with myself. Invariably all my everyday activities culminated at the moment when I would leave the office of the advertising department or when I would put aside my books to make the short drive to New-Isenburg. It was a pure pleasure joining a place where I could observe carefully and with due calm every day the different weather conditions and the slow changing of seasons without being forced to play my usual role, to fulfill the expectations of others and to engage in mediocre conversations. Besides, every angle of the town was full of inspiring memories. There was no need to travel far at all since the same place had every day a different smell and a different ambiance that prompted different reminiscences. Provided that it was not yet dark or raining, I would often sit on a bench on a cozy and small side street in Isenburg's western end, where I kept pondering upon the meaning of my life without Jana. The bench was surrounded by tall and healthy rhododendrons, next to a lovely villa with an open Japanese garden going to the street. I was often overwhelmed by a deep longing to be alone, hence whenever a rare walker came along, mostly accompanied by a dog, I felt disturbed in my intensity of meditations which were a loosed mixture of analytical thoughts, memories and dreams. And all that jumble of ponderings each time led to a radical quest for meaning, a kind of unyielding reflection that regularly led me to a cognitive dead end.

The result of my mental efforts was always the same: either everything was irrelevant, without the slightest meaning, suffused with the taste of an incomprehensible evanescence. This was the fanciless doctrine of the zeitgeist. Life as an accidental appearance before its total disappearance: the disappearance of deeds, of experiences and daily hopes, in short, the disappearance of everything which gave us the most compelling reason to go on living. And that conclusion hammered into my brain like a constant terror: Any reason to live will vanish into nothingness. Or perhaps life was yet the opposite of a dream, the opposite of an unreal and senseless illusion, namely a gate to eternity, a gate to a kind of absolute existence into which we would somehow drag behind all our experiences. I could not imagine further possibilities: a simple dualism. Life meant moving between the two options. The conventional approach to get through this existential tension and to adapt to the requirements of our present age was in my opinion artificially constructed to protect us from madness or dark despair. All the poetic ingredients had been deeply rooted at the bottom of my heart to sympathize with the conception that all our experiences would lead to a gate of eternity I would pass through and meet Jana again. There would await us the empire of fearlessness, a space of endless beauty that would be characterized by the total absence of hardship, a space without time and darkness. What a kind of outmoded and kitschy idea! And the more I thought about my thoughts the more I understood that I had to shun social life simply due to my unrealistic views. Besides, the more I thought about my thoughts the more I was able to advance further into the manifold dimensions of these ideas. The question, after all, would be finally one of morality. If nothing would remain of us absolutely nothing would remain of our deeds and intentions. That was the reason why I had been so deeply interested in de Sade's philosophy, a negative moral with totally nihilistic patterns of behavior and within a universe that did not deserve the name 'created', but was rather the random interplay of chaotic forces. Such a universe could have neither the slightest moral order nor provide a persuasive reason to continue living. Fortunately, de Sade's way of thinking was also only one of the huge range of ideas we had made of being and existence. Philosophical epistemes were characterized by permanent change and finally, most people would simply commit to the cognitive model prevalent in their time. And I understood better why Foucault had focused first of all on the history of epistemes as no episteme had ever been able to persist and to turn out as the correct form of knowledge. Hence, epistemes were nothing else than thought patterns to keep the social fabric in check, a means to control thoughts. That was my very personal reason I preferred to remain sitting on a bench in an unknown small town nearby the Airport of Frankfurt instead of speaking out or joining a research team at a university. Probably, it was only a cheap excuse to justify my lack of intelligence or even idleness. In short, I was not at all suited to pursue an academic career or integrate any philosophy into a kind of everyday life. It was very clear to me that philosophy could not be taught and for my part, I would never be able to tell others what should or could be the meaning of life, let alone derive a morally guiding principle from it. Who the hell was I, to have such ambitions? My conclusion towards the end of my studies of philosophy had been that academic philosophy was mainly limited to historical interest, epistemes were always changing and adapting to mankind's uncontrolled wills. A prevailing concept of reality was historically a fragile affair. In this context, I often remembered a sentence of the great French historian Paul Veyne, namely that the epistemes were at best the graveyard of dead truths. That was a real philosophical statement, absolute truth about the truth, so to say. But my fellow students totally disagreed and told me that philosophy, like mankind's social fabric, was in a permanent stage of development. I found it ridiculous because I never had enough faculty of abstraction to understand the progress we usually spoke about if we considered the development from ancient philosophy to the first half of our twentieth century with its total wars and devastating massacres: racial delirium, nationalist delusion, emancipation delirium and science delirium. How many dead souls, to put it with Gogol's masterpiece, lined the path to human sovereignty. And I thought of the tears that my mother still shed every week, seventy years after her father's senseless disappearance during the second world war. Rather than staying at home and taking care of his wife and three little girls, he was finally buried anonymously in the endless expanse and coldness of the Bristol Canal as one who seemingly believed in the end victory of that diabolic Nazi hubris. I had to treat my intimate and cynical thoughts mostly careful and I did never speak them out but the twentieth century's devastating massacres had been in my eyes the result of the so-called human progress, of the development of philosophical ideas. Simply an outcome of the proud yet illusionary conviction that man's intellect could provide final solutions to organize a sustainable lifestyle as humanity would use to say decades later. The apotheosis of man's yearning to *play God* had been an obvious feature throughout mankind's history. The pitfalls of freedom: riot or humility. What an endless tragedy. I had never forgotten how my sense of human dignity had been awaking for the first time at the sight of the conspicuous ugliness of socialist architecture during a field trip at school to East Berlin at the end of the eighties. I felt humiliated and totally lowered, although it did not concern me directly, seeing the endless rows of all these ugly apartment buildings. They were the negative highlight of dehumanizing dwelling places, considered by the communist ruling elite most probably as a culmination of the so-called progress in thought and deeds, instead, they symbolized the result of presumptuous ideas and a totally wrong interpretation of dignity. These loathsome buildings were in my eyes a frozen manifestation of the human will to power and corruption. Conjuring up all these impressions, it was ridiculous to see a linear-progressive development concerning human ideas. In which framework would this linearity unfold? What on earth would the climax be? It was probably the present-day dream of a universal comfort zone that we want to wrest from our natural environment for free, at least that was what our illusion told us. This was the pandemic utopia since the early nineties, especially after the enthusiastically celebrated Fall of the Wall.

People who had a so-called vision for humanity should be met with utmost skepticism I thought. Human progress was illusionary and mostly confused with technical innovations, dazzling our faculties of reason and leading to collective self-love with the result that man idolized his own intellectual splendor. I often thought back to Giuseppe, the charismatic Franciscan monk of Urbania's monastery with his charming German accent and his statement that human progress, or in his words, a timeless and comprehensive ethical awareness could be found only in a few individuals. For sure, I thought, everyone was eventually living in his own dream, his own reality that could never be considered as a reliable reality as such. And how different all our realities were at the end. While I was walking with Jana hand in hand through New-Isenburg's calm and tree-lined streets, a cruel war was raging only two flight hours from Germany in an until recently popular vacationland of Central Europeans: the Balkans. Warplanes of the NATO were bombing military positions of the Serbs and an opaque ethnic cleansing had again found its way into the heart of Europe. A controversial debate took place in Germany as to whether its warplanes should participate in this mission. At the time I did not pay much attention to the conflict and I followed the issue with the same interest with which I followed in reality much less relevant news. Our passionate love had isolated me and Jana from the problems and conflicts of the rest of the world. In that phase, we were completely depoliticized, instead, New-Isenburg's streets were calm and the sweet scent of the trees' lush leaves bewitched our senses. There was no room for others' distress. And could we really have changed something? Belligerence is a human constant.

The students at the faculty of philosophy organized many demonstrations those days, but I was totally indifferent to this political mobilization. Whenever students organized their sit-ins and gathered at the campus to take a stance against Germany's active participation in the aerial warfare, I took the subway to escape literally from all these young politicized and morally responsible people, heading to New-Isenburg or the southern outskirts of Frankfurt, where I usually had parked my car nearby the subway's terminus. Not infrequently, I was plagued by a bad conscience because a student of philosophy had simply to take a political stance and to attend such events, like Sartre did during the 68-revolution and also the far more unideologically politicized Michel Foucault did. This was more or less the attitude of all the other Parisian philosophers I admired when I had started my studies. But I had always been afraid of these masses which I considered as a dangerous and hysteric moralizing vector and whenever someone talked to me about political ideologies, I remained very insecure concerning my own political attitude and opinion. The widespread politicization of the student body seemed to me from day one at university as a new throng of inquisitors, of Manichean priests who would be merciless in their judgement whenever it came to politics. So, I preferred to read Kierkegaard's *either/or* in a quiet café, provided it was far away enough from the university to be sure that I would not meet other students.

Over time I got used to living without Jana, but considered all activities to be second-rate or at best as necessary in order to earn money and to maintain my relatively comfortable living standard. My sole pursuit was to muse about what my life was worth in a post-Jana period and it slowly dawned on me that I had perhaps overestimated Jana as a kind of absolute source of the meaning of life. And if everything would disappear what could have been the deeper sense of our passionate ecstasy? Perhaps only the romantic over-awareness of a biochemical reaction, of a serotonin rush, which would have assumed the same intensity with every other woman I would have fallen in love with? In addition to that, would death or dementia eventually obliterate also the sweetest and dearest memories? Me too, I was not totally immune to the temptations of nihilism. Would you really like to be immortal so that memories and experiences wouldn't make sense since you would be able to experience almost everything still in the future, my friend Mirko asked me one evening. I had no answer to it. But how could be a deed of moral value, or be called good or useful, in a context which is already destined to disappear as though it would never have existed?

In the meantime, the question of the meaning of my Jana-time had consequently expanded to the general question of the meaning of life as such. The idea of living a simple and relatively isolated life, dedicated to memories and the making of those a kind of counter-reality, attracted me with rising intensity. Already during my attentive reading of Dante at the small bay of Genova-Nervi, years before, I had the unmistakable foreboding that an anachronistic life would be a kind of asceticism against mass culture and communicative totalitarianism. So, it became clearer and clearer to me that the moments with Jana had been exclusively made to keep them carefully in my memory and to extol their entire beauty and integrity. The very task of my life was to save them from oblivion and to make them the meaningful background of my existence from which I could extract life's essentials. The rest of my biography, whether I would become a professor of philosophy or kitchen help, wouldn't matter anymore, it was of totally subaltern concern. I decided that my long walk towards disappearance should be accompanied by the memories of my time with Jana, of our moments of happiness, those moments when our surroundings seemed to transform themselves into the perfect setting of endless joy.

However, at the end of the day, I was a poor guy, unable to commit to higher ideals and to do something meaningful at least for others. A useless dreamer who was also writing a doctoral thesis in philosophy. Wasn't that ridiculous? Were my studies only studies for the studies' sake or rather to fill an enormous mental emptiness? And was the cognitive ability not at least the ontological difference between man and the rest of living creatures, a distinctive feature of his nobility through which man could establish a relation to being? But what was the use of such a distinctive disposition? That was the question that tormented me most of the time.

If reason had been given to us only for the sake of understanding the evanescence of our life, then it would be a totally masochistic and cruel faculty. In this case, reason would not even be an appropriate term since it would be nothing else than a strange accident of nature and could therefore not even be characterized as a punishment because punishment requires right and wrong as a reliable guideline. And if awareness was a purely accidental faculty too, it would be at best a pure and not less cruel instrument of understanding our own suffering. Since my intensive reading of Schopenhauer's ascetic and anti-Hegelian masterpiece *The World as Will and Representation* years ago, I had a better idea of the tensions between awareness, reason and will. Were perhaps Buddhists and Vedanta savants right, as Schopenhauer claimed, that the unique solution to soothe one's awareness was a total negation of the will in order to avoid suffering since it is obviously the will who determines our awareness which was consequently awareness of suffering; at least as long as we have passionate intentions. That meant not to love, not to buy anything and to eat and drink only moderately, in one word: abstinence. And as a corollary, it would most probably mean also not to remember Jana like I was doing it and not to stir longings, in other words, Schopenhauer's precept was to kill the elixir of life without killing oneself since suicide would have been still an expression of will. Such a noble stance would have been a futile experiment in our post-Nietzsche epoch which was totally characterized by a reversal of Schopenhauer's philosophical teaching: namely the claim for the absolute sovereignty of man's will. And still that outgoing century was clear proof that Schopenhauer was in a certain sense right with regard to the destructive outcome of human's will, especially when it is bundled in masses and given form in political awareness. All those broken dreams and utopias which had been transformed into the darkest dystopias, into inconceivable places of horror and I often had the impression that my beloved New-Isenburg which was carrying Jana's footprints and traces of her beauty, was surrounded by an unfriendly world. Could suicide be a solution? There were only a few moments I had thought about it. Once, after a strange phone call from Jana late at night. She asked me how I was doing and I told her with perfect feigning that I was very well since I was about to leave for Tuscany in a few days. In order not to fall silent, I immediately added if I could bring her anything she needed from Italy. To my surprise, she answered in the affirmative and demanded with her irresistible beautiful voice which brought my heart to an almost standstill, if I could bring her along with some Ray-Ban sunglasses. Sure, I said, then I silently thought: Of course, I will give you a pair of fashionable sunglasses so that you will be even more desirable for others. Yet my composure during the conversation was astounding compared to my inner turmoil.

After that strange phone call, I felt not only all the broken splinters of our bygone relationship once again, but also the irretrievability of all that we had experienced together. And it felt like I was fatally stabbed, so that I had to leave my apartment, to break out for the usual walk at New-Isenburg, to relieve my agonizing longing and to look if there was light in her apartment. During the short trip, I was stammering the whole time the same sentences aloud, namely 'I can't live without you, Jana! I can't live without you!'

This emotional shock made my short journey to Tuscany an extreme roller coaster ride since my inner confusion was persisting and I couldn't find a way to calm down. Italy, it was clear, was not the right place to distance me anew from Jana. I stopped my car at every small village after the exit Valdichiana, sitting for a while in any Bar to take a coffee and then to move on into the next village to continue that ritual until the end of the day. After my dinner in a simple trattoria at Pienza, I discovered an inviting eyewear shop and bought elegant Ray-Ban sunglasses as Jana had desired. I must have made a wistful face because the female seller asked me if I was okay which I replied with a warm and friendly yes, moved by her attentiveness concerning my emotional state. In the upcoming days I was meditating on a kind of peaceful and unspectacular suicide: to lay down on a snowy winter day on my well-known bench under the time-honored oak trees in New-Isenburg and freeze to death. It seemed to be a somehow reconciliatory and peaceful idea to simply freeze to death within a winter landscape and to accept silently the singularity of that beautiful time with Jana. To accept the premature end of everything. To simply accept evanescence. To put an end to everything. But that mood for suicide did not last very long and disappeared fortunately after a few days. I was still longing for memories as the decisive elixir of life.

Through memory and imagination, I quickly regained my vitality and will to live. And that was perhaps the deeper reason why I had been from the beginning of my passion for philosophy a keen reader of Nietzsche. His thoughts were life-affirming, despite many elements of discipline and asceticism. And in all his writings I could always find a sense for esthetics and beauty, for life's unmistakable grace and dignity. What Hegel was for Marx's philosophy was in a certain sense Schopenhauer for Nietzsche's philosophy for he made a total reversal of Schopenhauer's negation of the will and life force. It had always impressed me that Nietzsche clearly said yes to the phenomenon of life, he said yes to existence at all costs. But strange enough that I said yes to an existence which had so far characterized by a mixture of melancholic mood and steadily unfulfilled yearning. This kind of stance was the only one where I could feel existence in all its entirety, with all its dialectical beauty, comprising moments of suffering as well. Over time, I realized more and more that my deep love for Jana helped me to discover the still deeper love for life, for the world, for all the trees that surrounded me, for the sunset light sticking to the clouds. And I realized that I was losing my feeling for everydayness which was probably a healthy phenomenon to move on beyond the ordinary.

The modern age was undoubtedly the result of an unrestrained realization of man's will. Who was responsible for this false vision of man's destiny, since history had revealed itself so far for many people as a gloomy dystopia? Empirical research clearly demonstrated that the standard of living had never been higher or better. But at what price? Millions of dead soldiers and civilians were within the laboratory of technological progress during the First and Second World Wars. Both conflicts had been sold to the masses as the final and decisive ideological battles of mankind, moreover, haughtily characterized as anti-religious. What a comprehensive delusion. And the so-called concepts of progress and prosperity were most probably cynical ones, not only with hindsight but also with regard to the upcoming costs for these achievements. But what could I change about these facts? Instead of complaining, I should rather consider myself lucky that I was able to go for my daily walks and to chase my nostalgic daydreams. And fortunately, as a child of the second half of the twentieth century, I had been able to escape that ethnocentric collective madness. So, I kept pondering over the happy circumstance that I had been brought up within the peaceful era of the so-called end of history. Francis Fukuyama excluded more or less that there would be other forms of triumphs for political systems in the future, the present-day liberal democracy was its logical climax. Personally, I couldn't share Fukuyama's vision of the victory of liberal democracy due to the constant hunger for conflict which had characterized human nature throughout history, even though Fukuyama's premise certainly was that liberalism had put an end to man's contentiousness. Whenever I sat a few hundred meters north of New-Isenburg's train station at the edge of the forest next to the railway tracks, observing sometimes for hours the coming and going of the regional and long-distance trains, I fully understood how lucky my generation was: personal liberties, choice of an adequate lifestyle, let alone sexual freedom. The system's advantage was that it created at least the perfect illusion of freedom. Human desire had few constraints.

I came across Fukuyama's book during a lecture by the famous Professor Scharlau who taught theoretical philosophy at the University of Frankfurt. He was always up-to-date regarding social and historical research. While he was explaining historical materialism, he shifted to Fukuyama's new book and referred to it with a certain enthusiasm, even though he told us that the triumph of liberalism was for sure a Pyrrhic victory. Although more people would temporarily benefit from global prosperity, liberalism would eventually exacerbate again the social differences and create new forms of marginalization.

Only a few hours later I bought the book nearby the university and read it all at once in a shabby student coffeehouse next to the bookstore, while I ordered one coffee after another and yielded to my caffeine addiction. Fukuyama's book was fascinating and during that afternoon I experienced one of the rare moments of enthusiasm when I thought that the end of my relationship with Jana might open up an opportunity for my young life.

What a brave work I thought in between, although I was deeply convinced that even democracy would not remain in a state of balance and could also adopt totalitarian traits in implementing more and more intrinsic taboos. The overall and long-term objective of its doctrine would be perhaps the education of their citizens as sluggish consumers with a strong tendency to political apathy. Hitherto there was simply no historical experience and therefore no concrete idea in what kind of political system a tired and saturated democracy might transform itself. The general definition of development and freedom was so far depending not only on material and technological progress but rather on a continuous overstepping of moral limits and the dynamism of freeing man from his natural limitations would sooner or later unleash a new wave of destruction. I was convinced that the legitimacy of democracies would depend on carrying the so-called emancipation of mankind to its extremes. And what about those who were not willing to go in this direction. What about those who were not in the mood for total emancipation?

Hundred years after the fin de siècle our free European societies were entering a new decadence era, namely the fin de millénaire. And my blissful period spent with Jana was an unmistakable proof of it on a personal level. The earth and our surroundings had revealed themselves as a most friendly place for us, a place of unlimited consumerism and freedom of movement, provided one has the right passport. We had paradise on earth, even though a temporary one. And thanks to Jana my level of happiness hormones had reached a stable level for a constant period, so beauty and joy had filled my soul, no matter where I had been. As a result, I was not sensitive enough for a negative or critical eye on social or political reality. As regards my daily reading habits I continued to skim merely the feuilletons and the sports section. I was so emotionally focused on Jana and addicted to her that I was rather much afraid of all these controversial political debates. But protests were intruding even into our philosophical seminars for advanced students. Especially the conservative professor Radenburg was so much afraid when many students besieged his weekly lecture on Heidegger's *Being and Time* and started to insult him as a fascist who was ready to support German militarism on the Balkan. The poor Radenburg, a senior academic professor and specialized in Greek philosophy and German idealism, did not understand what happened and was on the verge of collapse. He had previously signed a petition of academics for military intervention, as genocide should not repeat itself in Europe. It was one of the rare moments where I forgot for a short while my relationship with Jana, taking a resistance attitude, telling the aggressive leftists, anarchists and Marxists that I wished to stay here and to continue listening to Radenburg's lecture on Heidegger. Even a young female Marxist immediately threatened me with violence, but they soon understood that I was ready to defend myself by all available means. In the meantime, Radenburg had fled the seminar room. The event confirmed my deeply rooted feeling of being scared of the ubiquitous over-politicization around me, and moreover, in this academic setting, I had never felt comfortable. The gathering of more than two academics had always seemed to me not only like a threat for the world's breathing rhythm but also like a fundamental threat for the poetic weltanschauung, a threat for beauty and dignity. Especially after delving into Fukuyama's essay, I thought that the decadence period which was propagated by parts of the Western political and scientific establishment as the age of the *end of history,* was not at all the climax of a liberal weltanschauung and fulfilling of democratic ideals. It was rather the outset of an era of scientific dogmatism and reductionism. Reality would certainly be sold in a more sober and unpoetic manner and I had the constant impression that a new army of soldiers of research was being established around me to conquer the earth a second time after the rage of industrialization. That era would be unmistakably more dogmatic, with an even stronger salvation mission, namely to save mankind definitely from darkness and to establish a new and real progressive age. The supposed end of history was not only characterized by the definite end of metaphysical hopes and longings, the latter were irreversibly replaced by immanent knowledge and the illusion to find sufficient meaning in material progress and individualism. Yet, I was convinced that this kind of weltanschauung would carry the same risk to patronize our thoughts exactly the same way former ideologies did. Manipulation of thought would not take place through ideology but through methodology. But I was also much aware of my thought's bizarrerie to assert that scientific methodology would bear the risk to transform itself into a new ideology which would mean a new culmination of mankind's self-esteem and eventually a new form of apotheosis of rationality. And in that haughty atmosphere, scientific research and economic growth would form a new alliance advancing in lockstep to sell their doctrine of salvation to mankind.

It had always been a typical feature of my approach to philosophy ruminating on books we did not really deal with at university. The further away I was from my usual academic setting, the more I was able to focus passionately on reading and contemplating. I loved to read and did not want to share thousands of arguments and opinions about a book I had discovered myself on the basis of purely individual interest. Fukuyama's bold essay triggered many digressive thoughts in me and I was convinced that a new revolution was taking place, much more comprehensive and complex than the Enlightenment of the late eighteenth century. And unlike the French revolution, it would unfold itself in a very different way, in a holistic manner, not only affecting the West since West was a geopolitical term which had anyway long lost its meaning. The transformation would be rather accomplished through creeping mental engineering, with the claim to be universal and non-ideological and with the dream to pave the way for an era of science as a new and auspicious individual and collective remedy. Yet already towards the end of the nineties, we had believed, encouraged by the historical turmoil and the end of socialism, to live in a new enlightened era, on the summit of awareness. Was not every period characterized by such consciousness and was it not a typical feature of the human mind to feel like the spearhead of evolution, since it was an existential axiom of every generation to look back and to blindly compare? This was our time, a heyday of awareness with its rising esteem of the environment and the establishment of a green party. Strange enough that we rediscovered our natural surroundings at the moment when we were living at a secure distance from it and under the impression of being able to dominate it. But this kind of classical awareness-raising would also run the risk to be illusionary since modernity as a whole had already been shaped by false promises from its outset. Nietzsche had predicted the modern epoch would be a mask, a theater, a pure stage play, in brief, sheer fiction. But what I knew for sure was that I had not the slightest intention to play a part on this stage.

What was also certain was that my sole and real personalized philosophy had been so far cowardice. To distance myself from other people, I did not shun them, rather I was generally a very friendly person, mainly due to my fear of conflict and to the overwhelming need for calm and composure. I quickly learned that politeness was the best way to keep a distance from others and to avoid senseless differences of opinion. For this very reason, the challenging and aggressive attitude with which I had approached the students of philosophy besieging the seminar room during Radenburg's lecture on Heidegger surprised me in retrospect. It had been most likely a personal aversion since I did not like the interference with individual freedom and that afternoon, I had really been in the mood to further deepen my knowledge about Heidegger's thought. Dealing with his complex philosophy was a suited remedy to get rid at least for a moment of my emotional fragility.

While I breathed my beloved November air and walked calmly towards the supermarket of New-Isenburg's West, I thought to myself that these over-moralizing troublemakers would certainly be the next generation of brilliant essayists and messengers of a new doctrine of salvation. As political opportunists, they would confuse the transient moment of existence with an immanent eternity and proclaim a new smart age, namely the real end of history, characterized by the dream of a redeemed life without metaphysics and longing. Heralds of new human creatures without humility, Gnostics of proud rationalism, disguised in modesty and ecological awareness.

Instead of constantly criticizing, I should have been grateful to live in this era of freedom, a relatively balanced age of consumerism and social democracy, regardless of a then so-called conservative-liberal government. Meanwhile, these terms had already become weak definitions with obsolete meanings. There were no social restrictions at that time, no private pressures from the part of Jana's family, not even moral objections. Rather, I lived for a while exclusively for a concatenation of moments of pleasure alone. For example, the enchanting period when Jana received me almost every evening in her apartment. And I still could not get rid of the always returning image: Jana as she wore her red high heels and black lingerie which accentuated her slim body and the smooth complexion of her skin. And every time an excess of so far unknown liberty regularly opened up to us, where political concepts and definitions of epochs made no longer any sense. My sole universe was my total devotion to her body and soul, to her soft voice and her beguiling fragrance. It was most probably a characteristic relationship for a typical decadent era. The only real threat to our love affair was the potential exhausting of our own feelings which would have been a purely natural process. Sensuality and passion would blossom and wither away, this was eventually all lovers' fate. And years later, whenever I felt loneliness, I was always longing for a meeting and conversation with Giuseppe, since I did not forget the last words of this humble, anachronistic person while bidding goodbye. *I should appreciate my time with Jana as a gift, as pure mercy of God.*

But I was longing not only for a dialogue with Giuseppe but also to sit alone in the Basilica of Sant'Ambrogio in Milan to finally kneel down and to thank for the moment when I touched for the first time Jana's fingers, just a few instants before our first kiss. It was a second birth for me, announcing at the same time the upcoming of the first death.

ESCAPISM (PART TWO)

I had been starting to further extend my walks. They became not only longer but also more contemplative. Yet my wistfulness had slowly begun to emancipate itself from Jana's image and reminiscences, transforming in a kind of pure, almost abstract longing, detached from the exclusive memories of my relationship with her. I set out crossing the railroad tracks at the western end of New-Isenburg, exploring parts of the great forest west of the town covering the entire area until the huge Frankfurt International Airport. Over time I strolled deeper and deeper into this forest of a very old stock of trees, a mixture of center European pines, old European beeches and oak trees. With the advancing of fall, a gorgeous play of colors set in and since my first long walks in this time of the year in the Eastern part of the airport forest, as I named it from then on, November became definitely my favorite month with its gentle farewell atmosphere. Only a few people lost themselves here, mainly commuters taking the bicycle to go to work at the greater Airport area, coming either from New-Isenburg or the nearby southern outskirts of Frankfurt. I became such a permanent guest on these forest trails that I recognized almost everyone in a short amount of time and sometimes we dared even to greet hesitantly each other. These endless and empty paths in direction of the airport exerted an irresistible attraction as they strengthened my longings and satisfied my hunger for freedom. I soon developed a kind of paradox feeling, on the one hand, I appreciated the usual tranquility, on the other hand, I sympathized with the abrupt end of that calmness, caused by the roaring noise of aircraft on approach. I would never have dared to dream that a new passion could emerge, a passion for planes even though I wasn't particularly interested in technological innovations and the art of engineering. The elegant wings of the different types of aircraft were soon intensifying my general feeling of liberty. It was a strange experience and I would never speak with anyone about it, but the companionship of low-flying aircraft gave me the impression of being in touch with the world despite this calm and isolated place which consisted of venerable trees.

I was very happy to be able to avoid academic hysteria from now on, moreover, professor Gardner at the University of Darmstadt gave me the unexpected freedom to explore at will the rebellious structures of thought of Kierkegaard, Nietzsche and Heidegger. The readings of those eccentric thinkers kept filling me with energy and I had the impression that I was staunchly writing against academic philosophy, therefore, producing an academic work on anti-academic and vital thought. It felt great, even though it was probably pure snobbism and no less the result of my chronic cowardice. In time, I had become a specialist in hiding my beliefs, being totally aware that these perspectives would not have the slightest meaning for others. Beyond, I did not believe that a philosopher could really produce an interesting philosophy within an academic setting and there were plenty of famous thinkers sustaining that assumption: Kierkegaard and Nietzsche who early left university. And in a certain sense, Schopenhauer as well since he was never able to attract a greater audience. Not to mention Heidegger whose thought blossomed in his self-imposed exile in the Black Forest after the end of the Second World War. And of course, the profane mystic Émile Cioran whose works were undoubtedly the climax of radical independent and paradoxical thought in the second half of the twentieth century. All of them were the best proof that academic activity was not conducive to genuine thinking.

The work on my dissertation took place almost exclusively deep in the night. It was a period when my longings for Jana finally weakened. I usually returned from my job in the advertisement department on Wednesdays and Thursdays early in the morning. Other days I came back late from my ritualized strolls in New-Isenburg and subsequently enjoyed working in the silence of the night. After making a lemon verbena tea, I first skimmed books that had absolutely nothing to do with my PhD. These were new discoveries, among them translations of Arab philosophy and Islamic thought which led me finally to al-Ghazali whose personal history impressed me. Hence, before resuming my academic work, I often travelled with al-Ghazali's *Deliverance from error* through the width of the Khorasan and solidarized completely with his solitude and his fervent quest for meaning. The thirst for truth prompted him to abandon his family and prestigious position as one of the most renowned Muslim jurists. Albeit an English translation, his words seemed to me like a personal message, the deeper meaning I could entirely grasp: either there is meaning in life because God had willed to integrate humans into the patterns of His creation or our existence is an illusory awareness, transitory and without the slightest sense. His staunch intellectual attitude ushered into a consequent search for God, without compromise, full of spiritual and physical tenacity. This book was absolutely admirable, especially his comprehensive attack on philosophy and its epistemological ephemerality. The personal description of his strict seclusion in one of the Minarets of the Umayyad Mosque in Damascus and of his radical ascetic practice until he had finally tasted the certainty of the Absolute Being left a tremendous imprint on me. As I sipped my tea within the nocturnal silence, I longed again for meeting Giuseppe since I was sure that he would have certainly known many details about the famous Arab intellectual he had already mentioned during our intimate conversation. Strolling through the bookstore a few weeks ago, I had immediately recognized the name of al-Ghazali, not hesitating a moment to acquire that pocketbook. And what the Minaret of the Umayyad Mosque in Damascus was to him, were exactly New-Isenburg's streets and majestic trees to me. While Ghazali was totally convinced that nothing else could divert him from his path to search for truth, I tried to translate his experience into my own, only with Jana as the very source of life's meaning. In contrast to the drunken mystics against whom al-Ghazali fervently polemized in order to establish a practice of sober approach to God, my mystical union would not be a self-abandonment in the Absolute Being, but would rather correspond to total submission to Jana. I certainly would never be able to go beyond that mundane dimension of union and that pure emotional state. I could only dream of the moments I put my head between her legs, telling her that it was better she had no idea how much I loved her. Then she always smiled tenderly and told me with her lovely voice that the truth was exactly the other way around.

The recent development of my personality, despite my relative serenity, was worrying, at least for outsiders as I supposed. I did always feel out of place unless I took my usual long walks and focused afterwards in nocturnal seclusion on new books acquired for my dissertation. The beauty of the natural surrounding and especially the solitude of the airport forest gave me a relaxing break from despair. In the meantime, my intense longing and melancholy sublimated to a purely esthetical level. I had started to buy all kinds of available Vogue editions, the Italian, the French, the English and the German Vogue. And in addition to the focused research on the common overlap of the philosophies of Kierkegaard,

Heidegger and Nietzsche, particularly on their assault on the reckless imperialism of modern rationality, I started skimming fashion magazines for hours. I looked for scenes that reminded me of particular moments with Jana, for example as we were lying silently next to each other, simply enjoying the other's presence, the other's beguiling fragrance, the other's mesmerizing tenderness. The subsequent drawing of these subjects was a pure mental necessity and I did not care if I had talent or not. The best and most timeless manner to represent these subjects was to draw them in black and white, charcoal on great white cardboard. All subjects, carefully selected, were sublime and represented passionate love with great decency since it was important to avoid vulgarity at all costs, no matter how great the passion was. The scenes were full of intimacy and isolated interiority. They were the perfect tranquillizer and the ideal projection surface of my own permanent longings.

The fact was that my small apartment on the outskirts of Offenbach along with the airport forest became my luxury retreat since both places made sure that not too many people were disturbing my reminiscences and attacks of wistfulness. And what could I wish more than being surrounded by these few pieces of furniture, floor lamps and thoroughly organized books as well as being calmed down by the melancholic universe of Portuguese fado and Spanish flamenco songs? The recently added drawings with the intimate motifs in black and white matched the interior perfectly. It was my own small empire where I could live undisturbed, sometimes interrupted by phone calls, mostly from my parents, sister or Olaf and Mirko. To this soothing setting were added my walks with direct contact to the beauty of nature, the countless trees and forest plants and I had been falling in love with the observing of the change of seasons, of the different colors of leaves and flowers. In January and February, the snow-covered and endless paths leading to the no-man's-land of the airport area isolated the entire landscape from the rhythms of seasons and from time in general. It became then a timeless setting for nearly three months which conveyed calm and peace for nature and mind. And if I had collapsed on a cold day and had been discovered lifeless by some driver of the airport security who regularly observed this huge forest and deserted landscape, who then would have dared to say that I had not had a beautiful life and death? After many years of suffering, I felt totally relaxed as though my pain had completely left my body for a while. So, my consuming longing and painful melancholy were medically speaking under control since I had found an adequate remedy to cope with. Most importantly, I accepted that my self-imposed escapism was the result of my weakness of character in a time of a primitive, but relatively balanced social Darwinism, tempered by a market economy which was officially called social. We were all forced to be more or less good consumers and had no alternative if we wished to live together peacefully.

The relentless passage of time also affected my friendship which hardly withstands the vibrations of fading youth. Only with Olaf and Mirko did I always have the feeling that crisis and periods of long silences could be overcome without harming our relationship. For the rest, we all were searching for our place in that new age of rampant liberalism and despite more or less distinctive traits of recalcitrance and non-conformism we were slowly becoming average and efficient members of our social context. It was irrefutably a great advantage of the prevailing zeitgeist to be very smooth and at the same time to make of outsiders eventually perfect fitting insiders. The period was colorful as never before in mankind's history and there was hardly one who was not able to find an appropriate place within society. Consequently, each of us was shifting interests and priorities, our emotional relationship became looser and replaced by the natural instinct for material wealth and the obligations of working life. Yet the most disruptive factor of our friendship was obviously the appearance of women in our lives. It quickly turned out that there was no way to maintain a post-youth friendship among us due to the very different characters and ambitions of the female partners. Astonishing was also to observe how quickly my friends changed attitudes when they were accompanied by their loved ones. Additionally, a certain kind of jealousy was rapidly arising among all these young women and it was strange that they tried strenuously to emphasize the advantages or the virtues of their respective partner, despite we all having known each other inside out for almost fifteen years or longer. As for my part, I had a special status as someone with a failed relationship and in the end, I was happy to be always invited to these exceptional get-togethers although I came without a partner. During my time with Jana, I had a totally sure instinct for not exposing us to a larger circle of friends, including my own friends, let alone her friends or fellows of the university. That was the reason for the uneasiness I had already felt many weeks before we subsequently spent our last summer vacations with her fellow students in her father's south Italian vacation home. In retrospect, my deep discomfort was not an a priori jealousy facing that upcoming difficult situation, but rather a foreboding of our upcoming end of the relationship since my love for her was so deep that it needed total intimacy, an unconditioned claim of mutual attention. And that had been indeed our commonly shared philosophy of intimacy, at least during the first two years of our love, until the relentlessness of the run of events had slowly eroded that tender attitude. The more people surrounded us later on, the more we were in an emotional downward spiral, a fall of our hearts into space where our feelings had been permanently attacked by the subaltern and meaningless affairs of others.

The topics of our tense conversations in these well-intentioned attempts to come together in mixed couples shifted from once cultural debates on music, arts, literature and soccer to more primitive matters like interest rates for real-estate credits or real-estate prices in Frankfurt's residential areas. In short, we had surrendered our young and unbiased approach to the world to a more conventional perspective, motivated by the urge to position ourselves slowly but steadily in our so-called free and prosperous society. Consequently, we had replaced the subjects of conversation dealing with cultural and immaterial issues with pure material topics. It was a spontaneous development since most of us now had university degrees and started professional life with the legitimate aim to acquire a certain social status. The sole exception was Emre who had recently been through with his divorce and continued to look unbalanced. He dreamt of living in Paris. All these typical topics of fresh couples only reopened old sores and he often stayed discreetly out of the talks during our rare gatherings, focusing on drinking and silently listening. We were all worried considering this sorry sight but there was nothing we could do because we were busy with our own life situation. The exigencies of our late modern society and its appeal to individualism was now clearly perceptible. Our once common interests, fervently debated, gave way to fragmented but purely mundane subjects which were at best suited to fill a conversational void or to maintain rather a shallow talk. We felt it, but were helpless and the female partners did absolutely nothing to maintain our strong friendship. They wanted to have their partners for themselves alone. Excesses of individual imperialism. Yet, remembering my days with Jana, I could perfectly understand it.

There were two decisive moments towards the end of the twentieth century which marked, strangely enough, also for me the end of an era, ushering smoothly in a post-post-Jana period. It was Kai and his partner Katia who took the initiative to invite their close friends to a New Year's Eve party on December 31, 1998. It was an immense joy to come together and to share meals, drinks and cool music. But there were many among the guests that I had not known so far. In the beginning, I had short conversations, especially with former classmates, the Greek fraction, with Konstantinos and Christos and with others of the wider circle of old school friends. Then Katia came to me and introduced me to a very good friend of hers, Naima. I was totally shocked when I looked into her dark eyes which were dignified to immediately compete with the beauty of Jana's eyes. We shook hands and gave each other a friendly smile, but I was not able to hold her gaze for long. She was smartly dressed despite tight jeans and had a soft voice. Only a short while later I took a seat next to her, offering to bring her a selection of the buffet. Her answer was a smile with the short remark she would not eat pork since she was a Muslim. Replying that I would offer her an excellent selection of a pork-free meal I also presumed that she would not drink of the excellent red wines carefully selected by the host, 'And no wine and beer, right?'

'Indeed,' she said with a natural smile, 'I am obliged to have fun without alcohol. Strange, don't you think so?'

For a moment I was surprised by her directness concerning the topic but was happy to intensify the conversation with her. 'I think that's pretty cool since especially males are always in need of alcohol to strike up a relaxed conversation, first of all with females,' I replied, gently smiling and further asking if she would mind showing solidarity with her. 'What about two non-alcoholic Mojitos, mixed by my ex-classmate Konstantinos?' She nodded kindly. Her natural beauty and elegant demeanor put me in an unusually good mood.

I walked over to the sumptuous buffet, lovingly organized by Kai and Katia, preparing attentively two dishes and asking Konstantinos for the two soft drinks. He took care of all drinks that evening since he had been always well-versed in that field.

'Two non-alcoholic Mojitos?' he said to me, 'what's wrong with you? Oh, I understand that something is looming, isn't it?'

he added with a wink and devoted himself to mix them.

'Not at all, I will just learn to have fun without alcohol tonight, something that you have never experienced,' I replied and we both laughed wholeheartedly, like in the good old schooldays.

While I was starting to arrange the plates, I perceived that my fingers started to tremble again years after the end of my relationship with Jana. And the reason for this was the presence of a young woman. Suddenly the unexpected hope for a new emotional life emerged. Konstantinos brought us the two drinks and I handed her a wide selection of tasty dishes. She smiled, slightly embarrassed and said:

'It's Ramadan right now, you might know perhaps. I haven't eaten anything in the whole day. It seems you have known it?'

'Really? I didn't know. I apologize for my lack of cultural knowledge. May I ask you where you are from?'

'I'm originally from Morocco, from Berkane, a city nearby the Algerian border you certainly have never heard of,' she said.

Morocco and Ramadan were both two keywords for me and my rising happiness quickly transformed into a total storm of enthusiasm. After my recent discoveries of eminent Muslim thinkers like al-Ghazali and Ibn Tufail, I intended to impress her with my knowledge of the late Golden Era of Islam, 'I recently discovered al-Ghazali's *Alchemy of Happiness* and Ibn Toufail's *The History of Hayy Ibn Yaqzan*. I am much attracted by the purity of Muslim thought and its absolute will to search for the truth.'

'Oh, my God,' she said, 'you are a strange guy,' but she looked at me for a moment full of sympathy before continuing the conversation, 'I don't know very much about Muslim thinkers, but I am sure they teach you the opposite of what we learn about religion and of how we were brought up within our families. For a girl, that means tacitly accepting unlimited male power. Please, don't misunderstand me. I love my religion and of course the fasting of Ramadan. But I am totally fed up with religion as a means of male dominance over women's behavior.'

'Wow! You are very tough! So how do you then manage to be here? Is this a problem?'

'Yes, it is, at least for my parents. I told my mother that I am only with female colleagues just around the corner. She will tell my father later. Imagine that even though I'm twenty-one years old. Neither of them knows that I am spending my evening with young und unmarried men like you who drink also alcohol. Though the most important thing is that she always reassures my father and brothers. My sisters of course do always provide me with an alibi,' she explained to me.

We started to look sometimes each other for long moments and were full of mutual sympathy. When I went to the toilette Olaf took me aside after he hugged me strongly since we had not yet had the opportunity to talk more intensely. It felt good, he was always a pillar in my life.

'That beauty will disarm you,' he said to me. 'I can see it from over there that you are admiring her. It is so good to see you in this kind of mood,' he added and smiled at me.

Naima corresponded exactly to the ideal type of woman as Jana had embodied it and it was likely I was still searching for a second Jana, for a double. Olaf was right, her black straight hairs, brought into shape by a hair barrette and falling behind her ears on her shoulders as well as her black great eyes with their piercing glance were driving me mad after a long time of emotional lethargy. And from the outset of this evening, it was clear that Naima was a young woman I could fall in love with again. My entire body was flooded by a sense of pleasure, giving me the necessary energy and tension to create a pleasant setting for our get-together. During the evening we talked about different topics, from our professional life to private details. It flattered me that she spoke to me bluntly, even regarding her difficult situation to get some free space and time and to elude control from her parents and brothers. She told me completely relaxed about the organization of her daily life, of her job for the city's energy agency and about her will to live as independent as possible.

At midnight we all celebrated the new year outside in the cold streets, looking at the fireworks and hugging each other warmly. It took only a few minutes until I found myself again next to her. Later we still ate the dessert at the buffet and continued to talk. She took the initiative in the conversation, giving me the opportunity to look at her and to observe the movement of her wonderful lips while she was talking and smiling. At a certain moment, we both realized that we were among the last guests and as Konstantinos and Olaf were bidding goodbye, we joined them. Outside the door, in the freezing cold of the early morning, we looked at each other without knowing what to do or what to say.

'Do you live far from here?' I asked her.

'Ten minutes' walk,' she said.

'Would you allow me to accompany you to your front door so that you arrive home safely?' I added shyly. 'It is too late to go home alone and most probably you will encounter many drunks,' I told her since a better sentence did not occur to me.

'Thank you so much,' she replied. 'I would indeed feel much better with you by my side.' The answer sounded like a perfectly composed piece of music.

We walked side by side along the avenue ushering into the inner city. It was icy but not snowing and it was really the first moment we did not talk to each other for a while. I heard the rhythm of the footfalls prompted by the noise of her high-heeled boots and I still did not dare to utter a word. Instead, I realized that my heart was full of sincere feelings which was a confusing experience after that long period in emotional no man's land, yet I tried to cope with that explosive cocktail of happiness hormones. We arrived in front of the entrance door of the house where she was living with her older sister on the sixth floor and lingered for a moment in silence before I addressed a few words to her with a touch of courage.

'Naima, I apologize!'

'You apologize for what?' she said with a tender voice.

'I am craving so much for seeing you again? Do you think it will be possible? And I apologize that I did not ask you if you have a boyfriend or not and that I am addressing you in such an outright manner.'

'No, I have no boyfriend, I wouldn't feel at ease! But don't worry, I can't find any reason why we should not meet up again. I think you are a peculiar type, reading Muslim thinkers and philosophers,' she said with an indulgent smile.

While I was looking into her eyes my heart seemed to stop. Nonetheless, I took off my black leather gloves and put my right hand slowly with utmost carefulness on her left cheek.

'Thank you so much, Naima! May I call you tomorrow at home?'

'Thank you for this unusual evening I didn't expect.' She took a ball pen out of her small, but elegant ruby colored purse and wrote her phone number on the back of my hand.

I took the hand with which she held the ball pen and we took up exchanges of caresses. My heart was filled with bliss perceiving she enjoyed it devotedly. Naima was so beautiful, she looked deeply in my eyes, her mouth was half-open, full of desire, almost expectant, but neither of us had the guts to kiss. Her expression and my clinging to her eyes burnt all my memories of Jana. We were not able to pause the exchange of affection, instead, we intensified the articulation of tenderness, starting to embrace us. Only the freezing cold of the night forced us to part.

Walking the long way back to my apartment through the

abandoned roads in Offenbach, I was reiterating permanently the same sentence: Love is possible! Love is still possible! A flood of tears was incessantly running down my frozen cheeks and I made not the slightest effort to hold them back. It was a perfect feeling. The essential was that I felt love. I really felt love again.

After I had called Naima the same first January in the afternoon, we started to organize carefully our meetings. I was amazed that she told me the best place to meet was my apartment on the outskirts of the town. There she could perfectly avoid the risk to encounter members of her extended family, especially her brothers and cousins. Moreover, she also explained to me in a very convincing manner and with the utmost kindness that I should not be upset or even sad when we would sometimes not see each other for a few days since she had always to be available for spontaneous family gatherings. It would be highly suspect to stay away from such events. The most important thing she wished was that our relationship, and we were both aware that we had to call it exactly that way, remained completely unperceived. Hence, she often took the bus directly from her office of the energy agency to come to me early in the evening and I did everything I could to impress her, preparing latte macchiato, different tea varieties and cooking later on mostly Italian specialties for her. Sometimes she stayed until midnight and took the last bus back, she asked me not to accompany her by car, to prevent she could be seen with me. I never disagreed since I quickly understood she went to great lengths to make our meetings come true. After sharing coffee, tea and dinner we always relaxed side by side, enjoying our mutual feelings and fresh love. But after she had left my apartment, I felt a terrible emptiness rising inside, prompting me to take my car and to set out again for my usual walks in New-Isenburg, passing Jana's former apartment house as well as her parent's house. Seeing the light of her father's reading lamp reassured me and filled me with strange optimism as well as the familiar setting of my former love story was still comforting me, even though I was totally in love with Naima. I was craving for that beautiful young Moroccan woman, but I was not able to give up a deep-seated yearning for the places where I had experienced so much happiness and where I fully understood the concept of Nietzsche's late philosophy now: The search for permanent bliss in the here and now because I was longing for endless immanence. I thought I understood what Nietzsche meant when he made the repetition of the highest emotions the method of his philosophy of eternal return. And from Zarathustra on it was the sole remedy in Nietzsche's philosophy against modern nihilism which would be in his eyes the prevailing philosophical mood of our modern world. Say yes to life, no matter what it offered. What a desperate escape from despair.

From the beginning, I had known that this love affair would go hand in hand with certain moments of heartache. Despite Naima's enormous courage and her unrelenting will to build up a real relationship, her daily life within her family structure was extremely complicated and challenging. As far as I was concerned it was rather a question of emotional disappointments due to exaggerated expectations from my side. And although I had thoroughly acquainted myself with this challenge and had inquired about the relationships of Arab women in our western cultural context, I became aware that it would be impossible to persevere with an ordinary being together. Perhaps because we had spent so many beautiful moments in a short period, I was definitely expecting too much over time, especially availability, at least on the phone. On days when she could not come to me, I tried to call her late in the evening, but I had already anticipated that no one would answer. In that case, I fell suddenly back into the desolate state I had experienced in the time after my separation from Jana, the entire world seemed to be made up of emptiness and senselessness. A dark place made for suffering.

Yet we made a wonderful trip to Milan after I had told her that Italy was a lovely country she would probably like a lot. She reacted surprisingly quickly to my suggestion and informed me that she had successfully asked for four days offs the upcoming week. The very next day I checked my bank account and booked immediately afterwards a five-star hotel nearby my once beloved church of Saint Ambrose in the Via Giosuè Carducci, not far from downtown and the most interesting places of Italy's economic hub. The day before the scheduled journey I withdrew all my available money, knowing that I had already paid the rent for my apartment and that my parents or sister would certainly help me out if I ran out of money. My aim for this trip was to show Naima how deep love could be and how love could change one's destiny. We agreed to meet at Frankfurt's main station, in front of the Illy café nearby the track and to take the train to Milan via Switzerland so that we could both admire the landscape, arriving slowly in northern Italy. The scheduled departure was at a quarter to ten, but I had already been there at half-past eight, drinking several latte macchiatos and trying to ease my excitement. I did not dare to call her the same morning, although I was permanently tempted to do so. Eventually, I convinced myself that she would come since she was also looking forward to going on that journey.

At exactly half past nine I saw Naima coming. She had an elegant trolley bag at her side, and I was totally overwhelmed by her appearance. Not dressed casually as it would have been appropriate for a longer trip, she had made herself beautiful in an unbelievable way prompting a rising mixture of erotic awe and happiness inside me. Her black half-long hairs were smoothly arranged by a side parting and on the other side adorned with two green sparkling barrettes. She had discretely applied make-up and used dark red lipstick. I had never seen her with such an elegant eyeshadow. Naima wore tight Jeans with an equally tight sweater and elegant black high heels with an ankle tie. As we met, I was left speechless for a while, but we happily smiled at each other. At the same time, I felt much flattered that she had made herself so beautiful only for our trip, yet I tried to be cool. 'Naima, hey, it's so good to see you,' I finally said.

'Let's go and catch the train, it would be a pity to miss it,' she replied, immediately adding that she just had to give her mother a quick call. She spoke from the callbox nearby and I listened to the rhythmic and fast explanations in Moroccan Arabic. After she had finished the call, she challengingly asked me with a smile if I had understood everything.

'Of course,' I answered, 'you know I am fluent in Arabic.'

'But not in Darija, the Moroccan dialect. Even if you knew standard Arabic you wouldn't be able to understand a Moroccan dialect,' she said amused as we headed towards platform seventeen.

'May I ask you what did you tell your mother? That you are travelling to Italy with your friend this morning?'

'Oh yes, that's what I said to her! With a very kind German guy! You must be totally crazy. I told her that I will attend a training my sister had already mentioned to her last week. Internal company training in Düsseldorf.'

'So, you are lying to your mother, isn't it?' It was a question I regretted immediately.

'Please, don't moralize. I thought I would enjoy the trip, since me too, I have the right to live, don't you think so.'

'I'm sorry! I thank you so much that I have the honor of being accompanied by such an outstanding woman as you. You are looking wonderful and yet again, pardon me!'

'Don't worry, things are extremely complicated for me, you wouldn't understand. But let's catch the train. Did you make a reservation so that we can be sure to have good window places with an adequate sight?'

'I did. It's wagon 27, just still a bit straight ahead.'

The time spent with her in Milan reminded me totally of my Jana period and the feelings of my heart experienced a holistic kind of *already experienced.* It was a surreal journey and seldom in my life had I been as happy as during these days, especially because after the bitter end of the relationship with Jana I was afraid I would never be able to be happy again. We spent entire afternoons strolling between Via Gesù, Via Santo Spirito and Via Montenapoleone to end up the early evening in the renowned Pasticceria Bastianello nearby Piazza San Babila. For hours we were sitting there drinking one café after another and tasting all kinds of sweet baked goods. The last evening, I suddenly took her hand and draw her almost impetuously into a store of luxury goods nearby, asking for two espressos and explaining to the seller that she would need time to look around. After we had spent almost one hour inside the store, laughing and amusing ourselves, I asked her if she would like to buy one of the elegant handbags on display. She did not hesitate and showed me a very small and distinctive black bag she found simple and stylish. I took it and handed it over to one of the sellers, asking her if she would kindly gift-wrap it. Although this exclusive gift exceeded, in reality, much of my budget it was a pure joy telling Naima that it was my present for the privilege of being with her. She could not believe it yet accepted incredulously, adding that she was just kidding when she selected that beautiful item, so we both continued to laugh and to be amused while strolling in love and carefree around the Piazza Castello and Piazza del Duomo.

There were moments in Milan where my feelings of the loss of Jana intermingled with the fresh enthusiasm of the new and deep love for Naima. Both sensations unfolded in an already known setting but immersed in an unknown light that was nourished by rays of a distant past. Gratitude and humbleness mixed up during our stay and when we decided to return separately home after our arrival in Frankfurt my demon of tears came back and overwhelmed me. And so, I spent almost the entire evening in the Illy café where I had been waiting for her before our trip and took the last subway back to Offenbach. There was no way to stop the relentless advance of time and I had to accept the bitter truth that the short but happy Naima-Milan period also came to an end quickly.

As if I had had a dark premonition, we should not see each other again for the time being. We sometimes talked on the phone, but she told me she would have no time to meet up, yet emphatically assuring me not to be worried. She intended to explain details later since it was a difficult matter. After a few days of silence, she called me once late in the evening while I was lethargically revising a chapter of my dissertation in the making, telling me she had taken most of her annual vacation leave because she urgently had to travel for a time to Morocco. Naima said she would accompany her two older sisters and her parents. I tried to hide my profound disappointment, acting as if I would take note of the news with certain aplomb even though my heart was shattered into a thousand pieces. I told her I couldn't imagine being without her for long before she abruptly hung up. Back at the desk, I stared at the papers I had written for the dissertation, being afraid that this news would mark a relapse or perhaps a mental crackdown that could negatively affect my work discipline and concentration. Fortunately, I had been working on my last chapter about Heidegger and *the zero hour of philosophy* for quite some time. My sole consolation now was of course to leave the apartment in the middle of the night and to park my car next to the old oaks in New-Isenburg's west. It was a mild night and I walked, as usual, several times through my beloved streets, passing the house of Jana's parents and her former apartment. Both seemed uninhabited and even her father's floor lamp nearby the window of the living room had already been turned off. I felt a threatening solitude deep inside as if an emotional death knocked on the doors of my heart. That night, the long nocturnal walk did not bring me the usual relief.

It wasn't until the end of the summer that I got news from Naima. In the meantime, I tried several times to call her, but no one answered and so I gave up quickly. But just like the last time I heard her voice she suddenly called me late in the evening, although I had not expected her call after such a long period of silence. I was convinced it would be Olaf since we had the habit to talk late. The surprise was perfect and my heart almost stopped. She unexcitedly apologized for her long absence and apparently without remorse, so that I immediately had the impression of having perhaps overestimated our relationship. Naima seemed quite distant on the phone, but not unfriendly, proposing to meet me in the coming days in Frankfurt, but not directly in downtown. Days later, after I had finished my tutoring, we met in a French coffeehouse chain in the northern parts of the city, in a very bourgeois neighborhood where she was safe as she added later, however, ambiguously. Her beauty impressed me anew and my feelings only confirmed that I had totally been craving for her presence. Almost all the guests inside the modern café looked around when she walked in like an Arabian diva, straightly heading towards the table where I was waiting for her. As usual, she never dressed vulgarly, precisely because of her extreme sex appeal. This attitude was certainly part of her Muslim culture. Yet it was unbelievable how her natural beauty suffused the entire room with harmony and brightness. My happiness was boundless, and I knew that I would forgive her the worst things, regardless of what had happened. Although she was kind as usual, I immediately perceived that her nature had slightly changed, something negative, a suffering aspect had crept into her natural disposition. It seemed to me she had lost a bit of her cheerfulness. I was hanging on her lips throughout the whole encounter. She told me that her parents had noticed during the summer something was different with her, and so they had insisted she had to come with them to Morocco. The pressure had been enormous and, although they were relatively liberal as she said, her three brothers unrestrictedly joined in her parent's idea that she needed a break. She had feared losing her job, fortunately, she had still much residual leave and her chief, a very kind and sympathetic head of office, signalized to her she should not be worried. What she told me sounded like an exciting short novel but was surely the opposite. She said her parents had rarely allowed her to leave the house in the city of Berkane where many relatives of them lived. Her father had also started to invite different family members who showed interest in marrying their son off to her. She fiercely resisted those initiatives but added that she was extremely exhausted, especially because she would not know whether the relationship with her family could ever be normalized again. 'You know, it was like an escape. Finally, I took my bag and went to the airport of Casablanca, after an eight hours train journey. Fortunately, there was a flight to Frankfurt the same evening. And fortunately, I have a job and my own money. But it is a gesture you have no right to dare in our social environment. This kind of disobedience to your family structure is a total taboo,' she told me in a surprisingly calm tone.

We agreed to meet from time to time with extreme caution and she asked me whether I would have the patience to accept such a difficult situation since she would accept if I wished not to see her again. Shocked, I replied that it was impossible for me not to see her again, at the same time, I was relieved that I had not completely lost her. I felt she had told me only half of the story, but I did not insist on further details as I totally understood the difficulty of her situation. So, we sometimes met up for a coffee in Frankfurt or went to the cinema or even we met again in my apartment to prepare delicious Moroccan dishes under her instruction. And we went through Morocco's landscape since I had bought a Michelin map of the Kingdom. I showed her proudly how detailed I had studied Moroccan geography, especially the surroundings of Oujda and the nearby Berkane with its Mediterranean coastal region around Saidia. It made me happy to see her so amazed by my knowledge of Morocco. I told her about my superficial reading of Ibn Khaldun who was in a certain way the founder of social science with his theory of the rise and fall of civilizations and his very elaborated concept of tribal loyalties. Thus, I could shine in front of her by knowing the original Arab term asabiyya. Since Ibn Khaldun had been called by the Marinid Sultan Abu Inan Faris in the fourth century to Fes, I fervently wished to visit this place of outstanding spiritual and architectural heritage as I explained passionately to her. In my enthusiasm to impress her, I added that the oldest university worldwide had been founded in this city by Fatima al-Fihri in the ninth century, stressing the fact that it had been a woman consolidating Morocco's spiritual and scientific life at that distant past. It was as if I intended to remind her of the forgotten richness and beauty of her own culture. She reacted extremely aloof to my suggestion to travel once to Morocco and to discover with her the cultural treasures of the country, instead, she replied that she would rather prefer to stay simply at home.

Over time and against the backdrop of our relationship's daily experiences I clearly realized that I was facing a cultural borderline, requiring much patience and unusual forbearance from me to avoid serious mistakes in dealing with her. Although Naima's cultural environment prevented us to build up a stable relationship, I steadily felt a growing interest in Moroccan culture. Despite some opaque modes of behavior and again periods of silence my curiosity to explore Morocco increased rapidly even though it took a considerable time to adapt to the emotional ups and downs of that adventurous love affair.

Some weeks before Christmas Mirko asked me what I

intended to do at the upcoming turn of the millennium. Widespread hysteria had been seized the masses throughout the globe and most people were only concerned with how to celebrate this event in an adequate manner. And precisely because I was tired of this mass mobilization, I told him that I had no plans so far, moreover, my other friends Olaf and Kai would be in Austria for having a one-week skiing vacation with their partners. He proposed to celebrate together discretely at his mother's estate she had bought two years ago outside of the small Portuguese village Aldeida de Juzo, not far from Cascais, in the western costal area of Greater Lisbon. She would stay there only from the midst of January on and celebrate with friends in Southern France. And with an enthusiastic voice, he added that there would be most probably no fireworks to hear, and still better, there would be not a soul far and wide. Mirko had always despised mass events and it deeply scared him to imagine that he had to celebrate the turn of the millennium in Frankfurt or its surroundings. The idea was amazing and since it was clear that I could not celebrate this event with Naima as the year before, we booked the next day direct flights from Frankfurt to Lisbon for December 29, 1999.

Already immediately after our arrival, I was extremely entranced by the colors of Lisbon and the azulejos I perceived everywhere on the walls of houses. These had been surely the remnants of Islamic culture, mainly of the Moroccan dynasties and the earlier Umayyad caliphate ruling there between the eighth and tenth centuries. All these traces interested me insofar I connected them with Naima and in a wider sense with my recent readings of al-Ghazali and Ibn Tufail. After renting a car at the Vasco da Gama Airport of Lisbon we drove on the A5 towards Estoril Cascais. Glancing to the left we sometimes caught the deep blue spots of the Atlantic Ocean. And from that moment on I felt that the light, coming from the West in the evening, or more precisely, from the endless expanse of the sea, was particularly beautiful, very different. We did not talk to each other during the entire trip towards the western outskirts of the city, rather, we were totally absorbed by the reconciling winter light covering the green landscape with a golden, almost magic veil. After an hour's drive, we went through the drowsy town of Aldeida de Juzo, driving northwards towards the national park of Sintra-Cascais. A few minutes later we turned right into a field path on which we drove on for a good while until we stopped in the middle of nowhere in front of his mother's white estate. Indeed, there were no immediate neighbors and day and night we could from then on listen to the different intensities of the mild December winds. On the famous New Year's Eve, we set out for a long walk into the national park after we had bought some firewood from a nearby farmer who had already been knowing Mirko and his mother. He was a silent man but nonetheless radiated much of human warmth. We started to use some Portuguese words, albeit dilettantish, but he appreciated our efforts, responding with a jovial smile. When I tried to explain to him that I loved the way Luis Figo was playing soccer, the eyes of the gentle farmer started to shine. It felt extremely good to breathe new air and culture, although it was an immense challenge to pronounce that consonant-heavy language. The same day we walked for hours in changeable weather across the National Park always in direction of Colares, through a very much changing fauna and flora with thousands of Agaves, lonely and wild olive trees as well as old and unusually tall yucca palms. The soft light of late December suffused both of us with a mixture of deep relaxation and melancholy. The only persons we met during that one-day walk were some Portuguese wanderers and a few Scandinavians lost like ourselves in this endless and breath-taking landscape. Both of us could clearly feel the beauty and intensity of our more than ten years old friendship. And precisely because of this mutual romantic feeling mixed up with a kind of timelessness and indescribable joy there was no need to talk about it. Mirko was happy after a period of extreme ups and downs regarding his exams in law, a course of studies he had chosen due to its promising social status and the prospect of earning money. He was all too aware of his inconsistency in this regard: blessed with creative talent in music and sports, playing for a while even as an ambitious percussionist in a jazz band he decided eventually to sacrifice it for an envisaged legal career. A decision his mother welcomed enthusiastically, although deep down inside him he was not happy at all with that existential choice.

Back at the white and snugly estate it seemed that the setting for a long night we would spend in complete solitude and isolated from the worldwide mass celebrations was perfect. We lighted the fireplace with the firewood bought from the friendly farmer and started to prepare the Raclette we bizarrely brought with us from Germany, accompanied by changing background music, from Miles Davis to Chopin and Debussy to George Michael. Looking back into the last century's history we totally agreed upon the cruelty and barbarism of especially its first part. Mirko was mostly in a pessimistic mood and the inclination to an occasionally emerging misanthropy had always been a strong common base of our friendship. He started to complain about his law studies and the greedy and superficial world of the law students surrounding him. His potential of frustration was very high because he had to repeat the second state examination, although the first was generally considered much more difficult. But I had recently noticed that the looming failure imbued his intellectual capacity with still more acumen.

'As always, we escape,' he started the talk.

'Cowards, as usual,' I replied and we both laughed relaxed sitting in front of the fireplace. 'Long live the cowards,' I still added. 'But I think coward as a character trait suits me better than you,' I told him. 'Look how unable I am to cope with the loss of Jana. You know best you were the only friend of mine she liked so much since you had always shown an honest joy in our happy being together. And look, how unable I am to engage in a sound and normal relationship. Instead, I am delving into books and philosophies that do not help me to put my life in order. A coward, isn't that the most suited attribute to me?'

'You are rather a wise escapist,' he replied directly and we both continued laughing.

'Wow! That's a real compliment!'

'You know that I had always been admiring your will for orientation, your will for doing things which satisfy you and correspond to your inner conviction.'

'I think the truth is that I only consoled myself with books and long walks in order to subtilize my inability of orientation, my uncertainty to understand the purpose of my existence,' I explained to him.

'But you know at best that few people strive for understanding the purpose of existence? Look what people are doing only to avoid a comprehensive reflection on life's meaning. How many people are distracted by activities that do not make much sense, to the contrary, they focus on subaltern distractions, our world has long since become a huge cinema, a bewildering entertainment park.'

'I see we are in a good grumpy mood to despise the rest of the world,' I added with an amused smile.

Mirko had remained silent for a while before he continued the conversation in a more thoughtful voice. 'Rather, I am also a good example for nowadays disorientation, and you are the friend who knows best that my pursuit of law study is exclusively intended to be a successful member of society and to satisfy the expectations of my ambitious mother. The law studies are boring me immensely. But there is still hope I will defend marginalized people from a precarious background. Perhaps it will give this work real meaning. Eventually, the purpose of existence must be answered by ourselves, on an individual level, we have to invent the meaning of life as

Nietzsche said. And you had taught me that years ago. We have to build up our happiness like a house since there is no happiness without meaningful deeds.'

'But even the so-called great German philosophers did not serve much to convey a deeper meaning of life, and Nietzsche isn't an exception, despite his precise analysis of modern mindset which is completely nihilistic according to him. Nihilism is, as Heidegger pointed out, not only the absence of real meaning but also a lack of comprehension concerning the concept of being. He named it oblivion of being which characterizes our modern existence. No doubt, philosophers have mostly good intentions, but they aren't able to prevent us from becoming disoriented or even bad persons. How proud humanity is of its rational tradition and ideology of emancipation, even after the great disasters of the two world wars. And how proud humanity is of its capability to invent sophisticated technologies and to dominate nature and seemingly destiny as well. Instead, at the end of these processes of rationalization, we still find ourselves immersed in gloomy barbarism. In the beginning, we are proud of our noble ideas, like that of communism, a typical idea of western thought which was missioned all over the world and left behind millions of obliterated people. The difference to fascism was insignificant in the end. I know it sounds extremely cynical. But millions of mass graves in the name of social equality and social justice. In the name of progress whatever that may be! In the name of this noble human race and its distinguished intellectual ability! This is total madness, isn't it?' All of a sudden, I was in the mood to philosophize.

'Death for all as the unique egalitarian principle, it seemed this had been the idea behind,' Mirko added with a slightly cynical undertone as well.

'Indeed. You see the result when so-called noble philosophical ideas become mental and social reality. May God help us,' I replied.

'But I think the timeless question of what we should do to be happy and how should we behave to realize our purpose of existence will be asked even in a sharper way within the upcoming millennium. The search for meaning will be an eternal repetition as long as there are mortal human beings on earth.'

'And it is better to keep distance sometimes from them and to sit in a vacation house in Portugal listening to the wind and breathing the salty air of the Atlantic Ocean,' I remarked and we both smiled while Mirko poured me more mint tea.

'We are a very much spoiled generation,' he resumed the talk.

'But, perhaps also more peaceful and reasonable as former generations, even though it sounds pretentious. We are saturated and therefore more peaceful, quieter,' I said before starting again a longer discourse. 'Take my example, a strange example, perhaps neither good nor bad. I have been immersed for years now into philosophy without the need to develop an idea that is worth to be realized in a concrete manner. I'm not a member of a political party nor I am committed to a civil society organization and worse, I have never worked as a volunteer except perhaps during a school festival. Instead, propensity for contemplation, for resignation and a lack of courage to face reality. Sitting at home and meditating on Jana's and Naima's beauty, again and again, wallowing in self-pity. I have been cultivating the loss of them and at a certain moment it ceased to be pure suffering, it was slowly transforming into longing, longing for beauty in general. Sometimes I am still surprised how this strange presence of longing filled me with peace of mind and tranquility of the heart, transforming into a form of permanent joy. But that state of mind has suffocated all my ambitions since I do not have any plan for what I should do after the time of my post-PhD. I'm so happy with my job in the newspaper's advertising department and with my afternoon private tuition. I am living in a kind of metaphysical tension without doing anything important. My gosh, it is most probably Baudelaire's attitude which Sartre, do you remember, my personal trigger for studying philosophy, despised so much. In his eyes, it was a completely anti-rational attitude. Weltschmerz, as an unmistakable sign of bourgeois existence. In the end, I didn't understand his harsh polemics against the bourgeoisie, although I knew that it had been due to his Marxist approach to look upon society in dimensions of class struggle and liberation only. But you remember perhaps the period when his excess of rationality and his tacit support for totalitarian regimes, especially the Soviet dictatorship, started to bore me. It is so ridiculous to support people to whom you do not belong at all. These Parisian intellectuals and academics of the state had most probably not the slightest idea of how factory workers and farmers lived in the Soviet Union. Today I am convinced that it is a form of political voyeurism and hypocrisy prompted by the bad conscience of a privileged class. The existentialists pretended to be fighting alienation, but they were deeply alienated from themselves. It's better to be silent and to live like an idiot which means etymologically to live in privacy. I know that sounds like political quietism or, worse, political nihilism. But, so what?'

'To live in privacy and to be happy as well?' asked Mirko.

'Happiness? This totally overused word in our present age! You know strange happiness overwhelmed me recently after having read a sentence on Shestov's philosophy in the literary encyclopedia, namely, that he continued in a tradition of Dostoevsky and Kierkegaard to attack the modern rationality's dictatorship. Then I jumped out of my reading chair and clenched my right fist like Boris Becker once did after a perfectly played ball. And I did this only because the prospect to choose his magnum opus *Potestas Clavium* and delving into it in the near future filled me with endless joy and enthusiasm, at least for a moment. And if one had observed me through the open window shutters, one would have thought me mature for the madhouse.'

'But you are at least enthusiastic and fervent, that's a good sign, you have blood in your veins when you deal with philosophy, something that I totally miss when dealing with legal cases. And you know that this boring life then pushes me to hunt women, to try to fall rapidly in love what doesn't make me happy either. It's just my childish manner of anesthetization and I am afraid of failing sooner or later and of having nothing in my hands,' Mirko replied directly to my remarks.

'It is only your way of searching deeper. Yet love as a sedative is indeed very effective. I think that the type of longing doesn't make us very different from one another. As far as I am concerned my longings can more and more be assuaged by a good reading or contemplation of nature, in short, by a journey in total solitude,' I went further on.

'My only longing is, unfortunately, an idolatry of the present, the idolatry of always new promises, new auspicious feelings, the longing to suffocate definitely my daily routine with its endless readings of boring law cases. I want to live! You know me! And you remember my passion for middle-distance running in combination with my passion for playing the drums. I gave up both passions for an impending career as a lawyer, with the hope to be well paid for it. There is not the slightest idealism in me, not even the childish to put evil people behind bars, perhaps as an attorney or judge later on. No ambitions apart from money. That job won't make me happy and I will leave this sector sooner or later, if I shall pass the second state examination, that's for sure,' and he started to smile and added, 'but what makes me happy is that we are both here now to escape the ridiculous mass hysteria of the turn of the millennium.'

Mirko approached the dining table on which he had been putting an open bottle of Barolo already the late afternoon. He sliced some pieces of Portuguese goat cheese and put them with big wine glasses on the table. We did not yet start the chess game we had aimed for that evening. It was a diversion we had thoroughly cherished since the beginning of our friendship, especially its socializing and at the same time contemplative character which always enabled us to address the most personal anxieties and solicitudes. Hence, a chess game would provide the perfect setting for that historical night.

'We will have an after midnight-Raclette like the so-called Spaghettata di Mezzanotte in Rome, what do you think?'

'Sounds perfect!'

Mirko poured the mellow Barolo into the glasses. He remained again silent for a while until he resumed the conversation teary-eyed. 'Will there be anything left of our friendship one day? Or will it burst like a balloon the moment we die? Do you remember the lightness of being when we met for the first time during the athletic school championships? The same evening, we went out as friends to attend a Fates Warning concert. I convinced you to come with me, even though I was only second behind you. Do you remember?'

A tear ran down his right cheek, but he was smiling. It was a tear of joy, a tear of friendship, a tear given that moment's happiness.

'How could I forget? I had immediately understood that you were an outstanding talent. And do you remember the training plan I wrote for you to tackle the challenge of the marathon? From the beginning, I had not the slightest doubt you would easily reach your personal goal of staying under three hours. Equally, I knew with certainty that you would become the next school champion in the city and throughout the region, if you would only start to train seriously,' I replied full of happy memories.

'But will all these challenges, all these profound and wonderful experiences, burst the moment we die? Does that make sense? I don't think so! You are the friend who knows best that I have no metaphysical inclinations, at least not pronounced or strong. Take only all our memories, all our experiences and what has remained of them together with our intentions and detailed plans of self-realization, and please don't tell me that all these contents of life should be at the end no more than a pastime.'

'Especially since being is above all time-consciousness as Heidegger clearly pointed out in his early work *Being and Time*,' I added briefly.

'I wish that evening could be a part of a frozen pattern of destiny, spreading out before us like a field of flowers when we die,' he further said. 'I know that so far I am only in love with the feeling of love. It bewitches me. As you said it anaesthetizes and distracts me from these bleak prospects to spend my life in an office, immersed myself in banal legal disputes, interrupted only by two annual vacations, regulated by law.'

'And I would wish to break away from my emotional attachment to Jana. Imagine, when I'm with Naima I sometimes have still the impression to cheat on Jana. Years after the end of our love affair, I cannot fight against this feeling. Can you imagine?' I asked Mirko.

'But I am so happy that you met Naima although it seems a very complicated matter.'

'Yes, it's much challenging, and yet it fills me with new energy.'

'New energy for the upcoming millennium,' Mirko added with joy. We laughed further and continued to be in the best mood despite the heavy existential topics we discussed the rest of the evening. A few minutes after midnight we went out into the darkness of the first night of the third millennium. 'What will be our motto?' Mirko asked.

'Let's avoid the idolatry of the present, the idolatry of velocity and the idolatry of forgetfulness. Let's protect our arsenal of memories!' I staunchly said to him. We hugged and squeezed us for a long time silently. This time I was the one with tears running down my cheeks. I thought of Naima and how I accompanied her home through the streets in the middle of the night after Kai's party last New Year's Eve. My personal time reckoning had already set in one year ago, since every end of history is unavoidably the beginning of a new history. In privacy as well as in dimensions of world history.

The only sound we could hear was the rustling of the nearby eucalyptus trees. We did neither see nor hear the New Year's Eve fireworks of Lisbon or Estoril. There was only the flickering of a dim light inside a distant villa with no signs of a celebration outside. A fresh breeze came from the Atlantic coast and seemed to gently blow away all characteristics of time.

'This is a dignified start to the new millennium,' Mirko said to me and we stood there for a while further listening to the wind and its play with the leaves. Then we went back inside and slowly started with the raclette. During our long meal, we made an extensive and detailed foray through our shared memories. It could have been the end of history concerning political ideas, perhaps, and it was for sure the end of the last millennium, but it was certainly not the end of our friendship that seemed to us the only worthy reality in the here and now. The rest was destined to disappear, but we were both aware of destiny's grace to live probably in the most liberal and saturated age mankind had ever seen so far, at least within the historical context of our hubristic and rebellious continent Europe. Many hours later we went out anew and stood once again arm in arm in front of the estate to contemplate the quiet early morning light of the third millennium's first day.

SAUDADE (PART TWO)

At breakfast the next day, I found that we were able to receive a Moroccan radio station. Despite my modest knowledge of Arabic, I was pretty delighted to understand a few words like akhbar and siyasiya, news and politics and ughniya jamila, a beautiful song. From then on, we listened to it every evening with its classical Arab songs that we could not understand, yet whose deep yearning we somehow felt. We continued to prepare sumptuous dinners and to take thorough stock of our youth that was definitely coming to an end.

Towards the end of the first week of the new year, Mirko told me he had to dedicate himself to a repetition of some exemplary legal cases regarding his upcoming second state examination, although he was not at all in the mood for it. I felt how hard he was working only to finish that history and to satisfy at the end more his mother's ambitions. This was a good opportunity to go to Lisbon and the following day I took a regional bus from the Café Jose Viana directly at the first traffic circle in the north of Aldeida de Juzo. The bus went southwards on the N9-1 through the white villages of Sao Gabriel and Cobre towards the relatively crowded Bairro da Asuncao where I took the regional train from Cascais to Belém. During this half-hour drive, I fell more and more in love with Portugal's vast landscape and its peaceful light.

My initiation took finally place in the monastery de Jéronimo in Belém. There had been no other building whose architecture shocked me more in my life than its late Gothic style. Only the Romanesque Basilica of Sant'Ambrogio and the High Gothic Milan cathedral had conveyed to me such perfection of architectural harmony and spiritual beauty. Both structures were extremely present in my mind the moment I set foot in Belém's monastery which made clear that architecture had more to do with a state of mind than simple construction. Fortunately, there were few tourists in that normally overcrowded place. I did not count how often I wandered through the cloister while I dreamt to spend the rest of my life in this place and finishing the search for an adequate partner or social position. Instead, I would prefer to read systematically the works of Dostoevsky and Tolstoy again, perhaps interrupted by a few tender memories of Jana and Naima. This would be the ideal place to find peace and to wipe out all the rest of my inner unrest. A real taste of paradise. The world's beauty had to be isolated, it had to be protected from man's hand, from his incessant need of destruction. The world's beauty I thought, had to be protected from the destructive masses of ambitious people and their vain yearning for recognition. And suddenly Giuseppe came into my mind again, that elegant man I remembered years after our talks in front of the monastery in the heart of the Marches. He reminded me of human frailty and transiency. I saw his stature and his face before me as I would have encountered him yesterday. His last sentences during our farewell meeting came also into my mind, these impressive and tender words, saying a deep love had much in common with fervent prayer. Take much care of you my inspiring friend, had been his concluding words. Now, it became totally clear to me that he was a man who had transformed a big personal disappointment and existential sorrow into positive resignation and melancholic, seemingly endless joy, full of attentiveness for the beauty of creation and for his fellow man.

My memories of that extraordinary journey with Mirko together with the enduring impression of Greater Lisbon's reconciling light and the spiritual experience made in the monastery of Belém triggered a deep craving in me for discovering Morocco. The relationship with Naima had also its due share in my new development of interests concerning Islamic culture. And it was the time when I was discovering repeatedly articles about Marrakech and Morocco in the new editions of the Vogue which I still regularly bought to look further for portraits to draw. As always, these were distinctive beauties who flaunted superfluous luxury items and were lost in reveries.

After another few weeks of silence, I finally met up again with Naima who had suggested watching a movie in a cinema center in the north of Frankfurt. She seemed happy to spend time with me and it touched me deeply that during the movie she took for the first time in public space tenderly my hand, albeit in a dark hall of a movie theater. This gesture finally made an even stronger impression on me than the first kiss with Jana, but perhaps the that first touch was too long ago to be properly judged now, and besides, the secret relationship between Naima and me made such a sudden tender gesture more exciting, more valuable. It was also the movie itself that intensified our longings to come closer to one another. Wong Kar-Wai's *In the Mood for Love* conveyed to us in an extremely melancholic manner how it felt not to come together despite a mutually shared deep love. The movie was thematically accompanied by Shigeru Umebayashi's mind-blowing waltz variation Yumeji's theme.

We left the cinema late and did not have much time for a long and relaxed talk about our recent experiences. The beginning of the new year had been rather a sad affair as she told me, adding with a very charming smile that no one had accompanied her to home, nor had she had an interesting conversation with an odd young man like during last New

Year's Eve. Instead, close relatives from north Morocco had come for a visit and they had spent the whole evening discussing boring matters like who had married whom or for whom the time was ripe now to get married soon. They had also talked extensively about the still young and childless women in their families. The entire evening, she had received admonishing looks from many of her relatives. Again, I refrained from asking for details. Although I wanted to accompany her back to Offenbach by car, she said to me in her gentle but unambiguous way that she preferred to take the last subway alone. So, there was no time left to tell her about my plans to travel to Morocco.

Fortunately, the doctoral committee consisted exclusively of polite experts. Professional philosophers are mostly grumpy or moody, at least this was my experience within the academic setting, yet in this case, my fears were quickly gone. Generally, they appreciated my efforts to show how a strong rationalistic stream had not only harmed philosophy in its traditional understanding but also engendered intolerance and totalitarian approaches to our political reality. This philosophical current was mostly disguised in terms like progress and development through scientific knowledge. I was quite aware of my shortcoming that sometimes I relied more on a superficial reading of Kant and Hegel, both my main adversaries so to say, but the committee recognized that I had thoroughly dealt with philosophers whose characteristic of thought was decidedly hermetic and singular. A member of the committee referred to de Sade and added that the worst among all philosophers who had been selected for this dissertation was undoubtedly Heidegger. We all laughed and continued to discuss the singularities of Nietzsche's, Kierkegaard's and Heidegger's ideas as well as the traits of their intellectual resistance against modern mainstream rationalism.

When I left the old building of Darmstadt's university late in the evening, I was overwhelmed by a feeling of happiness, albeit I understood well that with the beginning of the new millennium another period of my life had come to an end today: the kind of luxury life that had been dedicated so long to a calm two-days-a-week job at the daily's advertising department and to some private tuition. That rhythm had always given me enough time to delve into my books and daydreams. And I had asked myself many times before the formal end of my doctorate in which way I could further uphold this escapist life afterwards. As I went back home, I left highway 5 at New-Isenburg to have a long walk through its familiar streets in the middle of the night, as I had done it so often over the past decade. I wanted to pass by Jana's former apartment, although she had left the place years ago as I heard from a friend, and I wanted to see if at least her father would still sit reading next to the floor lamp late at night. I did not encounter anyone during this extended walk deep in the night and I went many times ever again through the same streets I was loving so much. It was a good sign that most of the time I thought of Naima, looking much forward to seeing her again.

At the end of my academic education, it was clear that I would never give up my passion for books and the formal end of my student days would not change anything concerning my reading praxis. But I had since long given up the illusion that philosophy or a particular episteme could provide me with due understanding regarding the meaning of existence. I felt educated, yes, but nothing more. Moreover, my resentment against empirical knowledge and positivism had undergone a significant increase during the last years. Philosophy, once the search for truth or the search for an enduring ethos of life, had been completely broken into unconnected splinters by the rush of fragmented sciences and their armies of nerds. So, the formal end of my studies and specialized research with all its tedious and inflationary footnotes immediately filled me with a kind of creative relief. The following day, I got on a buying frenzy of books in which I had been interested but had not the time to read due to my focus on the dissertation. It was a wonderful mélange of philosophy and literature, Ortega y Gasset, Shestov, Houellebecq and Le Clézio. These authors shared a common thread since they could easily be classified as staunch critics of modern rationality and the idolatry of the belief in progress. They all wrote in one way or another against the ridiculous premise of materialistic salvation. I knew that I would sooner or later come too into the predicament of a lifestyle dominated by material compulsions, but I vowed to fiercely resist as long as I would be able to do so. I hoped to compose of all my fragments of knowledge something that could provide me with a holistic principle of beauty and happiness. And if there were no such a principle to find, yet it would be a noble initiative at least to search for it; to simply search for something that even would not exist. Then, in the end, everything would be a pure illusion. These thoughts were an adequate consolation for me so that I could look ahead positively. At the same time, I was sure that I would not continue in the field of academic research although I felt that I could perhaps regret this decision later on. I did not have the slightest desire to become an expert in one or another field and with my final grade 'very good without distinction', I was certainly not a suited candidate for a professorial post. There were many doctorates who had finished their research with the highest honor. That was an easy and additional justification for me not to engage further in the field of research. My longing for intellectual liberty had vanquished all other considerations, even though my parents objected and encouraged me to continue research since they knew that I had found certain stability in my daily life. At least, I was able to make a living in the meantime, despite the odd choice of studying philosophy. But that was only a cautious and well-intentioned recommendation since they were totally aware of my stubbornness.

Both seats to my right remained vacant and as we approached the south-facing take-off runway I gazed at the endless rows of trees of my beloved airport forest. It was a sunny and cold late winter day. The trees were leafless, except for some Pinus sylvestris as green embedded particles connecting the airport area on the east side with the western outskirts of New-Isenburg. On these endless paths within that forest, I had always found the tranquility to cope with the existential pain I experienced, even though it was a luxury pain, a sign of mental decadence within a peaceful and saturated epoch without political persecution or conflict. But each era certainly had its own bubble of problems, regardless of its outward cruelty or peacefulness; the issue was simply not suited to compare. Walking for hours, ever and ever again, in good as well as in bad weather, I had always succumbed to the sweet illusion of being protected there from the quarrelsome masses, from the sophisticated predatory called human being. But in the end, I was aware that I would not have the slightest right to complain since I was simply whining on the highest level which was perhaps typical for individuals of an over-civilized period. I had a PhD, two jobs and enjoyed solitude. Moreover, I was in excellent health. During my recent deepening of knowledge on Islamic thought to which I was dedicating more and more time, I read the interesting statement that it was a question of predestination whether one would be happy or unhappy in life. It was probably like that.

Was I happy in the end? The time spent with Mirko in the seclusion of Aldeida de Juzo was good for me and I was in a pretty expectant mood, not at all unsatisfied, let alone unhappy. A certain emotional optimism imbued me and I was totally aware that the reason for my latent despair was either my insatiable longings for idealized love or perhaps in the meantime, a longing without a concrete object, a longing for something I was not able to define.

Naima had been extremely kind and loveable to me when I saw her the last time before my departure. We met at the outskirts of Frankfurt, in a small coffee bar after she had taken the afternoon off. She behaved with discretion as usual in public but made up for this lack of tender gestures by kind attentiveness and a look full of expectations and love. She was not happy about my idea of travelling to Morocco for three weeks and she was yet less happy when I told her that I had already booked a hiking trip in the High Atlas Mountains.

'You won't understand our society due to your lack of cultural experience, even though I know that the real intention of your journey is to understand my culture and eventually myself better,' she said to me. The sentence hurt me a lot, but I patiently accepted it, since her statement had not been expressed with an arrogant undertone. Finally, I was relieved that she seemed slightly flattered by the fact of my real interest in her provenance and culture. 'We are backward, do not expect too much. You won't even be able to find a path if you desire to hike in the Atlas Mountains. You need a trustworthy guide and I hope for you that you booked with a good travel agency,' she further continued the conversation.

'I don't really expect anything except that I may understand a culture better that I'm not familiar with but I'm very interested in,' I calmly replied.

'My goodness, please, do not expect to see that form of lofty Islamic culture you know from the books you recently read. These were idealistic thinkers of a once Golden Era that does not help us in facing all contemporary challenges in everyday life and education. Instead, if you will have a close look at the social structure, you will see most of the young males looking for a young girl they can marry, in other words, young males seeking to replace their mother with a young wife. And that young wife has to do the laundry and prepare three times a day a delicious meal as requested by her husband. Moreover, she must be available, if her husband has sexual desire, around the clock. Then she will bring up the children until she will be completely exhausted.'

'Naima, I think your judgement is too harsh. You sound like a right-wing orientalist. I noticed the moral quality and the courtesy of Muslim men towards women seem to be a very important issue of these thinkers throughout their chapters on morals and integrity. I think it's even a keystone in Islamic tenets, regardless of the historic developments of Muslim societies. The dignity of women was always stressed although the Golden Age of Islam occurred in the early Middle Age if we look at it from a purely European perspective. Of course, it was another time and family had been sacrosanct which is not the case in our free and consumer-oriented society of so-called autonomous individuals.'

'My dear,' she said now, 'you are so kind and so naïve. Don't speak of courtesy in this context. You don't have the slightest idea how young women live within the framework of their family, especially when they live outside a traditional context, here in the West, and when the level of education remains low.' Her voice was unmistakably clear but never rude.

'At least give me the chance to learn about Morocco. I recently read so many enchanting and positive things about Marrakech and its proud history and beauty,' I kindly replied.

'But don't take the reading matter literally. There is the risk to be very much disappointed. Believe me.'

'I can very well imagine that this country is not developed like our comfortable Europe. But this term does not have that redeeming connotation for me as usual in our Western context. A society that has still strong metaphysical values, and I presume Moroccans do have them, cannot focus exclusively on material and technological growth, let alone the greed to have at all costs its due share here and now, regardless of the

her passionately, but the craving for her was slowly mixing up with the tender and overwhelming souvenirs of my time with Jana. The truth I was always searching for and I would never find in philosophy or epistemology was perhaps that immense longing itself, that unfading saudade as the only constant hitherto in my life. I was wondering how could I relieve the desperate waiting for death which would come as the only conceivable certainty? And so, I headed straight into the old and ochre-colored city's labyrinth of narrow yet vibrant alleys. On foot, not by cab, and I dragged my bulky luggage after me with the impression it was loaded with all my heavy memories. Painful but also sweet memories without which I could not have lived.

The first night in Marrakech I fell into a deep sleep which was gently interrupted by the phonetic arabesque of the call to sunrise prayer. But I continued a restless sleep full of bizarre dreams and images, so it seemed that the unusual and mystical ambience had already unfolded its influence on my mind. I passionately made love to Jana and Naima as if I would have foreseen the subsequent and tragic loss of both of them.

Ultimately, I was woken up by the hysteric chirping of canary birds which had gathered in the lush green orange trees in the middle of a bright courtyard in front of the double door of my guest room in the heart of Marrakech's ancient medina. I got dressed quickly and went directly upstairs onto the rooftop terrace where I had a stunning view of the endless labyrinth of the city's houses and the majestic Atlas Mountains. There, a typical Moroccan breakfast was served, with pancake, honey and yoghurt, accompanied by a fresh mint tea and a tantalizing scent of orange juice and rosewater. The owner, a kind and middle-aged Moroccan named Khaled came by and asked me if everything was fine. I checked my booking, reminding him that I would already leave the next day for a hiking trip in the Atlas Mountains and again come back after eight days for another four days. He carefully inquired about the mountain guide and my equipment since there had fallen much snow in the region during this cold winter. I showed him my e-Mail I had still printed out before the journey and he confirmed to me that he had already heard about the man, moreover, the al-Balluti family was quite renowned throughout the entire region. A good choice, he said, but also added it was unusual to hike during this season and he warned me that bitter cold would await me in the small and high-lying Amazigh villages.

Marrakech immediately bewitched me. It was the mixture of different people, of modernity and tradition I had never seen before, the fragrance blend of spices as well as the sober Moorish architecture which suffused everything mundane with a natural spirituality. And there was the proud feeling of finally being in Naima's homeland. At the end of the first day, I was stunned by the jumble of these impressions: overcrowded mosques where elegantly dressed businessmen prayed next to dirty day laborers from the tannery, young women in revealing clothes with extreme sex appeal next to fully veiled women, luxury cars which had problems to pass by the many donkeys transporting different items through the narrow streets on the edge of the old town. I strolled across the Jemaa el-Fnaa place and around the majestic Kutubiyya mosque which had been built under the rule of the Amazigh Almohad dynasty and its puritan vision of Islam. Before I fell asleep exhausted in the evening, I packed up all my things again so that I could set off early for the mountains the next day.

My travel guide Abdelrahman had informed me via e-Mail that he would meet me at eight o'clock at the Café Dar Nzaha directly next to the gas station on the main road in the small town of Tahanaout south of Marrakech. As he had recommended, I took what is called a large cab for long-distance destinations from the Bab Doukkala, the gate to the ancient medina in its north-western part where the bus terminal for long-distance travels was located as well. Though it was still early and cold, the place was already crowded and full of travellers, a mess of people was running around from one cab to another while a cacophony of loud voices shouted wildly different city names: Casablanca, Agadir, Ben Guerir and Fes. From the first hours in Morocco, I was impressed by the careful manner even apparently poor people were dressing. Sometimes they missed several teeth, yet they wore an elegant Djellaba regardless of whether women or men. A young guy came up to me in a friendly way, as if he had only been waiting for my arrival and he asked in good French where I wanted to go. To Tahanaout, I said, which immediately prompted him to take one of my bulky bags and reach for my free hand, then he told me, 'Viens, mon cher frère!' We went through an endless accumulation of cabs until he stopped in front of an overcrowded old and rusty Mercedes 500 limousine and he told the driver that I wanted to go to Tahanaout too. The kind young man quickly gave my bulky bag to the driver who stood in front of the cab and made an unmistakable sign that I should also hand him over my backpack. He squeezed both into the equally overloaded trunk and invited me to take a seat on the passenger side even though two men were already sitting there. While I was still wondering how this should work, the two of them automatically slid further into the middle of the car so that one was already sitting with half of his body in the driver's seat. Both smiled invitingly at me. So, I took my travel seat, sandwiched between three men to my left side and the passenger door to the right side. We set in motion and meandered in dense traffic along the beautiful ramparts of Marrakech towards its south. The snowy Atlas Mountains shimmered like an immense mirage on the southern horizon.

As if all passengers were embarrassed with my uncomfortable situation, they started to take care of me. From the backseat where two women and three men were sitting squeezed as well, I heard a silent discussion in the Shilha language of the Atlas region as I supposed since I usually could make out Arabic. Then, they gave to the two men in front two pillows that a woman in the back seat had suddenly pulled out of the huge bag she had put between her legs. They tucked them carefully between me and the passenger door so I could sit comfortably. I was very touched by this gesture. The driver put a tape in the old tape recorder and we all listened to a powerful female voice accompanied by the typical Arabic rhythms I was already a little familiar with since I had listened with Mirko to the Moroccan radio station every evening in Portugal. While we were driving on a straight road lined with eucalyptus trees towards the first and lush green slopes of the mountains, my fellow passengers began to quietly sing along with the songs which was a clear sign of the singer's celebrity. The voices became louder and they started to clap their hands to the rhythm of the songs. I became curious for everyone was now completely absorbed by these tunes and their beguiling voice so I tried to find out who the singer was, addressing them in a mixture of French and clumsy Arabic. A sudden wave of enthusiasm swept through the car since they deemed the few words I uttered in Arabic as perfect skills of the Arabic language and I felt much embarrassed regarding the overwhelming kindness with which these people treated an unknown stranger like me. The cab driver explained to me in good French that this was Haja El Hamdaouia, the great singer of Moroccan popular music. 'You know,' he told me, 'she sings about love and longing, it means she sings about the reality of life, about the pain of unrequited love of which we all suffer isolated and alone. But that's the taste of existence. And you know that in our culture we never address things like lovesickness, longing and separation pain in the family. We share these emotions at best with our closest friends, but mostly with loneliness. That's the reason why Arabs had invented poetry long before Europeans dedicated themselves to this art of expression. And if you are interested in poetry in general you will certainly come across the great poets al-Mutanabbi and Abu Nawas. And you know, if I would turn one of the next roads left, we would arrive at the remnants of the ancient town of Aghamat. There you will still find the tomb of al-Mu'tamid ibn Abbad, one of the greatest poets in Arab history. It's just a stone's throw from here. You know, poetry is like an emotional outlet for our forbidden wishes and desires, dreams and longings. All passions take place within, in secret. The style of how Moroccan houses are built is a reflection of this. Look at them, they are unadorned on the outside, but passions blaze inside.' They all laughed and a woman in the back seat verbally took refuge in God from the devil while I was impressed by this short lesson in Arab poetry from our driver. 'And Haja El Hamdaouia is one of our most important voices when it comes to Moroccan intimacy. She is the mirror of our hidden reality,' he added in conclusion.

Without asking me a second time for my destination, he dropped me off at a large and busy gas station, with a Café right next to it, the name of which I could easily read: Dar Nzaha. The cab driver went out and handed me over my bulky luggage. He gave me a warm farewell putting his right hand on his chest and thanking me for the payment of fifty Dirhams that we had briefly negotiated at the start of the journey. All passengers turned their heads around and waved to me warm-heartedly. I did not have the time to sort out my feelings because a young slim man came straight up to me as if we had already known each other. 'Hi, I am Abdelrahman, it's a great pleasure to meet you!'

I was totally amazed at the ease with which he had identified me as his German customer. He was very handsome with noble features and spoke very good English. Abdelrahman explained to me he would first invite me to a large breakfast in the Café and then load the luggage on the donkey which would accompany us for the next eight days. The animal would be waiting for us right behind the gas station. As planned, we would both set off on our long walk to Ouirgane, the first destination. Almost in passing, he mentioned that the originally envisaged group of four had now shrunk to one person, as a family of three had only cancelled their journey the evening before. So, I would have to make do with him alone he said with a smile and ushered me into the coffee house.

The rest of the day turned into a mind-blowing experience. We hiked for hours over field paths through totally unspoiled nature in direction of the High Atlas Mountains, accompanied by our faithful donkey which carried our baggage and food. Few persons crossed our way. Men and women alike carried heavy goods on their back, greeting us softly with 'peace be upon you.' After a longer break around noon in which Abdelrahman served fresh bread with olive oil and tomatoes, grilled lamb meat and fruits with freshly made mint tea on an open fire he had lighted on a large and sunny meadow in the hills above Asni, we finally arrived at the wonderful and isolated valley of Ouirgane. There were spectacular views of the nearby three and four thousand meter high and snow-capped mountains while the valley seemed covered with an artificial light green around the deep blue and swollen river Oued Nfiss. At the end of the village, we stopped in front of a small and detached house on a hill, surrounded by a dense grove of olive and lemon trees where our donkey came also to its well-deserved rest.

'Welcome to my family's home, since you are the only honorable guest, I have the pleasure to invite you for the first night stop to our modest private home,' Abdelrahman said to me while he knocked softly on the metal door, which was painted with typical motifs of the Shilha culture of the mountainous region. It was a terracotta-colored house with scattered and small windows like all other houses around. Two young girls dressed in colorful Djellabas opened the door. They were immediately introduced by Abdelrahman as his younger sisters Khadija and Aicha. Both were strikingly pretty and were giggling all the time while carefully observing me. We took off our shoes at the entrance, then he led me into a large and tastefully decorated room. There was no furniture inside, but the entire floor was covered with beautiful carpets and equipped with many not less beautiful pillows along the walls. Due to space and inspiring colors, it was the perfect setting to rest. I was sitting between a huge pile of cushy pillows and tried to put an order in all the impressions of the day. Abdelrahman's mother came into the room and welcomed me with a warm-hearted peace be upon you, she then asked in fluent English about my journey with her son. Several times she stressed that I was obliged to feel at home and announced to serve now the tea with sweet pastries before we would have dinner with her husband later the evening.

'I apologize,' Abdelrahman observed, 'that my father isn't home yet but it's time for the sunset prayer. He is the Imam of the local mosque and will join us for dinner after the last compulsory prayer. You will surely know that our daily routine is still based on the intervals of the five prayers. They are the quintessence of our life. I look forward to introducing you to my father Hussein since as I learned from our conversation during the day you are a trained philosopher. And my father is constantly occupied with philosophical questions. It could be a very fruitful encounter for both of you.'

After we had taken an extremely delicious mint tea and tasted fine pastries Abdelrahman invited me to rest while he would help for a moment his family. And the next moment I fell into a pleasant half-sleep which was accompanied by low background noises from the kitchen and talks between his mother, his sisters and himself. In between, there was a babel of voices coming from the minarets which lulled me anew into a gentle sleep. It was the call to the last prayer of the day.

Approximately an hour later, I was sitting full of energy and curiosity with Abdelrahman's mother and sisters around a steaming couscous that was served in a huge bowl on the floor. The entire room was filled with a bewitching scent of fresh ingredients. Then in came a man whose handsomeness and nobility could immediately be perceived and his charisma was in no way inferior to that of his wife and children. He wore a dark green djellaba and had thick hair flecked with grey. His beard was shaved relatively short and gave him dignity and serenity. Deep circles under the eyes had dug into his face as if he worked a lot and slept little, but they matched his emaciated face with its healthy color. The man had a seat next to me and greeted me casually as if I was a daily guest. Abdelrahman introduced his father as Hussein al-Balluti who instantly addressed me in fluent English as well. My amazement continued in so far as the whole family, here at the outskirts of a small Amazigh town two hours south of Marrakech, spoke flawless English with me. The many travel guides on Morocco I had devoured before the trip had conveyed to me the opposite of my present experience, namely that the region south of Tahanaout was a structurally weak region with a high rate of illiteracy. A gas stove in the corner made the cold, slowly drawing into the house, bearable. Abdelrahman's mother handed him, her husband and me a spoon to eat, while she and her daughters formed the couscous into a dumpling with the right hand before putting it into their mouth. After they had sent ahead in the name of God, bismillah, we ate at first without exchanging words, only Khadija and Aicha continued to giggle from time to time. Finally, I broke the silence by inquiring about the family's excellent English skills I would not have expected this way. Immediately afterwards, I apologized for the question and said I had expected in particular French as a lingua franca for strangers.

'You are right,' said Hussein al-Balluti, 'French is mostly spoken here as the French make up the largest proportion of tourists in Morocco. Many of them bought new villas but also many traditional houses in Marrakech after they had cannibalized Tanger as their refuge in the 1970s. Furthermore, as you might know, Morocco was a French protectorate from 1912 to 1956 and since France is militarily and technologically a world power we are still being very much influenced by this country. And if you look at the details of our modern administrative law, you will see that we also have a structural legacy from France, even though we are inspired by German decentralization as well. But as you might have noticed, Marrakech and the rest of Morocco is not only full of French tourists but of visitors from all over the world. As an experienced guide of our majestic mountains my son Abdelrahman has mostly American and British clients who wish to discover the Shilha region. He has an excellent reputation as a mountain guide in English and you are right, he's indeed a bit an exception here in the region.'

'The person responsible for our good English skills is my father Hussein,' noted Abdelrahman and added, 'he studied at the famous Dar Al Hadith Hassania for Higher Islamic Studies in Rabat. There, besides the perfect mastery of Arabic, it was mandatory to learn a foreign language. Unlike most students who usually choose French, he opted for English since he understood that most of the contemporary literature on Islam is written in English. And due to his passionate relation to this language, he started to teach us daily at home. Later on, I studied economics in Birmingham on a scholarship, yet I went back home. I had no intention to be part of our country's immense brain drain which will be a real challenge for the future of Morocco. Don't misunderstand me, that's no reproach to those academics who leave the country. As a young and affected Moroccan, I am totally aware of what a big challenge it is for our young population to remain here and to build up a prospect for the future. But I'm too much in love with nature and I simply didn't want to sit for the rest of my life in front of a screen. And so, I did just like my father did as he was nominated to be one of the candidates to be the imam of one of the biggest Mosques in the world, the Mosque Hassan II in Casablanca which was inaugurated in 1993: he renounced and returned home to serve his native town after he had been the Imam of the great Sunna Mosque in the capital Rabat.'

'So, it means, that you are a very well-versed savant of Islam,' I addressed his father and continued to further nourish this absorbing debate.

'I don't know if I'm really a well-versed scholar of Islam,' he replied. 'My heart has been full of intentions to be it since my early childhood, yet my fellow Muslims have to judge this and finally, God will.'

'Dear father,' said Abdelrahman now, 'I think you can tell our dear guest from Germany a bit about our family history. I'm pretty sure he will appreciate these details since he had not only studied philosophy but recently read translations of al-Ghazali and Ibn Khaldun. The reason for his journey is not adventuring only, rather he is keen to get a profound idea of our culture. During our seven hours march, I had the impression that our dear guest is very much fond of Arabic and Islamic culture. Isn't that so?'

'Indeed, it is so!' I enthusiastically agreed and hoped to hear more from his father's mouth.

With an engaging smile, Hussein al-Balluti looked at me and said:

'But we are Shilha-people. You must first learn of our Shilha-Tradition and that many of the Islamic ruling dynasties in Morocco were of Amazigh origin. Of course, the founder of Morocco was our dear Arab noble Idris Ibn Abdallah who had to flee from the Abbasid dynasty's violent stripping of the Umayyad's power over a thousand years ago. After he had arrived in Morocco, he had obviously to forge an alliance with Morocco's then indigenous population, the Amazigh tribes. It was a fruitful alliance for the founding of our land. Thereafter came the time of Marrakech which was Morocco's capital under the reign of the Almoravid and Almohad caliphate. Both dynasties were essentially Amazigh, the purist Almohad dynasty had its origin even around the corner, some kilometers south of here in Tin Mal. It's worth visiting the remnants of the

Mosque from the twelfth century that gave style to Moroccan and Islamic architecture. The history of our country is a unique fusion of Arab and Amazigh culture, yet, as all history of people, full of bloody rivalries which we have fortunately overcome. Our last King Hassan II fervently defended our political and cultural traditions from falling prey to the former colonial powers. Fortunately, unlike many other neighboring Arab countries Morocco had not to adopt chauvinist and socialist ideologies. It was a real tragedy and these countries will still be wrestling for their identity for decades to come. Unfortunately, I fear the worst for countries like Yemen, Egypt, Iraq, Libya and Algeria. And we Moroccans know this also very well since the bloody coup attempts, fueled by the foreign powers thirty years ago, deeply divided our populations in the aftermath. Moroccans should have become slaves of a so-called secular military rule and all that violence was justified by the euphemism of a necessary modernization of reactionary states. There is still much to be done today for our new King Mohammed VI in terms of the political legacy of that time, especially with regard to domestic reconciliation and the implementation of real solidarity, let alone prosperity, among Moroccans.'

In the meantime, we had finished the amazingly delicious couscous while Abdelrahman helped his mother and two sisters to clear dishes and to prepare dessert. Then fresh fruit was served with tea, especially oranges from the area of Marrakech. With the dessert, they brought in more blankets since the wind blew through the closed windows and doors while the gas stove struggled in vain against the cold of the night. We sat in silence for another moment, wrapped in brightly colored blankets, and sipped the lemon verbena tea with relish. Driven by my curiosity, it was me who broke the silence again.

'And your son earlier spoke of your family history. May I ask about it? Perhaps your family was part of the Amazigh dynasties?'

Hussein smiled with amusement and made a defensive gesture. 'Fortunately, not. To exert power over others has never had a good reputation in our Islamic environment, even though it is not desirable to have a power vacuum. But traditionally, we don't deem a man or a woman able to exert power if he considers himself to be capable of it and advertises it. I think this idea is hard to understand in the context of democracies in the West since their approach to political participation and power is exactly the opposite. We consider it a heavy burden to decide over the destiny of others and to approve laws for man and his destiny, no matter how innocuous and fair they may seem. How many errors you can make here that lead whole nations into misery and destroy people. Therefore, we don't envy human beings exerting power, rather we feel sorry for them. And believe me, we don't mean this disparagingly or out of arrogance, but in case he will be held accountable for his deeds. Back to your question, our family has never been directly involved in political affairs, yet the al-Balluti family can look back on a long line of Muslim scholars. In the past, a Muslim scholar had always to be close to the ruler as an advisor. Besides, he was closely observed by the ruler's officials. A balanced judgement was therefore required with regard to the understanding of the religious text sources and the needs of the community. This virtue was essentially bestowed on a famous al-Balluti, namely, Mundhir ibn Sa'id ibn Abdallah ibn Abdelrahman al-Balluti, the chief judge under the rule of the renowned Umayyad Caliph of Córdoba Abdelrahman III, undoubtedly the golden age of Al-Andalus and a very civilized epoch in the global context of its time. Parts of the Balluti family left our mountain region towards Al-Andalus most probably at the beginning of the eighth century with the first Muslim expansion into the Iberian heartland. It seems that they did not take part in the Amazigh uprising against Arab conquest, rather, they most likely contributed to the establishment of the Arab Umayyad rule in southern Spain since the Umayyads had been overthrown during a bloody revolution by the Abbasids in AD 750 in the then heartland of Islam, in Damascus. But Umayyad rule continued still for more than two-hundred and fifty years in exile, in Al-Andalus. And during the rule of Abdelrahman III which lasted half a century, the city of Córdoba became what Muslims describe today as a perfect model of civilization, particularly if we take into account the medieval timeframe: tolerance, prosperity and a real sense of community due to stability of rule. According to history, Abdelrahman al-Balluti seemed to have been an exceptional scholar during that era, well-versed in Arabic grammar and poetry besides a perfect mastery of the science of the Koran and the Prophet's tradition. Muslim historians characterize him as a role model of a Muslim intellectual and a ruler's chief judge for all his vast knowledge was gained through God-consciousness and humility. It is said that his intellectual keenness and spiritual integrity obliged him to always tell the truth, especially to the ruler, no matter how bitter the truth was. And so, he became famous for having rebuked harshly the Caliph Abdelrahman III when the ruler furnished his monumental palace Medina Azahara outside of Córdoba lavishly. Yet, he was a controversial figure since it was said that as the chief judge he did not follow the official school of jurisprudence, the Maliki law school which came from the great Muslim jurist, theologian and hadith scholar Malik Ibn Anas. Imam Malik lived in Medina, the Prophet Muhammad's city, in the eighth century and, therefore, rapidly gained a reputation for being profoundly familiar with the social and legal framework of the young Muslim society. In short, he became one of the most famous authorities in Islamic law throughout the Muslim world. And here in Morocco, the Maliki law school has been prevailing for almost a thousand years, it's a part of our Islamic identity in questions of Islamic law and ritual. Moreover, it has been strongly connected to our ruling dynasties and their legitimacy. The same holds for the

Umayyad rule in Andalusia, yet authentic traditions report to us that al-Balluti followed the Zahiri school of law. It is of particular interest since that method of approaching issues of Islamic law arose during a time when the new Muslim society faced her first wave of disintegration due to different interpretations of textual sources with legal references. It's a big mistake to design that approach as a school of law. The deeper intention of al-Zahiri was to prevent Muslim jurists to enact religious laws by individual deducing from the text sources, which we denote as analogical reasoning, and therefore, to prevent declaring a law as to be religiously binding even though it goes back to fallible human reasoning. And in a certain sense, Muslim history shows that he was totally right, since especially from the eighth century onwards a strong wave of over-legalization set in which rapidly became dogmatic and hampered for many centuries the intellectual creativity of Muslim jurists. Worse, it made Islam a science that was comprehensible only for experts and less understandable for the average Muslim. It was one of the greatest yet most controversial figures of Muslim scholarship, Ibn Hazm, that half a century after al-Balluti grasped the real problem of analogical reasoning within the context of Islamic law, namely the Muslim jurist's risk of apotheosizing himself. Many jurists were tempted to enact religious laws without reference to the primordial text sources. Ibn Hazm simply feared a lack of humility of Muslim jurists in their approach of delivering legal opinions or so-called fatwas. We Muslims normally have a natural aversion to drafting and enacting laws if they are not to find in the relevant text sources, the Koran and the Prophet's tradition. And Ibn Hazm advocated to be very careful with juristic speculation and to refer to the exact wording of legal passages in the text. Only this method could prevent a Muslim jurist from making laws that are subsequently labelled as God-made laws for Muslims. He considered this in his monumental book al-Muhalla which is an entire encyclopedia of Islamic jurisprudence as the worst failing in the sight of God apart from idolatry and disbelief. It's crystal clear that Ibn Hazm was a so-called literalist who granted legal validity to approximately eight percent of the verses of the Koran. His literalist approach was soon misunderstood as narrow-mindedness regarding the ability to the interpretation of legal sources. He was not against the interpretation of the true spirit of Islam and the figuring out of our texts' deeper intentions but simply against arbitrary religious law. Ibn Hazm's heart was filled with the spirit of holding the Muslim community together and avoiding a cult of personality, moreover, he was totally aware of the permanent risk Muslim jurists were facing, namely that their rulings could easily be considered as infallible. Traditions suggest that our ancestor al-Balluti also made this legal approach the basis of his personal reasoning in Islamic matters, yet as a judge, he concealed it and officially professed Maliki law. It's an anecdote of our family's history, but you should not deem it as the pride of our ancestors since pride has no place in our religion. God tells us: Verily, the noblest of you in the sight of God is the one who is most deeply conscious of Him.'

Hussein al-Balluti remained silent for a short while, then he said kindly, 'Our dear guest, take another cup of tea and taste these homemade Moroccan cookies. I don't want to overstrain your patience with dry lessons on Islamic law and family anecdotes dating back a thousand years.'

But I had listened to him like to a storyteller who bewitched me with his quiet and assuring voice and so I replied that the opposite was true, directly continuing with another remark, 'So, allow me to say you did the opposite of the chief judge al-Balluti who served a powerful Caliph because, after all, you renounced your appointment of being the Imam of the greatest Mosque in Morocco. It's a very humble stance, isn't it?'

'Not at all,' he replied directly to my question, 'look, Casablanca is a very huge and extremely complicated city that I know very well. It's the most liberal place in Morocco, people are open and polite, yet it is a place where all our Moroccan contradictions and problems come to light in an extreme, in a dense way. We are facing many social problems there, and for me, as an Imam, I would have to do my part in mitigating these dire social tensions. The city is not only a simple point of clashes between liberalism and religious conservatism, it is also a city where Muslims have so different visions of Islam that you run the risk of constantly getting caught between the fronts. Modernism has undeniably brought a disintegration of the Muslim community. This is an irreversible tendency. In many so-called modern Arab nations, the fragmentation of society is even worse than in Morocco since we have still a relatively stable and traditional structure of society and ruling, thanks to Islam. But the modern spirit, along with superfluous consumer goods, keeps hammering on the mentality of Muslims, seducing them to strive for power and to use Islam to achieve that goal. This thirst for power generally occurs under the euphemistic disguise of political participation but such a term had a totally different meaning in Islamic society. Islam is particularly a religion of social participation which means indeed political participation in the community yet without the connotation of power. Within an Islamic framework, political participation means social responsibility and every Muslim is obliged to do so the best way she or he can. And I apologize my dear guest from Germany, but today's concept of political power is the corollary of modern and post-Enlightenment thought stemming from the Western world. It presupposes first the emancipation of man from transcendent connection to his Creator and the destruction of metaphysical concepts. Furthermore, it appeals to a form of rationality that considers itself able to give an adequate answer to the question of the meaning of existence. Both do not fit our Muslim setting although we always try to reconcile Islamic principles with the principles of democracy, progress and consumerism, even though we know that these do not really go together. Yet worse are those who claim that even a country like Morocco was not

Islamic enough since its ruling elite would not implement Islam in society. My dear friend, you can imagine what kind of Islam they want to force onto people only to assuage their own ambitions and to come to power. Unfortunately, we have many of them, especially in greater cities and they are very much influenced by the so-called political Islam which is a hybrid version of democratic spirit, hunger for power and moral tyranny. Believe me, we will have many problems with these groups in the years to come. They establish political parties as if to be a good Muslim was a question of belonging to a political party. Moreover, they claim the prerogative to set up real Islamic principles for society. Some of these groups had been used by Western states to fight against Soviet communism and for the independence of national states. These groups will soon change their image of the enemy and neither Western states nor our own Muslim society will be safe from them. Look, these socio-political phenomena are very complex, but they are prevalent in Casablanca. I deemed a dear colleague of mine much more suited to this position. We had studied for years together and he became later Imam in a history-charged mosque in Fes. He is a brilliant scholar and very well-versed in understanding totally different social contexts and problems. I advised the commission at the Ministry of Religious Affairs to rather appoint him instead of mine. Last but not least, I missed my home village and the pristine countryside after years of life in Morocco's capital Rabat. You will literally taste the beauty of our majestic landscape during the next few days. I am sure you will understand me and my son. Coming back from Birmingham to live at home again in the Atlas Mountains is a huge step. Do you feel how the cold wind is whipping into the house? It's not an easy surrounding, but it's worth living here, beyond the hustle and bustle and the smog of a big city.'

Indeed, it got colder despite the mass of warm blankets that covered my body up to my neck. Hussein's wife brought another tray with an ornamented teapot and said smiling, 'It will be a long evening. My husband loves to discuss and is never able to put an end to his verbal stream of knowledge. It's good you will leave tomorrow early in the morning with my son for the Igdet Mountain region, otherwise, I'm afraid you will end up as a Muslim scholar if you would spend an entire week with him.' We all laughed heartily.

'It sounds complex and as if your country were caught in a field of extreme tension between tradition and modernity,' I resumed the thrilling discussion.

'It's correct and, at the same time, worse than what you said. We are caught between tradition, modernity and false traditions as well as false modernity,' he said with a thoughtful look while sipping his tea.

'Morocco is in a catching-up process vis-à-vis the so-called developed countries of the northern hemisphere. It's a merciless dynamic with regard to our traditions since the wave of modernism streaming into our country is clouding our consciousness and negatively shifting our priorities. So, life slowly gets a different orientation. Our region, rough and dry, is fervently resisting the influences of a materialistic lifestyle, mainly due to money shortage but also to a strongly rooted spirituality. Therefore, you can't say that people here have a bad life. They have a pure heart and they live in harmony with their natural surroundings, like their ancestors for hundreds of years. Beyond, they are not yet infected by ideologies like consumerism and progress or other promises of happiness. People here know well that the so-called progress is a grey area one has the price to pay. They also know the striving for the power of certain Islamist movements does not match easily to the pristine teachings of Islam. These groups subscribe to a false tradition, distorted by modern claims of people's sovereignty. But in the Shilha area between Asni and Taroudant, most people live still beyond ideological inclinations and seductive ideas of ephemeral prosperity, due to a deeply rooted Muslim spirituality and strong ties to the natural setting. Humility is the essence of their existence. While our big cities are being conquered by the end product of late Western thought, namely the will to power with its cynical emancipation of mankind, people here are strongly committed to adapting with gratefulness and humbleness to their given setting. That's, at first sight, unspectacular, but look what material our houses are built of and how our mosques are designed, they will never be outdated, they will always reflect the timeless adequate answer to the people's daily material and spiritual needs in this region. We have been facing more and more public awareness campaigns by Western development agencies for years, advocating for change and a better life. These people from Europe or the United States who cooperate closely with our indigenous population are generally very educated and highly cultivated people with excellent intentions and they often know our history even better than we know it. They usually appreciate our culture and outside of working hours, they enjoy our treasures of nature or play Golf. So, they have an extremely good life in Morocco, profiting from their status and our deeply rooted tradition to care for the poorest, taking them as domestic servants. And yet they strongly believe that their advocated weltanschauung will sooner or later be shared by all who have sound common sense. This is perhaps one of their greatest errors. I'm pretty sure that in a few years you will have still stronger environmental movements in Western countries since you will slowly understand that the Western lifestyle is a kind of strong aberration of man's primordial nature and his real longings. Western or modern lifestyle will have been nothing else than a systematic stress program for the individual, the community and especially for nature, for the whole creation. And the West will sell us this insight most probably as the next step in its linear progress ideology. So, how should we be able to catch up with industrial countries? I presume there will be a moment your agencies and ministries of development will tell us: Stop! We in the West had prosperity, but with our progressive rational approach, we were able to understand that this kind of prosperity and affluence did great harm to the environment and our surroundings of nature. You have to stop, they will say, you have immediately to switch to a sustainable lifestyle. This form of prosperity was a kind of interlude of progress and modernity which has to be corrected. But in reality, this interlude my dear friend was a great illusion brought about by man's haughtiness and orthodox rationalism. And with the same paternalism, they will then explain to us that this prosperity is now outdated and not suited anymore to imitation. These conclusions of the developed countries are nothing else than the hard empirical confirmation of occidental thought's false premises.'

I listened carefully to what he said while I was clasping the small glass with lemon verbena with both hands to have another source of warmth. 'Your argument seems to follow Heidegger, occidental thought's last philosopher. He set forth in his entire work that philosophy had neither grasped the concept of being nor the meaning of existence from its beginning. Perhaps you have heard about him?'

'Of course I've heard of him. During my formation at the Dar Hassania in Rabat budding Imams had to attend specialized lectures in philosophy, ancient philosophy, philosophy of the enlightenment or modern philosophy. I studied one and a half years of Heidegger's work *Being and Time* as well as extracts of his late thought on the turn in metaphysics.'

I was totally amazed and felt like in an endless dream while the noise of the cold wind outside seemed to be the adequate background sound of this extraordinary evening. For a moment the wonderful conversation with Giuseppe, the Franciscan monk, came back to my mind. And now, in the small Amazigh village of Ourigane, two hours south of Marrakech, surrounded by mountains nearly four thousand meters high, I was sitting again with a scholar, albeit from a different culture, and starting anew a discussion on Heidegger and philosophy. Fate is a wondrous affair.

Thoughtfully, Hussein al-Balluti took up the argument again. 'It's impossible to think on Heidegger's philosophy without connecting it to Nietzsche. As far as I understood, Nietzsche's philosophical concepts of the will to power and the eternal return were the final outcomes of occidental metaphysical thought, but also an idealization of Renaissance ideas with ingredients of early Greek thought. And the entire philosophy of Heidegger is finally a result of a thorough analysis of Nietzsche's philosophy. We used extremely good translations since Heidegger was a key reference for French modernity in philosophy. All these complex theories of deconstructivism and structuralism of Derrida and Foucault are not easy to understand without knowledge of Heidegger's philosophy. But, to tell you the truth, I have always been fascinated by Heidegger's thorough analyses and his extremely deep knowledge of the history of thought, yet I never understood how he could speak of the oblivion of being without presuming a Creator behind all Creation. He himself speaks of thrownness, namely that man is thrown into the world, a very important concept of his early thought, but he lacks the courage to think that out of nothing there can hardly be thrownness. So, what about the one who throws and creates? In the end, his thinking is not so different from any other modern thinker, insofar he thinks the concept of being without a Creator and intention. Existence without meaning. And doesn't his own thought reflect the meaninglessness that Heidegger himself considered as the logical corollary of occidental philosophy? Well, thinking without a pivotal point is really a difficult undertaking that we are not used to in our context of ideas. Yet what is inspiring in Heidegger's late thought, also for Muslim scholars, is his idea that man is not the center of creation, he is not the standard of being rather an opening of being as he presented it in his *Letter on Humanism*. Since Muslims are theocentric this critical view of occidental humanism is extremely stimulating. But in the end, he doesn't know how to get out of the dilemma of a philosophy of being without God. Most probably Heidegger remains a great nihilist and seals the destiny of occidental philosophy. But most likely, I'm not well-versed enough in occidental philosophy to understand his entire thought,' he said with a warm smile, immediately adding, 'I always had great respect for people who could run into a totally black abyss that devours everything. Moreover, he too wasn't able to resist the temptations of an overbearing political ideology, at least for a short while around 1933.'

'The abyss that devours the great movie of life, all these sequences, a flood of wonderful images, and I think even the bad ones are covered with the veil of beauty at the end,' I interrupted him.

'Your worldview is poetic rather than scientific,' he chimed in, 'my son told me that he had an extremely good conversation with you during the entire trip from Tahanaout to Ouirgane, about the beauty of nature, the beauty of life and the suffering of love, isn't it?'

'Indeed, it was a real pleasure to have a long conversation with such a noble and educated young man who knows, moreover, every flower and herbs at the edge of the pathway,' I said.

'I know, he did never lose his passion for this rough but beautiful landscape and his longing to be surrounded by all these treasures. His fellows at the Birmingham School of Business were impressed and wondering when he decided to return to Morocco and to work as an alpine guide in a relatively unknown region,' continued Hussein al-Balluti. 'He's a strange guy, they thought, since he could have got a quite well-paid job in Greater London, Liverpool or Manchester, right?' he kindly asked his son Abdelrahman who listened attentively to the conversation.

'Well-paid is a relative term, especially in London. The pressure as an economic or financial analyst would have been high and the salary would have been spent for rent and the use of public transport. And believe me, I love London so much, the open-mindedness of the people living there, their politeness and ability to solve complex things in an uncomplicated way. I will never break the ties to Great Britain and to the good friends I still have there. But for me, it was a question of priorities in my life. It's important to earn money but what matters is how you earn your daily bread. It's eventually a question of principles of what to do with your precious lifetime. First of all, I did not want to spend the rest of my life in front of a plastic screen, looking into an artificial world of facts and data. The revolutionary process of digitalization that will speed immensely up during the next decade I guess, threatens us with a so far never experienced atrophy of social life and anarchy in opinion-making. So, I made up my mind since I simply yearned for oxygen and social interaction in my job. And I am convinced it was the right decision,' he explained.

'May I ask you,' said his father while turning to me, 'what will you do with a finished study of philosophy? I suppose you will focus on a position in the university. But, if you allow me, I am more interested in your philosophical positions.'

'I think I have to disappoint you since philosophy was a kind of occupational therapy for me, even though I've always tried to extract wisdom for everyday life. Therefore, I focused on Schopenhauer, Nietzsche and Kierkegaard and on Heidegger as well. Just in search of the meaning of life. But you can't find it in occidental philosophy, Schopenhauer is amazing and sometimes comforting with his stance to negate every sense of life and to be therefore totally relaxed at the end. Waiting for death in a relaxed manner, without will. Fascinating to read at first, but after careful thought, totally depressing. And I'm not convinced at all if Nietzsche's search for the eternal return of happiness must be the result of a realized will to power. He remains too much a Greek philosopher under the disguise of modernity. Kierkegaard's leap into faith opens the horizon of the original search for truth, that's most amazing, perhaps the Danish philosopher was the most uncompromised. Yet modernity has abolished the notion of truth, it's an outdated term. And so, I live in a total vacuum since I'm not able to fill the cart with one of the illusionary products that promise meaning in our supermarket of stimulations and seductions. For several years I was convinced that love could effectively appease that desperate search for meaning since my heart had been filled with happiness and ease. But no state is permanent, especially not an emotional elation. So, I noticed with bitterness that love is as disappointing as philosophical epistemes,' I concluded my answer.

'But you told me that a glimmer of hope appeared, namely that Moroccan young woman Naima who finally triggered your trip to Morocco?' resumed Abdelrahman.

'Don't tell me that our dear German friend fell in love with a Moroccan woman! What a wonderful history! Is that really true?' asked Hussein al-Balluti.

'It is,' I replied embarrassed. 'It was a strange coincidence because I met her at a time when I discovered al-Ghazali and Ibn Tufail and I started to brush up on my Arabic I had learned in university many years ago. So, from our first meeting we had always a good basis for discussion on Muslim and Arabic culture. I enjoyed these moments very much.'

'But you seldom agreed, I suppose, especially when the subject of discussion was your personal impression of the Golden Age of Islam to which al-Ghazali and Ibn Tufail undoubtedly still belong,' Hussein al-Balluti remarked briefly.

'It is so, she had in my view a totally negative attitude concerning Arab and Muslim culture,' I admitted.

Now, Abdelrahman interfered and said, 'You have to understand her attitude and perspective. Instead, you had totally different access to Muslim culture through our noblest and most brilliant intellectuals. Al-Ghazali, Ibn Tufail or Ibn

Khaldoun are, let's say, the pride of our history. They give you an idealized version of Islamic culture. But she, as a young Moroccan woman in a very advanced and extremely liberal society suffers from the discrepancy of everyday life in Germany and the strong expectations her family will undoubtedly project on her. In general, Moroccan women have to endure a lot of pressure, sometimes unbearable, be it here in Morocco or abroad. Within our modern world, they became a projection surface for social discrepancies and fields of tension. And they have, unfortunately, to master this challenge alone because men often disappear and avoid facing these issues. Still, in our culture, a woman is strongly associated with motherhood and later on with the very nucleus of family life. A mother is considered as the cement that always holds the family together. The men, on the other hand, are poor wretches who have to look out for their daily wages in order to provide for the whole family. This is certainly not a modern vision of family and works as you are used to in European countries. But we Moroccans are very reluctant when it comes to change, sometimes with good reasons, sometimes not. And all these tensions are carried out even more on the backs of these Moroccan women in a Western context. You need a lot of patience and forbearance with her to shun misunderstandings and further burdens on her. It will be the same challenge for you as for her if you aim to establish something like a stable relationship in your social context. She has a lot to lose, perhaps everything, you know what I mean. You should have the grit to speak bluntly with her about all these challenges and to make it clear to her that you are totally aware of her complex situation. This is the best way to show your love for her. Be sure, she will appreciate so much your sense of responsibility. That's just a little piece of advice on the basis of what you told me today during our trip.'

'Now, we have shifted our discussion from the aspect of the disappointment of philosophy and love to Naima. So again, if

I understood well, the quest for your life's meaning is bound anew to, let's say, a passionate love? Isn't it?' asked Hussein.

'I'm afraid so,' I said.

'Please, don't misunderstand me, I already think you two could make an amazing couple in the future taking into account her efforts to meet up with you and your efforts to deepen your knowledge of her original culture. It's a wonderful story. But does it mean you are again full of hope that love will provide you with a kind of holistic meaning of life, albeit you said that love is as disappointing as a philosophical episteme?' Hussein al-Balluti asked further while he ran his hand thoughtfully through his short and grey beard, assuming a very reflective stance.

'Yes, I think so,' I said, adding with a hint of a smile, 'hope out of despair. Oh, it sounds too much like Kierkegaard.'

Hussein al-Balluti smiled too. 'I heard of Kierkegaard. He was the al-Ghazali of Christendom, albeit six hundred years later. A totally fervent searcher for truth and a great esthete. His estheticism was triggered by his passionate yet failed relationship with Regine Olsen he abandoned for the sake of his spiritual life. It's been always a bit disturbing for me, whenever I came in touch with texts of the Christian context, that spirituality and physical love are rarely compatible. I considered the negation of the body in medieval Christianity almost as blasphemy since we are not able to imagine life without a body that is dependent on everything, water, food, love, feelings. We cannot even dare to speak of a soul without a body, at least with regard to our earthly existence. However, in al-Ghazali's work, erotism and esthetics are prompted by the beauty of nature and the majesty of creation which are signs of the transcendental unity of their Creator. I apologize, we are digressing from our topic. Love is the most beautiful wonder two souls and bodies can experience and its intensity can easily erase the sense for space and time and even the sense that one needs a stronger and more enduring source of meaning for life. I think your disappointment with philosophy and love is unfounded and rather the result of false expectations. Both can never provide you with a holistic meaning of life, let alone inner peace, which we call mutmaina and is mentioned explicitly in verse twenty-seven of Sura eighty-nine in the Koran. It's a very complicated term concerning its precise meaning. Complete mindfulness and gratitude at the same time which can only be achieved through permanent practice in worship. Instead, philosophy can never create sense. Real meaning has to be found by searching for it. I don't believe that one who lacks humility might ever be able to gain real knowledge. And with regard to philosophy and speculative thought, it can show the way, at best. The same holds for love. Even the most beautiful flower withers one day which is not at all an argument against the flower's beauty. Therefore, love can never be the source of the meaning of life, it must rather be embedded in it. Then love has the chance to be healthy and unfolding. Unfortunately, your generation, especially in Europe, is obliged to be emancipated from man's natural disposition, entering a gigantic realm of emptiness being full of illusionary meanings, which are superficial and exclusively connected to sensuality and passion. This kind of meaning is rapidly consumed and usually leaves a bland taste of transience, creating a fervent longing for permanent stimulation which is easily mistaken for liveliness. But in a context that has abolished a transcendental and holistic approach to life, you might be tempted to take philosophy or love as exclusive sources of meaning. Yet the meaning of existence must be found in transcendence and spiritual practice. I know it's strange to hear this since such concepts are totally outdated in the Western world. It seems that scientific progress and the new fascination with technology are enough to provide sufficient meaning for the life of future generations. So, the so-called developed countries still have a religion, even though they don't want to admit this fact. Most of all it's a substitute for religion. A syncretic mix of prosperity, materialism, science and democracy, the latter as a promising illusion of man's sovereignty, regardless of the fact that a human being is but a hurried traveler on earth,' said Hussein al-Balluti with now downcast eyes.

There was a moment of silence and he served the rest of the tea with a thoughtful expression. His wife Khadija came in and wished me a good night. She kindly informed me that my room upstairs was already prepared. 'It's late,' she said to her husband and her son, 'you know that our guest will have a challenging day tomorrow. It's a very long hike to the Jbel Igdet and there is still a lot of snow.'

Before we went upstairs Hussein al-Balluti looked at me tenderly and said calmly, 'Who knows the Shilha region of the High Atlas Mountains certainly has an idea on Morocco's heart, its secretes, beauty and stubborn resistance to all pernicious influences brought in from outside. Your secret partner Naima will understand that your love for her is as sincere as your love for Morocco. My dear German friend, since you are a trained philosopher, I don't have the slightest right to recommend you a book or rather a timeless masterpiece on love. *The Ring of the Dove* from Ibn Hazm was written at the beginning of the eleventh century and has not lost its topicality. People find it strange that especially a devout Muslim could write about the different forms of love and affection as well as their impact on the heart. That thorough analysis of Ibn Hazm will unmistakably remind you that love can easily tear up your heart in pieces or give it inner peace and balance. Don't be unfair to love and don't mistake it for blind passion, no matter how seductive it is. So far as I'm informed Arthur John Arberry's translation from 1951 is still the best available edition in English. The book is so timeless and distinguished that it has not been buried under the trash of mainstream entertainment literature, at least not yet. Just let fate simply speak to you and you will always be on the right track because fate has nothing illusionary. Enjoy your days with my son, dear friend. Our home is always your home.'

It was a clear and cold morning. The first rays of the sun with its blinding light suffused the strong contrasts of the lush green valley, the always terracotta-colored soil and the snowy mountains against the backdrop of an unreal blue sky with a gleaming veil. We went along the valley of the river N'fiss with our faithful donkey that patiently dragged our provisions. A stunning view opened permanently to our left side to the four thousand meters high mountains Toubkal and Ouanoukrim. In the small Shilha village Imigdal, a hospitable family made us a simple but delicious second breakfast. Unlike the Ballutis nobody spoke English there, but you could feel an unusual human warmth in every gesture. Inside the simple mud-walled house it was cold and we took a seat on the only real piece of furniture, a large and impressively beautiful carpet of the region. We did not dare take off our jackets, yet the traditional lemon verbena tea warmed us quickly. Abdelrahman talked and laughed a lot with the man of the family, both were obviously well acquainted with each other. He explained to me that the man would lead the donkey to the small Amazigh village Arg where another family would host us after our long trip over three peaks at the end of the day. He had taken some alpine equipment items out of the huge bags hanging over the donkey before we set out for the Jbel Gourza on a constantly rising mountain path. We walked at a steady pace and Abdelrahman regularly asked me if everything was okay. I felt like I had lost an immense burden despite my own heavy backpack and the physical efforts I had to make. The lush and green slopes that were dotted with brightly colored spring flowers quickly turned into a landscape of eternal winter, yet the intense North African sun was still warming. We put on our snowshoes after another small break and headed towards the Jbel Gourza. During the entire hike Hussein al-Balluti's sentence hammered constantly into my mind, again and again: *Just let fate simply speak to you and you will always be on the right track because fate has nothing illusionary.* Regardless of its meaning, it was a sentence with an incredibly beautiful resonance. We reached the third peak of the day, the majestic Jbel Idget, already towards the early afternoon. Abdelrahman always went ahead although there was no pathway to be seen. There were neither footprints nor did we meet anyone since we had left Imigdal. There was complete loneliness and I followed his footsteps with concentration. Jana and Naima kept coming to my mind, but without the pain of loss when I thought of Jana und without all too longing expectation when I thought of Naima. Both were beautiful and I felt their beauty calm me down. I would always love both of them, that was clear and that was okay. Where would love end with our disappearance? Probably just burn out.

After eight exciting days, my trip with Abdelrahman through the proud and wild Shilha region came to an end at the ancient city of Taroudant, called the smaller twin of Marrakech south of the Atlas Mountains. The last descent from an exposed peak into the Sous region exhausted me, yet I was happy about the flood of beguiling impressions I experienced during this week. Not far away from the gate Bab Sedra in the city's ramparts where the big overland taxis waited for customers, we shared a delicious lamb Tajine and happily recalled the past days. After he had ordered a tea and apologized, he left me for a few minutes to discuss with a cab driver who was hanging around nearby. I saw them laughing and joking in a familiar way before Abdelrahman came back and told me that my return trip to Marrakech was well organized. I didn't have to worry. After we had finished the tea, he gave a sign to the cab driver waiting in front of his wagon. He greeted me warmly and took my two heavy bags which he rapidly loaded into the trunk.

'He will accompany you to the door of your Riad in the ancient medina of Marrakech,' Abdelrahman kindly explained to me.

I was completely surprised and we stood face to face for a while then he put his right hand on my chest. 'My dear friend, thank you for your trust in me and the honor that I could spend my time with you. Thank you! Please, don't forget that the home of the Ballutis is always your home. That's not a saying. You know where you find us. And I think you will come back, Inshallah. Take much care of yourself! Bislama!' he said and hugged me long and tight.

'Thank you and your family. It was my honor to be hosted by the Balluti family. Dear Abdelrahman, thank you so much and take care! Bislama!' I replied quickly and teary-eyed, with a lump in my throat

'And you will pass by all these wonderful places again on the winding road back to Marrakech. Always on the left side,' he added and waved to me.

I put my hand on my chest and said goodbye one last time. Then the driver opened the back door and invited me kindly to get into the car. He had put some pillows on the seat so that I was comfortable and he had covered the panes with towels to protect me from the sun. With a gentle smile, he also handed me over a cloth bag with fresh fruits and a bottle of water. I felt disproportionately cared for and much flattered.

The way back to Marrakech was an emotional highlight of my stay in Morocco and a dignified closure of these enchanting eight days spent with Abdelrahman. We drove the winding road 203 via Talat N'Yaaqoub and Ijoukak towards Ouirgane always along the river Nfiss which carved itself a troubled path through the massive Atlas Mountains. The deep blue water was surrounded by green and fruity banks while the snow reached as far as the upper valley floor. The sunset bathed the four-thousand-meter peaks Toubkal and Ouanoukrim in a magical red on my right. Men and women in long djellabas, fluttering in the wind, from time to time strolled lonely along the road and I tried to imagine to where they would go or from where they would come. As with the outward journey to Tahanaout this driver was also in an extremely good mood. Initially, he listened to classical Arab music with another beguiling female voice and he too seemed to know all the texts by heart. Later, at dusk, when we had already the Atlas region behind, definitely approaching Marrakech, he switched to the Koran. His name was Amin and he told me about his four children, Salma, Ouafae, Hamid and Muhammad as well as about his hometown Ouarzazate in Morocco's south he had left ten years ago to look for work. Marrakech was a totally different place he said. People were open-minded and the city was blessed by abundant tourism. They had a good life he stressed, saying all praise is to God alone, alhamdulillah. Finally, we arrived at the Bab Doukkala and he accompanied me on foot to the entrance door of the hidden guest house in the labyrinth of the medina's mysterious alleys. He said goodbye and asked me if I needed an airport transfer in the next few days. We agreed that he would pick me up at six in the morning in two days since my departure to Frankfurt was scheduled for nine.

Amin, this kind and slender man, had already been waiting for me in front of the door when I left the hotel with my luggage a few minutes before six o'clock in the morning. He took one of my huge bags and we went on foot through the still abandoned streets of Marrakech's medina in the direction of his cab. Only the doors of two mosques were open where people recited the Koran aloud after they had finished the dawn prayer. The main roads were still empty and so we headed quickly towards the Ménara Airport, leaving the ancient town through the Western gate, the Bab Jdid, passing by the Koutoubia Mosque and the luxury Hotel La Mamounia. On the Avenue Prince Moulay Rashid, I could see the Atlas Mountains where the first dawn hung on the snow-capped peaks. A strong and very warm wind was blowing, casting a sand-colored veil over the endless rows of olive trees to the left. Amin told me it was the Chergui, a hot and sandy wind coming from the desert that usually blew in mid-August, but sometimes heralded a hot and dry season already in February or March. But at this time of the year, the sandstorm seldom came directly from the south, instead, it rather took a circuitous route along the coast and then swept across the country from the West, he added. Bewitched by the sand-colored light in the plain and the steel-blue sky above I spontaneously asked what Morocco's West Coast was like? A most wonderful place said Amin enthusiastically and he told me that the Shilha region of the Atlas Mountains stretches further into the plains of the Atlantic Coast, especially between Essaouira and the Sous Valley north of Agadir. The area was as lonely as the mountain region and seemed not to know any limits due to its endless expanses that were suddenly swallowed by the eternal blue of the Atlantic Ocean. His words seduced me and without further thinking, I asked him if it was possible to drive me there and to show me the region. I did the math quickly and was sure to still have money available. In his good French, he inquired incredulously if I meant it seriously, pointing at the same time to the Marrakech Ménara Airport sign. I wanted him to make me a price offer for a three-day trip and his prompt suggestion of two thousand dirhams with two nights and food seemed totally fair to me. 'Forget my flight,' I told him full of enthusiasm. And we drove straight ahead on a long road into a vast ocean of blazing light and sandy soil. We alternately listened to classical Arab and Moroccan popular music while Amin revealed to me all the details of each singer's life. Suddenly I felt that pain and despair had been washed away from my heart. As if they had simply been consumed by longing.

ABOUT THE AUTHOR

Jochen Lobah

was born in Germany. He studied philosophy and later lived in Morocco for many years. Janamania is his debut novel.

Made in the USA
Columbia, SC
27 September 2022

68013648R00136